SARA
BLAEDEL

"THE B[...]
—MICHAEL CONNELLY

THE
MIDNIGHT
WITNESS

MORE THRILLING BOOKS IN SARA BLAEDEL'S ACCLAIMED LOUISE RICK SERIES

AVAILABLE NOW

AND LOOK FOR HER NEW SUSPENSE SERIES

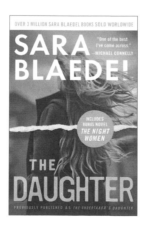

AVAILABLE NOW

PLEASE TURN TO THE BACK OF THIS BOOK FOR A PREVIEW.

EXTRAORDINARY PRAISE FOR
SARA BLAEDEL
AND THE LOUISE RICK SERIES

"Blaedel is one of the best I've come across."

—Michael Connelly

"Crime-writer superstar Sara Blaedel's great skill is in weaving a heartbreaking social history into an edge-of-your-chair thriller while at the same time creating a detective who's as emotionally rich and real as a close friend."

—Oprah.com

"She's a remarkable crime writer who time and again delivers a solid, engaging story that any reader in the world can enjoy."

—Karin Slaughter

"One can count on emotional engagement, spine-tingling suspense, and taut storytelling from Sara Blaedel. Her smart and sensitive character, investigator Louise Rick, will leave readers enthralled and entertained."

—Sandra Brown

"I loved spending time with the tough, smart, and all-too-human heroine Louise Rick—and I can't wait to see her again."

—Lisa Unger

"If you like crime fiction that is genuinely scary, then Sara Blaedel should be the next writer you read."

—Mark Billingham

"Sara Blaedel is at the top of her game. Louise Rick is a character who will have readers coming back for more."

—Camilla Läckberg

THE LOST WOMAN

"Leads to…that gray territory where compassion can become a crime and kindness can lead to coldblooded murder."

—New York Times Book Review

"Blaedel solidifies once more why her novels are as much finely drawn character studies as tightly plotted procedurals, always landing with a punch to the gut and the heart."

—Library Journal (starred review)

"Long-held secrets and surprising connections rock Inspector Louise Rick's world in Blaedel's latest crime thriller. Confused and hurt, Louise persists in investigating a complex murder despite the mounting personal ramifications. The limits of loyalty and trust, and the complexities of grief, are central to this taut thriller's resolution. A rich cast of supporting characters balances the bleakness of the crimes."

—RT Book Reviews (4 stars)

"Sara Blaedel is a literary force of nature…Blaedel strikes a fine and delicate balance between the personal and the professional in *The Lost Woman*, as she has done with the other books in this wonderful series…Those who can't get enough of finely tuned mysteries…will find this book and this author particularly riveting."

—BookReporter.com

"Blaedel, Denmark's most popular author, is known for her dark mysteries, and she examines the controversial social issue at the heart of this novel, but ends on a surprisingly light note. Another winner from Blaedel."

—Booklist

"Engrossing."

—Toronto Star

THE KILLING FOREST

"Another suspenseful, skillfully wrought entry from Denmark's Queen of Crime."

—Booklist

"Engrossing...Blaedel nicely balances the twisted relationships of the cult members with the true friendships of Louise, Camilla, and their circle."

—Publishers Weekly

"Blaedel delivers another thrilling novel...Twists and turns will have readers on the edge of their seats waiting to see what happens next."

—RT Book Reviews

"Will push you to the edge of your seat [then] knock you right off...A smashing success."

—BookReporter.com

"Blaedel excels at portraying the darkest side of Denmark."

—Library Journal

THE FORGOTTEN GIRLS

WINNER OF THE 2015 RT REVIEWERS' CHOICE AWARD

"Crackling with suspense, atmosphere, and drama, *The Forgotten Girls* is simply stellar crime fiction."

—Lisa Unger

"Chilling...[a] swiftly moving plot and engaging core characters."
—*Publishers Weekly*

"This is a standout book that will only solidify the author's well-respected standing in crime fiction. Blaedel drops clues that will leave readers guessing right up to the reveal. Each new lead opens an array of possibilities, and putting the book down became a feat this reviewer was unable to achieve. Based on the history of treating the disabled, the story is both horrifying and all-too-real. Even the villains have nuanced and sympathetic motives."
—*RT Times* Top Pick, Reviewers' Choice Award Winner

"Already an international bestseller, this outing by Denmark's Queen of Crime offers trademark Scandinavian crime fiction with a tough detective and a very grim mystery. Blaedel is incredibly talented at keeping one reading...Recommend to fans of Camilla Läckberg and Liza Marklund."
—*Library Journal*

"*The Forgotten Girls* has it all. At its heart, it is a puzzling, intricate mystery whose solution packs a horrific double-punch...Once you start, you will have no choice but to finish it."
—BookReporter.com

"Tautly suspenseful and sociologically fascinating, *The Forgotten Girls* demonstrates yet again that the finest contemporary suspense fiction emanates from Europe's snowbound North."
—*BookPage*

"Sara Blaedel's *The Forgotten Girls* is an emotionally complex police-procedural thriller set in Denmark. With a gripping premise, fast-paced narrative and well-developed characters, *The Forgotten Girls* is an incredible read."
—FreshFiction.com

"Tightly knit."

—Kirkus Reviews

"*The Forgotten Girls* is without a doubt the best the author has delivered so far...strikingly well done...The chances are good that *The Forgotten Girls* will become your favorite crime novel for a long time to come."

—Børsen (Denmark)

"[*The Forgotten Girls*] is gripping when it depicts some horrific crimes...[An] uncompromising realism...distinguishes this novel at its best."

—Washington Post

THE MIDNIGHT WITNESS

BOOKS BY SARA BLAEDEL

THE MIDNIGHT WITNESS

SARA BLAEDEL

Translated by Mark Kline

GRAND CENTRAL
PUBLISHING

New York   Boston

Copyright © 2018 by Sara Blaedel
Translated by Mark Kline, translation © 2017 by Sara Blaedel
Excerpt from *The Daughter* © 2017 by Sara Blaedel
Cover design by Elizabeth Connor
Cover image © Vadim Krupnov / EyeEm/Getty Images
Cover copyright © 2018 by Hachette Book Group

Grand Central Publishing
Hachette Book Group
1290 Avenue of the Americas
New York, NY 10104
Hachettebookgroup.com

First Edition: September 2018

Grand Central Publishing is a division of Hachette Book Group, Inc.
The Grand Central Publishing name and logo is a trademark of Hachette Book Group, Inc.

The Hachette Speakers Bureau provides a wide range of authors for speaking events. To find out more, go to www.hachettespeakersbureau.com or call (866) 376-6591.

The publisher is not responsible for websites (or their content) that are not owned by the publisher.

Library of Congress Control Number: 2018939702

ISBNs: 978-1-5387-5979-0 (trade paperback edition); 978-1-5387-5978-3 (ebook edition)

Printed in the United States of America

LSC-C

10 9 8 7 6 5 4 3 2 1

To Gitte and Kristina
—because you're there

THE MIDNIGHT WITNESS

1

The cell phone buzzed from the windowsill. She'd set it on silent mode, making the stubborn vibration the only sign that someone wanted to get in touch with her.

Louise Rick opened her eyes. The foam in the bathtub had disappeared, and the water was now closer to cold than lukewarm.

Nine thirty a.m. The bright March sun filled the courtyard. Her thoughts were in another world, one she didn't want to leave.

For a moment, she thought about emptying the tub, filling it up again with hot water and lots of fragrant bath foam, and sinking back in. But her daydreaming had been interrupted, and she'd never find her way back. Even if she did, it wouldn't be the same.

Her funny bone rammed into the faucet when she stood up, and instinctively she pulled her elbow into her ribs.

She checked the time. Five hours earlier, she'd crawled into bed, and in just over two hours, she and the rest of her team would gather in the Department A conference room at Police Headquarters. She'd give anything to get out of the briefing. She sent a small prayer skyward that her plea would reach Homicide and Suhr would postpone it until later in the day.

Louise grabbed the dark blue terry cloth towel before stepping out of the tub, then wrapped it around her hair and reached for her bathrobe behind the door. Her body ached and her eyes stung, and she was so exhausted that she felt she could stretch out and fall asleep right there on the floor, no problem. Yet she couldn't keep from thinking about last night's conversation.

Her sorrow was still lodged in her gut. Not a personal sorrow, but the type that crops up when you see other people's lives torn apart. When you find yourself in the middle of disaster and death instead of just reading about it.

Out in the kitchen, she put water on for tea and reached for a large caffe latte glass in the cupboard. She'd begun drinking tea in glasses, which held more than mugs but less than a pot. Perfect for her.

She stared through the window into the courtyard, her mind emptying. Which was how she felt, too. She'd snap out of it, though; like so many times before when in this mood, she thought back to the day she'd been called out to Østerbro, one of Copenhagen's posh districts.

Two men in their late twenties had been assaulted on the street. One of them, Morten Seiersted-Wichman, was brutally hurled through the plate glass window of a clothing store after being knocked down and kicked in the head six or seven times.

The forensic pathologist said that Morten had been unconscious when the glass severed his carotid artery.

The other victim had been Morten's brother-in-law, Henrik Winther. A tall, lanky guy. He was luckier. The police guessed that the assailants had taken their anger out on Morten, and presumably, they'd also been unnerved by the blood streaming out from Morten's neck. Winther escaped with only a broken nose and a bruised rib.

Back then, Louise had been in the Criminal Investigations Department. Morten's death had left its mark on her, though less from the killing itself than from what happened when she informed his wife of the tragedy.

A half hour after the ambulances had left with the two men, Louise rang the doorbell of the apartment where Morten and the young woman lived. When the door opened, Charlotte Winther looked surprised.

"Oh, hi," she said, "I thought you were Morten and Henrik. They forgot the keys…"

Louise couldn't recall the exact words she'd spoken, but Charlotte's expression etched itself in her memory, the way it shifted from joy to confusion and puzzlement—why was a policewoman standing there in front of her?—and finally to total despair.

Before Louise's words sank in, Charlotte nodded several times and said she was terribly sorry to hear what had happened, that it was horrible, but it couldn't be Morten. He'd just stepped out with her brother to pick something up at the 7-Eleven.

She stubbornly maintained that Morten and Henrik couldn't have been assaulted, that there hadn't been enough time. And besides, no one gets attacked in broad daylight in Østerbro. No way that happens, she said, over and over, with desperation in her voice. Louise saw it in her dark eyes, though, when the truth began to settle in.

Louise heard her partner coming up the steps behind her. She wanted to lead Charlotte farther inside, into the living room, where they could sit down. But suddenly she froze, terrified at the sight of the young woman. She literally couldn't move.

Then something in her chest loosened, giving way to a wave of anguish. Her throat tightened; she'd barely been able to breathe.

Louise stood in the kitchen holding her tea glass, with echoes of the wretched taste in her mouth back then after throwing up on the neighbor's doormat. She felt again her humiliation, from the tears streaming down her cheeks and how she reeked of vomit.

Her male colleague had been watching her. He closed the apartment door to block off all view of the hallway. Before she could speak, another wave of nausea rocked her. Yellow bile rose up in her throat, through her mouth. She wiped her lips on her sleeve; she was shaking all over.

What was happening to her? She should be comforting that poor woman, but she couldn't even take care of herself. It felt as if she'd left her body and entered Charlotte Winther. She wanted to open the door and slip in beside the young woman and cry along with her.

But her disgusted colleague led her up a few steps and shook her angrily. "What the fucking hell do you think you're doing?" He kept his voice low enough that Charlotte couldn't hear from the apartment. "If you're sick, go home. If you can't handle this, get back in the car, do your crying there. The last thing we need here is someone who can't be professional."

She'd felt so small. Small and insecure, and still paralyzed when she got to the car. Trembling, as if she were the one who'd been given the horrible news. Later she'd thought some new age type could explain how she'd suddenly taken on Charlotte Winther's emotions—something like an out-of-body experience.

Louise added sugar and milk to her tea, something she did only when she was tired or hungover.

She walked into her bedroom, threw off her robe, and climbed into bed. Just to be safe, she set her alarm. Forty-five minutes. She grabbed the paper she'd laid on her night table when she came home.

Her experience in Østerbro had cost her a week in bed and a session with Jakobsen, Department A's crisis counselor at the National Hospital. She'd also had to deal with the realization that she might not be as hard-core as she'd thought.

Jakobsen explained that there was nothing mysterious about what had happened. It was an emotional breakdown, brought on by the intense feelings connected with this part of her job. He described how she had abandoned her role of messenger and identified emotionally with the receiver, which wasn't at all professional. No one in the department needed to say it; police officers had to distance themselves when working on savage cases involving murder, violence, and child abuse.

There was both good and bad in what had happened, Jakobsen said; of course, you must maintain your professionalism in stressful situations, but it's healthy to be able to sense what another person is going through.

It took a year before Louise stopped worrying about literally bursting into tears when notifying family members of a death, but her anxiety about badly handling those situations never disappeared.

Louise put down the newspaper; the letters and words were a jumble to her. The moment the paper slid onto the floor, her phone began buzzing again out in the bathroom. She felt like ignoring it, but after a few moments she swung her legs out of bed. It might be Suhr. He might have heard her prayer and delayed the briefing.

"Louise Rick."

"Have you seen the papers?"

Camilla sounded upset.

Louise thought about saying she was on her way out the door, but Camilla had been her best friend since second grade. She couldn't just brush her off.

While in journalism school, Camilla Lind had declared her

intention to be the first female journalist to win at least two Cavling Prizes. She'd dreamed about becoming a famous war correspondent, had seen herself as a counterpart to Åsne Seierstad, the Norwegian journalist who as a young, blond-haired woman had reported from the front lines in Afghanistan and Baghdad. But something always seemed to sidetrack Camilla, and she had yet to reach any of the world's hot spots. On the other hand, several editors and many readers appreciated her human-interest stories, and she might have gained recognition for that if she hadn't switched horses in midstream and decided to cover crime. In a straight and serious manner, as she put it.

"What are you doing?" Camilla asked, reproach in her voice. "I've been calling Police Headquarters every five minutes, your cell phone, too."

"The paper's right here, but I haven't read it. And I didn't answer because I was in the tub when you called. I guessed it was you anyway."

"Lounging around in the bathtub never stopped you from talking with me before," Camilla shot back.

"I've been sitting all night with a father and mother in crisis," Louise said.

"Karoline Wissinge? I heard about that on the morning news."

"It's almost unbearable. She was twenty-three, and last year her little brother died in a traffic accident. Four young guys drove into a tree out on Amager Landevej. But you know that; you wrote about it," Louise added. Sometimes she forgot that Camilla had left *Roskilde Dagblad*, a small paper, for the crime desk at *Morgenavisen*.

"I remember. Was that her little brother?" Camilla sounded interested. "My God, parents should never have to go through something like this."

Louise could hear her friend was shaken up. She'd also had to pull herself together when the parents told her they'd lost their son only a year ago. The mother had wept softly as the father spoke about the accident. The news had come the same way, completely out of the blue.

Sunday afternoon, someone walking a dog had found the body of a young woman in Østre Anlæg, a hilly Copenhagen park. The rain had been pouring down all day long, and the park was nearly deserted, which is why the man had let the dog run around unleashed. At first, he thought nothing of it when the dog began barking loudly, but when it ignored his calls, he went over to see what was wrong. He spotted the body in the bushes behind one of the park benches. It looked as if someone had tried to hide her, though the leafless bushes were barely dense enough to shield her from the sight of people strolling by. But those in the park braving the weather had presumably focused on the gravel path to avoid the worst puddles, so it wasn't strange she hadn't been seen earlier.

"What actually happened?" Camilla asked.

"She was strangled."

"Raped?"

"Stop asking! You know I can't talk to you about it."

"So, one of the four was her brother?" Camilla said, referring to the accident.

"Yeah, Mikkel Wissinge. He wasn't the driver; he was only seventeen."

Louise could almost hear Camilla trying to conjure up the images of the four boys.

"I think I remember him," Camilla said. "Blond hair, very good-looking kid from the photo we had of him."

"That sounds right. He was in the back seat. He died from his injuries the next day."

"It's a good story. You think anyone has a line on it?"

"No, and no one will if I have anything to say about it," Louise snapped. She swore to herself for even mentioning the connection. "When am I going to learn to keep my big mouth shut? I keep forgetting you're one of them. Promise me you'll leave this one alone, really. The parents can't take any more. Karoline was living with her boyfriend, and he's in shock. They have more than enough on their plate right now; they can't deal with their son's death again."

Camilla grunted something.

Louise could hear herself pleading. Too much so for her taste. Hopefully her friend would do what she asked of her; she didn't want to get into journalism ethics. Yet she knew that if Camilla didn't write the story, someone else would.

That didn't stop her from getting mad, though, when working on a case Camilla was covering. Louise felt that journalists turned her work into entertainment, that they showcased victims' families during their sorrow. It annoyed her to no end, and seeing Camilla's name on such an article's byline provoked her even more. It happened often, too. At the same time, having a reliable contact in the press was to Louise's advantage. It worked both ways, of course.

She glanced at the clock; time to get going. "What was it you wanted me to see in the paper?"

"Remember Frank Sørensen, from back when I started at the *Roskilde Dagblad*? Curly hair, wrote a lot about the bikers taking over the town back then. He left a few months after I got there, got a job as a crime reporter here in town."

"What about him?" In her mind, Louise saw a face that had seen better days. A boyish smile, though. Strong lines around his mouth, deep crow's-feet shooting out from his eyes, a large mane of dark curls. She'd met him one day when she picked Camilla up at the paper in Roskilde. He and several others had gone with them to a bar, Bryggerhesten, and drank beer until they closed.

"He's dead," Camilla said. "He was found in the bike shed of the parking lot behind the SAS hotel by Vesterport Station."

"The Royal Hotel?"

"Yeah, in the courtyard behind Hertz. The paper mentions it, but without his name. They told me when I came in this morning. It's so strange."

A few moments went by; Louise sensed her friend was close to tears, and she felt a bit rattled, too. Even though she hadn't known Frank Sørensen well, it was always sad when someone you knew suddenly died. It was totally different from a death in connection with her work. She could deal with that, despite being moved by the sorrow of those left behind.

"How did it happen?" She spoke a bit matter-of-factly to keep Camilla from crying.

"Actually, I don't know yet. That's why I've been calling you. To ask if you knew something."

"If it's not a homicide, I wouldn't hear anything about it." Louise was out of bed now, rummaging around in her closet for a pair of jeans and a sweater. "Who found him?"

Mentally she was already on her way to the briefing. She decided to take the bus to Central Station and walk down to Police Headquarters. She didn't feel like biking.

"One of the hotel's waiters going to work, parking his bike. Or so I heard. Terkel drove by on his way here. You know, Terkel Høyer, our managing editor. Part of the courtyard is blocked off; your people are there. They wouldn't do that if he'd just keeled over, would they?" Camilla said she'd called the dispatcher at Station City, who would only confirm that a dead man had been found at that address.

"Take it easy," Louise said. "You know very well it doesn't necessarily mean a crime has been committed, just because the officer confirms a death."

Of course, the techs had been sent in, she thought, but there could be many reasons for that. She tried to sound chipper.

"Listen, Ms. Crime Beat Reporter! There's always a report to be filled out when someone dies on the street. You know that. Look, I've got to get going."

"I don't understand it," Camilla said, ignoring Louise. "A man in his mid-forties doesn't just fall down and die. At least not very often. Would you do me a big favor and ask around? Discreetly, of course. I promise not to do a thing without your permission. I'd just like to know what the hell happened."

"Okay. Privately, for you, and don't open your big mouth about it at the paper. I really don't know how much I can find out." Louise glanced at her watch. The briefing would start in less than a half hour, and she had to pick up some of her papers. "Camilla, gotta run. I have to grab a taxi to get to work on time. But I'll ask around. Okay, bye."

2

Camilla sensed someone watching her when she hung up. In the second it took to whirl around in her chair, she flashed through what she'd told Louise, what the person behind her might have heard.

"Hi, Terkel, I didn't know you were standing there." She tried to keep her voice light.

"Did she know anything?" he asked, not even trying to hide his eavesdropping.

She almost flared up at him, but then she noticed how gray and hollowed-out he looked. Suddenly she feared he was going to start sobbing.

"No," she said. "But she promised to see what she could find out. I just don't know when; they're working twenty-four seven on the case with the young girl found yesterday."

Høyer obviously wasn't listening. He walked over to her desk and slumped down in the chair, as if someone had pulled the plug on him.

Camilla went out for two cups of coffee. How should she tackle her boss falling apart in her office? She didn't really know him all that well.

She set the coffee down in front of him. "You use cream, sugar?"

He shook his head.

She sat down and looked at him expectantly, but he simply stared at the photos on her desk. "How old is he?" he said, pointing at the photo of Markus.

"He'll be six this summer."

He seemed lost in thought while gazing at her son. Finally, he said, "Frank's the one who called and told me about you when he heard Laugesen was quitting. He said it was obvious from day one at *Roskilde* that you'd make a name for yourself."

Camilla didn't know what to say.

"How long did you two actually work together?" he said.

"A few months."

"What did you think of him?"

"I wasn't around him much. He focused on the biker stories. One time he asked me if I'd go with him to talk to an ex-biker who'd gone underground. The guy agreed to tell his story if we kept his name out of it."

"He always got so involved in whatever he was covering," her managing editor said. He straightened his glasses. "One time the police offered him an anonymous address, but he wouldn't take it. If someone had a bone to pick with him, they were welcome to stop by."

"It seemed to me he was always working," Camilla said. "Did he even have a life?"

"He got married three years ago. Helle was the first girlfriend he had that I know of, and I've known him since journalism school. Liam was born two years ago."

He reached for his coffee and then slumped back again. "We were going to get together this evening, but when I called to hear when, Helle answered. She was crying. Yesterday morning two police officers came by and told her Frank was dead. He'd been found early Sunday morning."

Camilla nodded and noticed a cuticle she was scratching had begun bleeding. She dabbed some spit on her index finger and wiped off the blood. "That's damn strange, too. Louise says she'll call when she's had time to ask around. But surely they told his wife something?"

"Not much. She went in yesterday evening to identify him, but that's just a formality. He had his driver's license and press card on him; they had his name and photo."

"Hmmm."

Høyer stood up to leave. Before he reached the door, she promised to let him know as soon as she heard from Louise.

"I'll keep checking with the dispatcher, too," she said. "And with Department A."

He turned at the doorway. His expression had changed. "We also need to find out about that girl they found in Østre Anlæg yesterday evening. Did your friend know anything about that?"

So much for Mr. Sensitive, she thought. "No, not really. But the officer said the Homicide chief is sending out a press release this afternoon."

After he left, she had the feeling he'd been standing in the doorway long enough to hear her talking to Louise about the girl's brother.

Louise Rick handed her debit card to the taxi driver and waited for a receipt to sign. The briefing started in ten minutes, and she still had to pick up her files.

After signing the receipt, she crumpled it up and threw it in her bag along with her billfold. Then she jumped out of the taxi, hurried over to the broad entryway, and took the steps two at a time. She was winded by the time she tossed her bag and coat on the chair in her office.

The files were on her desk. She forced herself to slow down; she didn't want to show up at the conference room down the hallway all out of breath and stressed out. No one was going to get on her case for galloping in at the last second. Everybody had been hard at it since being called in yesterday, after the girl's body was found.

Louise ducked into the kitchen for a cup of coffee before sitting down at the oval table. She still felt cold.

"Hi, Louise, how'd it go with the parents?" Henny Heilmann sat with her papers neatly piled in front of her, a bottle of water beside her.

"It went fine, but it got late. It hasn't soaked in for them yet. They were with their daughter and her boyfriend Saturday afternoon, and a day later she's dead. I'm driving over again when I'm finished with the report, so they can sign it."

Heilmann nodded. Normally people associated with a case were questioned at Police Headquarters, but when the immediate family was involved, it wasn't uncommon to go to them.

Louise smiled. She'd quickly realized that her boss's stony, insensitive front had nothing to do with her. She liked Heilmann, who was in her mid-fifties and had been detective chief inspector for several years. The way Louise understood it, she had no ambition of moving up the ladder, because she liked heading up Investigation Team 2. The police chiefs and detectives were very welcome to duke it out at the top.

The briefing started at ten past twelve, even though one officer hadn't shown up yet.

Besides Louise, the members of the team were Thomas Toft,

Michael Stig, and Søren Velin. Velin was Louise's partner, but he'd been sent on leave for two and a half months. Lars Jørgensen, a new man at Homicide, had been filling in; he was the one missing. Together with Forensic Services and the Criminal Investigations Department at Station City, they would be investigating the murder of Karoline Wissinge. The head of Homicide, Hans Suhr, wasn't at the morning briefing, either.

"We're starting one short," Heilmann said, explaining that Willumsen had nabbed Jørgensen for a few days to work on a new homicide. No one said anything, but they were all annoyed. Detective Superintendent Willumsen headed up an investigation team when a vacation or leave of absence required it. And he always got what he wanted. When he needed an extra body, he took it, and when anyone else was lacking an investigator, he never gave one up. But no one called him on it.

"All right, let's go through what we have," Heilmann said. She grabbed the top sheet of paper from the pile in front of her. "At four ten p.m. on Sunday, a dog walker discovered the body of a twenty-three-year-old woman under some bushes in Østre Anlæg. Initially we couldn't identify her. She had no bag, no identification on her. She was taken to Forensic Medicine, and at that time a Martin Dahl reported his twenty-three-year-old girlfriend missing. The woman in the park matched the description he gave. Later, around nine p.m., he showed up and identified her as Karoline Wissinge."

Louise was having trouble concentrating on what her boss was saying. A monotonous clicking sound distracted her; as usual, it came from Michael Stig. He'd tipped his chair against the wall and stuck his feet up against the table. The ballpoint pen was hidden by his arms, which hung between his bent knees.

"At present we know Karoline was in town with two friends Saturday evening," Heilmann continued. "According to them she left the café they were in, a place called Baren, with a man..." She grabbed another sheet of paper. "Lasse Møller, around one. No one saw her after that."

"Michael. Would you please stop!" Louise snapped.

Nonchalantly he tossed the pen on the desk without looking at her.

She relaxed and focused on the case again. She was familiar with the basic facts, but she jotted down the times in her notebook.

Heilmann looked at Michael Stig. "You spoke with Martin Dahl yesterday?"

"Yeah." He took his legs off the desk and scooted his chair forward. "He said he was home alone Saturday night. It's in my report."

Dahl had gone to Karoline's parents after Stig left, and Louise had met him there, but she'd formed almost no impression of him. He'd sat silently on the sofa, lost in his own world, while she was occupied with Karoline's parents.

"Fine." Heilmann checked something off on her list. "CID is helping us knock on doors in the neighborhood; I'm organizing that with them. Wissinge and Dahl lived in the Potato Rows; they had the ground floor of a house on Skovgårdsgade. It runs into Lundsgade, which is the street that leads to the park where she was found. We're looking for witnesses in the area from Silver Square to her home and then over to the park."

Heilmann looked over at Toft. "What did the pathologist have to say?"

Toft thumbed through a pile of yellow documents with the Department A logo in the corner and pulled out a sheet. "Flemming was the one out there last night."

Flemming Larsen was Louise's favorite forensic pathologist. He was professional and easy to get along with.

"He wouldn't give a precise time of death. It was cold Saturday night, the body temperature was screwing up his calculation, but hypostasis was evident where she was lying, and there was full rigor mortis. She'd been dead between twelve and twenty-four hours."

"He's got to pin it down better than that!" Stig said.

Toft laid a hand on his partner's shoulder. "I twisted his arm; finally he said between nine p.m. and seven the next morning."

"And we know she was alive after midnight," Louise said.

Toft nodded and turned back to his papers. "He was sure about his conclusions at the crime scene, though. The marks on her throat were obvious, and her eyes were visibly bloodshot."

"Was she raped?" Louise asked.

"Right now, it doesn't look like it, but of course they'll check that during the autopsy. By the way, Flemming said to tell you hi and thanks again."

Louise smiled; the shift in mood was a bit absurd but welcome.

Last Friday they'd been out bowling with several forensic technicians and pathologists, along with a few CID officers. They'd been talking about going out together since last summer, because though they knew each other superficially, there was never enough time to sit down for a really good talk. Louise didn't feel like she had to socialize with her colleagues, and she didn't want to ruin their professional relationships, but it had been fun. They actually got along together without blood being involved.

Louise told about her night with Karoline's parents. "They're in their mid-fifties, really nice people. They said that Karoline and her boyfriend had been living together for a year. She'd just finished nursing school and had a temporary job on the neurosurgery ward at the National Hospital. They also said they lost their son last year. Karoline's younger brother, Mikkel, died in a traffic accident."

Heilmann nodded. "Of course, it's tough for them to handle another loss, so soon after the first one. Has anyone suggested they talk with a crisis counselor, with Jakobsen? It might be good for them." She made a note of that. "I want you to stick with the parents, and we'll have to bring the boyfriend in for questioning. Can you take care of him, too?"

Before Louise could answer, Heilmann said, "I can try to find a partner for you until Søren comes back, if you want."

Louise shook her head. "That's okay, I can deal with the parents and the boyfriend myself."

"Great. Toft, Stig, I want you to focus on Lasse Møller, the guy who left Baren with Karoline, and her friends she was with that night."

The briefing broke up, but Louise stayed in her chair.

Heilmann gathered her papers until Toft and Stig left, then she asked what was wrong.

"What happened behind the Royal Hotel?"

"The dead man, you mean. They thought it was natural causes, but they found out it was a homicide at the autopsy this morning. Someone stuck a small knife blade under his skull."

"I knew Frank Sørensen. He was a crime reporter."

Heilmann nodded.

"How in hell didn't they see it was a homicide?" Louise said.

"Initially there was nothing to see. He had stumblebum trauma and he stank of alcohol. Which is why they didn't call us in at first."

Louise sighed. Stumblebum trauma. The label given to heavy drinkers who fell.

"He had scrapes and scratches here and there, bruises from falling, a cut on the back of his head," Heilmann said. "The doctor they called in concluded he was an alcoholic who had too much to drink, and he put that down as cause of death. He assumed that Frank Sørensen had staggered around and maybe knocked into a few of the posts holding up the bike shed."

"So, the doctor didn't call us in?" Louise was incredulous.

"No, he just sent the body to be autopsied. That's what they do in deaths like that."

Louise's hackles rose. What the hell did that doctor think he was doing? Just because a man looked a bit scruffy and stank of booze didn't necessarily mean he'd drunk himself to death.

Heilmann broke into her thoughts. "There's a team of techs over there now, going over the area. But it's been twenty-four hours since he was found; there's probably not a lot left."

They sat quietly for a few moments. "It looked like a heart attack," she said. "He was lying there with a bike key in his hand. The key fit the bike he fell over."

Louise knew she was filling her in on how Frank was found, not making excuses for the doctor. She shivered and felt the cold creep under her skin.

"His wife immediately claimed he'd been killed; she refused to accept that alcohol caused his death."

She could already imagine Camilla's reaction. She felt sorry for her, but she probably should call Willumsen; it was his case. She needed to find out if it was okay to tell her friend about this murder.

Louise rounded up her things and returned to her office. She wanted to try to catch Peter before writing her report about the parents last night. They hadn't seen much of each other lately. Not that that was so unusual. They'd been a couple for five years, but only within the past two years had they talked about living together so they could at least sleep in the same bed. So far it had all been talk.

She pulled her phone out of her bag. It was still on silent mode, and she switched it back to ring before texting Peter to call her when he had time.

She turned on her computer, but before she typed in the password, her phone rang.

"Louise Rick."

"Hi, hon, good to hear you're still alive. How are you?"

The sound of Peter's dark voice warmed her. She missed him. Peter was the European product manager for a large pharmaceutical company, and there were periods he was out of the country half the time. Sometimes even more than half.

"I didn't make it home until early this morning." She filled him in on Karoline Wissinge and her conversation with the parents. "Did you get anything done?"

He laughed for a second. "That would be an exaggeration. I had the pleasure of Thora's company last evening. You remember her, the Finn we had dinner with? She insisted I take her to a buffet with all her Finnish friends."

In her mind Louise saw the stout lady with the infectious sense of humor. "Is it Wednesday you're coming back?"

"Yeah. I'll be home late in the afternoon. You want me to shop for dinner?"

"I don't know how things are looking here. The investigation's just started; there's going to be quite a bit of overtime until we find the killer."

She sensed that she needed to talk about it. "There's another homicide. One of Camilla's former colleagues was killed. I haven't told her he was murdered yet."

Pause. "We can invite Camilla and Markus over on Wednesday," he said. "I'll fix dinner, and if you don't make it home, I'll save some for you."

"Great idea. Her mother is coming to town that day, but she's taking some New Agey course with her spiritual friends, so I don't think that'll be a problem."

Peter had never tried to come between Louise and Camilla, and he was wild about Markus. Camilla and the father, Tobias, had split up several years ago, and now the boy was with him every other weekend. Camilla's mother lived by herself in Skanderborg, and Camilla's father wasn't someone she could just call when she needed help with picking Markus up at day care, so Peter had stepped in to help several times.

"I'd better call her," Louise said.

"Tell her hi. I'll call you later tonight."

She sat for a moment holding the phone after Peter hung up.

Louise punched in Willumsen's number while the computer started up.

"Detective Willumsen." As usual, he sounded gruff.

"Hi, Willumsen, it's Rick."

"I'm busy," he said. Make it short, in other words.

It had taken Louise a long time to figure out how to speak with Willumsen. Her tone had to be a mixture of jaunty and tough. She couldn't sound too vague or hesitant, either, and not at all girly-small-talk-ish. Otherwise he wouldn't give her the time of day.

"I understand you have the Frank Sørensen case," she said.

"That's correct."

"When are you going public with the fact he was murdered?"

"It's no secret, not really. We informed the family. First, we had to find out it was a homicide, you know," he added, his voice about as close to jolly as it ever came.

Louise sensed his good mood. Sometimes he was unapproachable, while on days like today he was friendly enough, but you never knew which man would show up. And he could change at the drop of a hat.

"Camilla Lind from *Morgenavisen* asked about the case, but I didn't know then it was a homicide. What can I tell her?"

"Not a goddamn thing," he thundered. "She's been calling me every five minutes, the duty officer, too. She's a pain in the ass."

Louise held her breath and waited. A few moments, after calming down, he said, "Is it that Camilla? The one with the blond-haired kid?"

He'd met Camilla and Markus one day. Louise had taken them over to the police garage so the boy could sit on a police motorcycle. Willumsen had run into them on the way. It had been one of his good days, and he'd stopped to say hello. Louise was nearly shocked when he patted the boy's head and suggested she take him for a spin in one of the police cars.

"Tell her someone stuck a shiv in the victim's neck, a long knife that severed his spinal cord. But they were kind enough to more or less put him under before."

Louise bit the inside of her cheek as she took in what he'd said. Death occurs quickly when the spinal cord is cut, she recalled. "Okay."

She told him Camilla had worked with Frank Sørensen in Roskilde, which explained her interest in the case.

"That's fine. We might need to speak with her. Bye." Willumsen hung up before Louise could thank him.

She needed to start her report, otherwise she wouldn't have time to get it signed by Karoline's parents and bring the girl's boyfriend in for questioning. Yet she picked up the phone and punched in Camilla's number.

"*Morgenavisen*, Camilla Lind."

"Hi," Louise said.

"Something's wrong. I've had the pleasure of talking to old grouch Willumsen all day; he's always a bastard on the phone. What's going on?"

"Frank was killed, that's what's wrong. They're going to announce it at a press briefing this afternoon."

"I knew it," Camilla cried. "I could damn well figure out he didn't just fall, with the barrier tape and all the techs running around."

"They did think it was accidental death at first, but the autopsy showed a knife wound in his neck that severed his spinal cord. If it's any consolation, it looks like he'd been anesthetized first."

"Jesus, that's gruesome. Who the hell would want to kill him?"

"You can ask the same question about Karoline Wissinge," Louise said, with an edge of sarcasm.

"How's that case going? I'm supposed to cover it, but there's almost nothing about it yet. Did you say you were with her parents all night?"

"Yes."

"You have any idea who killed her?"

"Not really. Not yet."

Louise smiled inwardly at Camilla's optimistic questions while thinking about all the hours of work ahead of her. Suddenly she felt it. All morning she'd been worried it wouldn't show up.

The rush.

The energy came like a wave, a familiar feeling that usually came on at a crime scene. It was like an injection, adrenaline shooting up her body and into her chest, ending with her scalp prickling. She was ready. It happened every time; she doubted she could handle a case, her anxiety would be simmering just below the surface, when all of a sudden, she'd feel the rush. Peter liked to say it transformed her from Louise to Detective Rick, Homicide, Copenhagen Police.

3

Camilla hesitated before knocking on Terkel Høyer's door. Usually it was open; the only time he closed it was when he absolutely did not want to be disturbed.

"Come in," he called out.

Camilla waited at the doorway until he waved her in. She sat down in the chair facing him. "I just spoke with Louise Rick." She took a deep breath and went on. "Frank Sørensen was murdered."

"Oh God." He stiffened. "I had my suspicions."

He ruffled his long hair until it stood straight up. Camilla watched him struggle to think rationally, hold off his emotions. "We have to find out what happened; we're going all out on this one. What did you learn?" He eyed her expectantly.

"The way I understand it, he was anesthetized before someone stuck a knife in his neck." She paused for a moment. "And cut his spinal cord."

She knew how gruesome that sounded. This was the type of

story they discussed at their morning meetings, but now the words felt strange.

"It doesn't surprise me one bit they'd have to anesthetize him first," Terkel said.

"They?"

"Yes, or him, or whoever the hell did it. Was Frank aware of what was happening?"

Camilla knew he was trying to form a picture of the events. She could almost feel it, how he wanted her to say that Frank had been unconscious when the killer finished his work.

"I don't know, really I don't. There's a press conference this afternoon. I'll attend if you want me to."

"No, I want you to cover the girl in the park. I'll go in with Søren Holm."

"Isn't he more than busy with that drug case?"

"He is. Last night the police raided an apartment in Østerbro and found almost a kilo of heroin. But if I know Søren, he'll bite my head off if I don't let him cover this case. He and Frank knew each other for years, they worked on the same kind of stories. That can be an advantage; Søren might know something useful to us."

He's sidelining me, Camilla thought.

"There's plenty of work for everyone," he said, "because Søren is sticking with the drug case, too. Someone tipped him off about another police raid on Wednesday, and he's trying to get the green light to go along. Otherwise he'll show up immediately after."

Camilla nodded. Holm had been with the paper for seventeen years. She guessed he was in his mid-forties, Frank's age. He had a nice wife and two teenage daughters; somehow that didn't fit with him knowing the Copenhagen underworld as well as the most experienced narcotics officer, but he'd always kept his work and private life separate. That's why he was still married, he claimed.

Among other things, Camilla respected him for that. When he

was off work, no one even thought about calling him in. Those who had tried understood why. But when he worked he went all out, even when the hours were long.

She stood at the door, antsy to get going, but her managing editor ignored her eagerness. "Kvist is coming in later. He'll be doing all the calling; Jakob is gone this week."

Jakob was the intern responsible for calling around to the country's major police stations for their activity reports. So, Ole Kvist was filling in for him. That suited Camilla just fine; she hated calling duty officers, going through the daily reports of various police experts, even though she'd found out it was a good way to dig up news.

"Maybe we should gather the troops in the conference room when we get back from Police Headquarters," he said.

"Fine with me." Camilla smiled a bit stiffly, then she walked out and closed the door behind her.

What the hell happened! she thought as she marched back to her office, her high heels clattering in the hallway. I'm out of the loop!

She stood in front of her window. Apparently, the story was so important that they had to send Holm in to make sure everything was done properly. Who the hell did he think he was! She sat down and stuck her legs up on her desk. He doesn't think I can handle it. Thoughts buzzed around in her head like angry bees knocked out of their hive. She realized she was getting all worked up.

"What time is the press briefing?"

Camilla jumped when Høyer slammed the door behind him. "Three o'clock," she said.

"This is the first time I can remember that a Danish journalist has been killed, at least this way. There could be a connection between the murder and his work; that's obvious. Maybe some psychopath just randomly chose Frank, of course, but I wouldn't be one damn bit surprised if it was someone shutting him up."

"Yeah, and they can't count on getting away with it; it's too obvious," Camilla said. Surely the police see it that way, too, she thought.

"Talk to Holm. He'll know who might do a thing like this. Maybe Frank mentioned something." Her boss turned and walked back to his office.

Camilla felt bewildered. Hadn't she just been told to keep out of this? She shook her head and grabbed her notebook on the way out the door. She walked past the intern's office and stopped outside the crime staff's first office. The door was open a crack. Holm was on the phone, but he waved her on in when he spotted her.

"Hi," she mouthed.

"Hi," he mouthed back.

Camilla sat on the red two-person sofa and studied the crowded bookshelf on the wall opposite her. A cigarette smoldered in an ashtray on the desk, the blue smoke snaking up toward the ceiling.

"Hi, Camilla. So, what the hell's next, now that they're stabbing a person for doing their job!"

His attempt at lightheartedness couldn't hide his despair. He took a deep drag on his cigarette, the glow at the end longer than what was left of the butt.

"Who do you think is behind it?"

"Damned if I know." He crushed the cigarette out. "All I can think of is, he stuck his nose too far into somebody's business, and that somebody is probably involved in the drug case."

"It's insane."

He smiled and nodded. "You're right, but there's a lot at stake for these mobsters; they'll do anything to protect themselves."

"Isn't it too risky to start snooping around right now?"

She knew she sounded motherly, and she grimaced in apology.

"Yeah, it's not a good idea to push things too hard. But if his death is connected with the drug thing, he must have uncovered something. And I fucking want to know what."

"It doesn't necessarily have to do with drugs. It could be the bikers, all the articles he wrote back then. Maybe they've been waiting for revenge until someone else would be suspected."

He studied her as he thought about that. Shrugged his shoulders, knocked another cigarette out of his pack. "Maybe!" He stared up at the ceiling. "It can't be ruled out. But I'll probably know more sometime this evening."

"Watch out for yourself."

"Don't worry, I'm not going out there to track down some murderer, but there are some guys who usually have a good idea what's going on. I'll look them up. The police will have to take care of the rest. That's what they're paid to do."

Louise's office chair sank when she sat down. In her head she ticked off everything she had to do. She'd already printed out the report about last night, and she'd stuck it in a plastic folder. Karoline's parents would have to read and sign it before it could be scanned and filed away. And she needed to get hold of Martin Dahl. The best would be to speak with him at his and Karoline's apartment. It was easier to form an impression of people when she was familiar with their homes.

The phone rang five times before the voice mail message kicked in. "You've reached Martin and Karoline. We're out right now, but leave a message and we'll get back to you. Bye!" The young woman's voice was chirpy and light.

Louise hung up before the beep. Karoline's happy voice rang in her ears. Maybe she could drive by on the way to the girl's parents.

She put on her coat and was on her way down the hallway when she heard her office phone ring. Shit! After hesitating a moment, she ran back. "Department A, Louise Rick."

"I am so goddamn stoked. I'm going out to talk to Frank Sørensen's wife," Camilla said, her voice shrill with excitement.

"And?"

"It's really incredible. She won't talk to anyone from her husband's own paper, but she wants to talk to me."

Louise realized it would take a while for her friend to calm down. It was a big thing for competing journalists, a big victory; that much Louise knew. It was exactly this type of situation when she doubted Camilla's noble intentions: Her friend insisted she wasn't prying. She was giving someone the chance to speak out! What the hell was the difference? She wasn't one bit better than the others when she saw an opportunity. Louise suspected her friend was intent on becoming the most hard-core of all crime reporters—the woman who could get her foot in the door anywhere.

"You're making too much of this. Get a life!"

"This is a life, damn it. I'm making a difference when a woman who just lost her husband would rather talk to me than anyone else." Camilla sounded as if she'd been slapped.

And, of course, in the end, Louise had to agree with her. "You're right, congratulations. It'll be great to read what you write about it. I've got to run. Talk to you later."

Strange, she thought. She talked ten times as much to Camilla as to Peter. There was something about a female friend, one you could share your happiness and here-and-now frustrations with. She'd never dream of calling Peter up to tell him she'd snapped at Michael Stig again.

She shook her head at herself. Three thirty, time to hit the road.

Louise ran down the steps and jogged through the courtyard, determined not to be waylaid if she met someone. When she had that look on her face, very few people dared approach her.

She found Svendsen in the garage. "I need a car. I won't be back until sometime this evening."

Svendsen reigned over the fleet of police cars. Heilmann had already reserved two unmarked cars for the team, but when Louise went to get the keys for one of them, they were already gone.

Svendsen made sure the cars were filled up and running well—no one at Police Headquarters had to worry about that—but it wasn't always easy to squeeze a car out of him without a reservation.

Come on, come on, Louise thought. She crossed her fingers in her pockets; she didn't want to have to argue.

"Here, take this one," he said, handing her the key to a white Focus.

"Hey, thanks!" She was surprised, and she gave him a big smile as she got into the car.

Before starting the car, she plugged her earbuds into her phone.

She drove past Central Station and up to Palads, the nearby movie theater. She thought about getting a hot dog at Nørreport Station, but she knew parking spaces were hard to come by. Instead she continued down Øster Farimagsgade; she could stop along there for a bite to eat before checking if Karoline's boyfriend was home on Skovgårdsgade. She parked and crossed the street to a produce market, where she bought four bananas and a large bag of raisins. On the way back to the car she ducked into a kiosk for a Diet Coke.

She adjusted the seat back for more room to eat. After two bananas and a few handfuls of raisins, she wiped her fingers off and pulled her phone out of her pocket. She found Martin and Karoline's phone number in her bag and called, only to get voice mail again.

The curtains were closed on the ground floor. She rang the doorbell and heard its shrill clang, then pressed the button again and held it in for five seconds. After waiting a few minutes, she gave up.

Karoline's parents lived farther out in Østerbro. Three cars were parked outside the large house—the media, maybe? Louise checked before pulling in behind the rear car. No one was sitting in the cars or standing outside; the cars belonged to family or friends, she decided. There to support the parents.

The door opened before she reached the porch. Karoline's mother, Lise Wissinge, must have seen her walking up the sidewalk. Louise shook her hand.

"Please come inside. And thank you for your help last night; it was so very kind of you to sacrifice a night's sleep for us."

Her red eyes were dull, heavy. She was clenching a white handkerchief.

"You're very welcome. I'm glad we had the opportunity to talk."

"My sister is here, also Karoline's grandparents, but please come inside."

She led Louise out to the spacious kitchen. Last night they had sat in the living room, and Louise had sensed they were a very conservative, very respectable family, perhaps a bit strict and old-fashioned. But that impression didn't fit the mood in the cozy kitchen. Karoline's father, Hans, wore jeans and a dark turtleneck sweater, while Lise, as Louise only now noticed, was dressed very casually. She realized the stiffness and formality the previous night had been a shield protecting them from reality, a buffer to help distance themselves from what had happened. That distance was gone now.

Pots of coffee and a large teapot stood in the middle of the table. Candles were lit all over the room; a peace hung in the air, the type that comes only when the crying is over. A younger version of Lise, her sister no doubt, sat on a bench with the grandparents, looking through a large photo album. Karoline's father commented when they turned a page. At the end of the table sat Martin, Karoline's boyfriend. He nodded politely when Louise walked in.

"Hi."

"Hi, Martin."

Louise shook his hand. She hadn't paid much attention to him the night before. He was taller and much more a man than she'd thought.

She fished the report up out of her bag and asked the parents to read it. Then she walked over and sat down beside Martin.

"I was wondering if we could have a talk," she said. She nodded when Lise offered her a cup of coffee. Martin stiffened. Louise hoped he wouldn't make a big deal out of this. It would be awkward if she had to force him to come in for questioning; this relatively relaxed atmosphere would vanish the second the parents realized something unpleasant about Karoline's boyfriend might come out. Something they really didn't want to know.

Louise wasn't listening to the conversation around the table. She heard only fragments of stories about Karoline and her little brother when they were small, about family vacations and Christmas evenings, because she was focused on Martin. She wanted to know more about him before they reached the point where he might be added to the list of suspects—a thought that clearly hadn't occurred to Hans and Lise. Louise sat back in her chair and sighed.

"Would it be okay with you if we went into Police Headquarters now?" she asked, leaning toward him.

"Are you going to question me?"

"We have to talk to you." She stood up, hoping he would follow.

"He's already spoken with someone," Karoline's mother said.

"We just need to know a bit more," Louise said, trying to make it sound like a mere formality.

Hans sat hunched over the papers Louise had brought along. He'd been nodding occasionally as he read, and now that he was finished, he signed on the dotted line. An elegant signature, Louise noted. He walked over to Karoline's boyfriend and laid a hand on his shoulder. "Lucky for you it's Louise Rick taking care of this. Go along with her before they send someone else."

He gestured for Martin to stand up, and they walked out to the hallway. Lise was reading the report, but she stopped and looked up. "All he has is his mother, and she lives over in Frederikshavn. So, we've suggested he stay with us as long as he wants." She caught Louise's eye to make sure she understood: It was important to them to take care of Martin.

"Of course," Louise said.

Lise skimmed the rest of the report and signed her name beside her husband's. Then she followed them out and stood in the doorway as they walked to the car.

4

Is this something I need a lawyer for?" Martin asked on the way to Police Headquarters.

"Oh no, you haven't been charged, it's really not necessary. I just need to talk to you about Karoline and go through what happened Saturday night."

She smiled at him. "It's completely unofficial for the time being."

He turned in his seat and faced her. "For the time being? What do you mean?"

"Nothing, I was just trying to be funny."

He annoyed her. He was twenty-seven, and she didn't think it should surprise him that he would play an important role in this investigation.

She parked on Otto Mønsteds Gade. Their footsteps rang out on the stairway. Martin trudged along several steps below her, falling farther behind all the time. She decided to keep things light; hopefully he would loosen up a bit.

"Would you like some coffee, or something cold?" she asked after they hung their coats up. He looked uncomfortable as he glanced around the office.

"Water's fine. We've been drinking coffee all day."

He stooped a bit as he walked over to the chair at the end of the desk. Louise headed for the kitchen and closed the door behind her. Sitting alone and thinking about what to tell her would do him good.

The lunchroom was empty. She poured water into a pitcher and grabbed a cup of coffee. On the way back, she stopped out in the hall and listened for voices. Silence. She walked over to Toft and Stig's office. In the car on the way there, she'd thought it might be smart to look up Stig, since he'd been the first one to talk to Martin Dahl. The door to their office was closed. She laid the pitcher and coffee down on the floor, knocked, and checked the door. Locked—damn!

Back in her office, she set the pitcher and a glass in front of him. "Here you are." She sat down at her computer.

"Can you tell me a little bit about yourself and Karoline?"

At first it looked like he was going to argue, but then he leaned back in his chair, crossed his arms, and tilted his head an inch or two. "Sure, what do you want to know?"

Louise took a deep breath. There was an arrogance about him, along with a resistance she couldn't figure out. Was it that he didn't want to talk about what happened, or did he just not like cops? She might as well get right to the point. She straightened up in her chair.

"I want to know everything about you and your girlfriend. She was a sweet, sensible young woman, yet she was found murdered in a park less than twenty-four hours ago, and to put it bluntly, you don't have an alibi for the time of her murder. And that, my friend, isn't all that great for you."

Louise sighed heavily and sank back in her chair. Now it was out in the open, and the effect on Martin was obvious: He was white as a sheet.

He stared at her. "I knew it," he whispered.

She raised an eyebrow. "You knew what?"

"I knew I'd get the blame."

That riled her up even more. She rolled her chair over to him, not stopping until they were six inches apart. "We're not talking about blame here. Someone is going down for this murder, and you risk being that person if you keep behaving like this is a matter of some stolen scooter."

He straightened up as her words began to sink in. "I'm sorry, I really want to help. But no matter what you find out, I didn't kill Karoline. I loved her, I dreamed of starting a family with her. The plan was that I'd work less at the shop, and eventually we'd—"

"How did you meet each other?"

"In town four years ago; she'd just turned nineteen. I had a small apartment, and she was still living at home. I have a clothing shop on Nørrebrogade; I'd just opened up back then. At first it wasn't anything serious. She helped a little at the shop on Saturdays, she had the weekends off. She was in nursing school."

Louise began taking notes. The sound of her keyboard trailed his words.

"After six months I knew I wanted her to be the mother of my children. We were always together, either at my place or out at her parents'."

"Did you ever take any breaks in the relationship? She was very young; it wouldn't have been at all strange."

"Once." He bit his lip. "She broke up with me because I got mixed up in something really stupid."

Louise sat stone-faced and silent. If she waited long enough, he would come out with it.

"It wasn't actually me, it was one of my friends. I helped him out, and Karoline lit into me for getting involved even that much."

Louise kept waiting.

Martin slumped a bit and held his palms up in resignation. "He was an old friend from Frederikshavn. He was dealing a bit out on Østerbro, mostly ecstasy I think, but once in a while he forgot to pay for what he was selling. Things got really hot about a year ago, right after Karoline and I moved in together, so I loaned him the money he owed. That was it."

He looked as if he expected Louise to demand more details.

"Do you take drugs like ecstasy?"

"I did, but that was a long time ago. Karoline wouldn't put up with anything that had to do with drugs. That's why she got so mad at me for even thinking about helping him."

"How much did you loan him?"

"Fifty thousand."

"Did he pay you back?"

He smiled and nodded. "Two months later. I didn't even need to twist his arm. He's okay. We were in school together from first grade, and I've tried to talk some sense into him, but it doesn't really seem to sink in."

Louise thought about her friendship with Camilla. She would have loaned her fifty thousand, too, if she'd really needed it. She knew from experience that ending a friendship wasn't easy, when a friend began running around with the wrong crowd, doing things she considered to be wrong. She cleared her throat and looked at Martin. "Did anything like that happen again?"

He hesitated just long enough for her to notice. "No, just that once."

An hour and a half later, Louise felt she had a good picture of Karoline and her relationship with Martin. She knew about their habits, and she'd dug things out of him, like how he partied more than her, how it was hard for him to let go of his bachelor life; he'd still gone into town with the guys sometimes when Karoline had a morning shift the next day and went to bed early.

Martin had been out with two friends Friday night. One of them sold clothes, the other was the Frederikshavn friend. They hung out at Konrad until four in the morning, and he came home drunk. He and Karoline spent Saturday afternoon with her parents, which hadn't been easy for him to do.

"But it went okay, it wasn't like she was mad at me for coming home late. Occasionally it didn't go over so well, but she didn't really notice I wasn't feeling great. I didn't work that day, and anyway, she'd been looking forward to meeting her parents in town."

He stared off into space.

She felt for him. The cool and somewhat arrogant attitude had vanished. The person underneath turned out to be a nice guy, a small-town boy living in the city. A smart-ass who wasn't all that smart, who on the surface loved the big-city life yet dreamed of having a wife and kids outside Copenhagen. A bit out of place, she thought. She reached in her bag, brought out a pack of Kleenex, and pushed it over to him.

"Thanks."

"You're welcome."

He blew his nose and took a sip of water. "Was she raped?"

Louise thought for a moment. Maybe she shouldn't tell him too much before she knew his whereabouts on Saturday evening. On the other hand, it felt odd not to talk about it. If he really was the killer, it wouldn't be news to him, and anyway, there wasn't much to say before the forensics report came in.

"There's no indication of it. The coroner's inquest is finished, but the autopsy hasn't been performed yet, and we can't be sure until we get the report. Shall we go on?"

He nodded.

"You two were with Lise and Hans Wissinge Saturday afternoon until when?"

"They went home at four thirty. Karoline had a few hours before she was supposed to meet up with her girlfriends. They get together for dinner a few times a year. She doesn't like going into town that much."

He closed his eyes for a moment. He'd realized he was speaking in the present tense.

"She'd really been looking forward to it. They were going to fix dinner together and have fun; sometimes they went out later for drinks, sometimes Karoline just came home."

"What did you do?"

"I crashed on the sofa. I must've been really drunk the night before. I didn't feel like moving a muscle. So, I called out for pizza. I watched a couple of films on DVD."

He thought about it for a moment, then he said it had been three films, not two. "I woke up about three and went to bed, slept till about ten. That's when I realized Karoline hadn't come home."

"What did you do then?"

"I waited for her. I expected her to walk in the door any minute. I called her several times, but her phone was turned off. And I called Trine and Heidi, her two friends she'd had dinner with, but they didn't answer, either."

"Had she ever not come home before?"

"No, but sometimes things happen..."

The awkward silence told Louise that he'd probably done just that to Karoline—not come home after a night on the town with the boys. "Did she say she might not be home until the next day?"

"No, but I assumed she was staying with one of her girlfriends, or..."

Jesus, Louise thought. She reminded herself how happy she was with Peter. That *or* didn't exist in their relationship, thank God. "When did you really start to wonder why she still hadn't come home?"

"I called Heidi around three. She couldn't understand at all what I was talking about; she said Karoline went home before she did. I had to really twist her arm before she admitted that Karoline had left with another guy. And she worked really hard to convince me it wasn't some guy she'd been with." He didn't sound convinced.

"Weren't you worried then?"

Louise was completely focused. At this point, every reaction, every detail had to be noted. Why the hell wouldn't someone react immediately when their girlfriend didn't come home? Either it had happened many times before, or else he knew why she hadn't come home. In her head, Louise ran through all the possibilities and tucked them away. They would sharpen her intuition when she went through his statement later on. What did he react negatively to? Why did he wait so long before contacting the police, when Karoline never stayed out all night? She also made small notes to herself on the notepad beside the computer.

"Just before eight that evening you called the National Hospital to find out if she'd been admitted. Why did you do that?"

He looked confused. "Well, she didn't come home, did she?"

"No! But why were you suddenly worried? When you weren't all day, at least not so much?"

"It was getting late, her parents had called a few times, and I couldn't just tell them she hadn't come home."

"So you thought she'd gone home with someone else, and that's why you waited so long before searching for her?"

Louise held back. It wasn't her job to judge, but it irked her that he could imagine his girlfriend was cheating on him, when she so obviously wasn't the type.

He stared at her as if she'd slapped him. "Yeah, that's probably why. What the hell was I thinking?" He began sobbing.

She drove him back to his apartment at six thirty. She told him she wanted to have a look around, but she emphasized that it wasn't a search. He nodded and said to go ahead.

The crowded apartment was only forty-five square meters. There were things everywhere she looked. Several cute knick-knacks blocked off some of the light from the windows. White bookshelves, a console table, and a buffet were crammed in the living room, along with a large, plush leather sofa and an enormous TV and DVD player.

Obviously, the TV area was Martin's realm. It must be what they called a home theater, she thought. And everything that was white was Karoline's. The techs had been there earlier that day, so she knew she was free to touch things.

She didn't have a search warrant, so she didn't dare look through cupboards and cabinets, but she opened the sliding door of their wardrobe and looked inside. Karoline's clothes were neatly stacked; much of it was black and gray, classic, nice. She had definitely been organized. Eight ring binders were lined up at the bottom of the wardrobe. Louise glanced around the apartment. No piles, everything in its place. Except for Martin's clothes and two pizza boxes. The type of stuff that cluttered Louise's apartment was put away—presumably in the ring binders.

Several family photographs in old as well as new frames stood on top of the white buffet. Louise recognized the grandparents and the aunt. There were also photos of Martin, and of Karoline's deceased younger brother. He had longish blond hair and a broad smile.

Louise shook Martin's hand when she said goodbye, adding that they'd probably need to talk to him again, that it was normal to be called in several times during this type of investigation.

He nodded. "I understand."

He smiled weakly and handed her a card with numbers for his cell phone and store.

It bothered her that she didn't really have him figured out.

She checked her watch. The seven o'clock briefing was definitely over with. She needed to call Heilmann to hear if anything had come up that she should know about.

As she walked to the car, she wondered if it was too optimistic to stop by Sticks'n'Sushi for dinner. She decided that food was the top priority, even if she had to take it back to headquarters and eat in the office while the others shamed her for buying only enough for herself.

Louise patiently waited almost a half hour for her sushi. Back at the car, she called Heilmann. "I'm finished at Karoline's boyfriend's apartment. Anything happen while I was gone?"

"We have some names, some people to bring in for questioning."

"Great," Louise said. She couldn't work up any enthusiasm, though. Suddenly the tray of sushi in the paper bag annoyed her.

"The boss just stopped by. He wants us to do the interrogations this evening. And by the way, he's certain you'll come in with something strong enough to charge the boyfriend."

"He must be out of his goddamn mind. Why would he think that?"

"My best guess is he's emphasizing to everyone that he expects a breakthrough very soon. The journalist's murder is drawing a lot of attention from the media; he'd like to see everyone concentrating on that."

"No problem, let's just stop investigating the murder of Karoline Wissinge. Now that she's been dead for over twenty-four hours."

The words flew out of her mouth, she couldn't stop herself,

though she tried to make a joke of it. She was so, so fed up with how some murders were more important to solve than others. She'd discussed this with her boss before, but Heilmann had patiently defended the head of Homicide by saying that as long as the public took an interest in what the police did, extra resources had to be allocated to higher-profile murder cases. Other cases had to make do with fewer personnel.

"Christ!" Louise sighed. She knew the murder of a crime reporter was more interesting than that of a twenty-three-year-old nurse. If Karoline had been a fifteen-year-old schoolgirl, Suhr would probably have given her priority.

Heilmann broke into her thoughts. "Did you get anything out of Martin Dahl?"

"Not really. He still claims he was in his apartment during the time frame of her murder. And he says that he wanted to marry her and have children, that he loved her more than anything. Nothing in particular made me think he was lying, or that they were having problems."

She considered whether to mention his odd behavior when his girlfriend hadn't come home Sunday. But it wasn't really anything new; she could talk about it in the morning. "Who are we bringing in for questioning this evening?"

"Some of her girlfriends. Toft and Stig have already started. I think you should go home and get some sleep, you had a long night."

"Are you sure?"

"Tomorrow you can find out which of her colleagues at the hospital we should talk to. A few of them have already contacted us, but talk to the head nurse."

"Okay, I'll see you at the morning briefing."

Louise leaned back in the car seat and sighed in relief. She had to return the car to Svendsen, but she gave herself permission to

take a taxi home. She pulled out and headed for Police Headquarters.

She caught a cab just outside Copenhagen's central post terminal.

"Hollændervej, Frederiksberg," she told the driver. Carefully
she laid the tray of sushi on the back seat. It had been a strange day.
Department A took on a lot of non-homicide cases, so of course
they would get two homicides, one right after the other. And the
most difficult type of homicides, to boot. Usually murders were
committed by someone who knew the victim—a married couple,
for instance, or a dispute between friends. They were simpler to
deal with. When the killer's identity is known from the start, it's
just a matter of collecting evidence to support a potential confession. But these murders were apparently committed by unknown
outsiders. Two major investigations of this type were a lot to handle at one time.

Louise caught herself hunching her shoulders. She forced them
down where they belonged. A massive pile of work lay ahead, but
strangely enough she loved it. She liked the pressure, enjoyed concentrating on a case. And lack of sleep didn't really bother her,
either. Short-term, at least. The worst part was the junk food she'd
ended up eating because of the long hours, but lately they'd been
better at ordering from places other than McDonald's.

As the taxi neared her apartment, she began looking for her
billfold. For a moment she panicked; had she left it at the sushi
place? But she found it in the outer pocket of her bag. She sighed
in relief and paid the driver.

"So long." She slammed the door behind her.

After opening the door of her fifth-floor apartment, Louise froze.
Something felt wrong. She stood perfectly still and listened, then she
backed out into the hall and set her bag and the tray of sushi down.

She still couldn't hear anything. Should she go down and call for a patrol car? Or just walk inside? If this had been some Hollywood film, she would have pulled out her gun. But this was the real world.

To hell with it, she thought, and stepped inside. "Hello? Anyone here?" Something clattering startled her; the door to the kitchen's back stairs was open a crack, and she ran over and pulled it open. She heard footsteps below on the stairs, not the rapid-fire tapping of someone running down, but heavy, slow steps. Someone on the way up. It confused her, and she stepped back and pushed the door shut.

She struggled to control her breathing. The footsteps were closer now—one floor below, it sounded like. And they kept coming. Quickly she grabbed one of the big knives on the magnet above the kitchen counter, then she flung open the door, ready to fight.

It was Peter. "What the hell are you doing here?" she yelled.

"Taking the trash out."

"But why are you here?"

She was still pointing the knife at him. He looked a bit sheepish, but then his smile took over. "So, were you going to attack me, or what?"

"You're goddamn right I was." A wave of relief washed through her, and she stopped shaking. She lowered the knife and laughed. "Honey, you nearly scared me to death! When did you get back?"

He came inside and closed the kitchen door behind him. "I left a few hours after I talked to you. The German buyers were called home, some sort of emergency, so there was no reason for me to stay."

She sat down on a chair at her round dining table.

"I called and left a message on your phone when you didn't answer at the department. I talked to somebody who thought you'd be getting home late."

"You scared the crap out of me."

Louise couldn't shake it off. Peter came over and put his arm around her, and she buried her head in his stomach.

"I'm really sorry, I didn't think about you being surprised."

He stroked her hair. "Have you eaten?" He walked over to the refrigerator.

"I brought some sushi home with me, how about you?"

"I did some shopping. There's a bottle of wine in the living room, if you'd like."

She stood up and decided to take a hot bath before they ate. She fetched the wine and poured two glasses, then she took one with her while Peter handled the food situation.

This was what Camilla meant when she whined about not having a man to come home to—though she didn't mean one who scared the daylights out of her. Louise smiled as she stepped into the tub and turned on the hot water full blast. Water exploded out of the showerhead when she raised the knob on the faucet.

The hot stream felt incredible as it ran off her shoulders and down her back. She lost track of time, then suddenly caught herself thinking how she'd been looking forward to an evening alone. She missed Peter when he wasn't there, yet she valued her solitude. When he was out on the road, she liked to listen to music or go to bed early and read. Immediately she felt ungrateful and pushed her disappointment aside.

She'd forgotten her robe in the bedroom, and her towel from that morning still lay on the floor. "Peter," she called out after turning off the water.

A few moments later she heard his steps. She had goose bumps, and her nipples stuck out. Hopefully that wouldn't encourage him; she was too exhausted for that. She covered up with the shower curtain when he came in.

"Hey, you're modest all of a sudden," he said with a grin on his face.

"Be a hero and bring my robe in from the bedroom and a clean towel from the drawer. Please."

When he returned he handed her the towel and held the robe open for her. She stepped into it as quickly as she could and tied it carefully.

"Plates and silverware are out on the coffee table." He kissed her on the cheek.

"Thanks! Was your trip okay, apart from having it interrupted?" she asked over her shoulder.

"Yeah, it went fine. Something interesting came up. I was contacted by our branch office in Scotland. They want me to help introduce one of their new major products."

"That sounds great. What's it all about?"

"They didn't give any details, but they'll get hold of me when I get back to the office."

The wine was just what Louise needed. While they ate, drowsiness began to take over. "Wasn't it in Scotland that it poured all day on you?"

Peter nodded thoughtfully. "But it's beautiful there," he said, after thinking about it for a moment.

"Gray on gray, I believe, is how you put it," Louise reminded him.

"The nature there is absolutely fantastic. Magnificent landscape." He made a sweeping gesture with his arm to describe the expanses.

"Is that the tourist brochures speaking?"

He shook his head. "Really, it's beautiful, even when it's rainy and gray."

She smiled at him. "You must have made quite an impression on them, since they contacted you."

They stood up and cleared the table. Louise had eaten too much; she felt bloated, heavy. Peter couldn't walk into the specialty food stores on Gammel Kongevej without bringing home a little bit of everything. And then there was all the sushi she'd bought. She was yawning even before she crawled into bed.

5

Department A met in the lunchroom at eight the next morning for coffee and a briefing. Besides the regulars, several detectives from Bellahøj and City had been brought in to assist them.

Louise found an empty chair and dragged it over to the corner of the table. When everyone had settled in, Hans Suhr, the head of Homicide, stood up at the end of the table. "Do I need to say we have visitors?" He gestured toward the two long tables in the middle of the lunchroom.

"Visitors we're happy to see, I might add." He smiled. "We have more than enough to do. Right now, there's not much to go on with the murders of Karoline Wissinge and the journalist, Frank Sørensen. We've established that both victims were killed where they were found. Sørensen was lying in the courtyard behind the Royal Hotel, in the shed where the hotel employees park their bicycles. Karoline Wissinge was strangled and shoved behind a bench in Østre Anlæg."

He paced a bit in front of the wall with the large whiteboard. "It's not often we're in a situation like this, working on two major cases at the same time."

Louise stared straight ahead. That was exactly what she'd been thinking, but how did he plan to deal with it?

"Lars Jørgensen is on the team working on the Wissinge murder now. Willumsen and his team will continue with Frank Sørensen."

Suhr straightened up with his back to the wall. "I might as well make it clear, there will be no days off until we wrap these cases up. They're top priority, and I'll make sure your shifts are canceled indefinitely."

Louise brightened. She hated taking duty shifts at Station City. Once a month she had an evening shift, every seven weeks a weekend shift, and she swore like a sailor when her time came.

"Here we'll be running two team shifts a day, at least with the murder of the journalist. We're getting a lot of heat from the media, and we need something to give them."

Suhr raised his voice at the end, making it clear that otherwise there would be hell to pay. He was about to sit down, when he remembered something. "We'll be holding briefings internally for the two teams. Separate briefings. I'll be running them, as much as possible," he added.

"Good," Toft said. "It's too much to be involved in both homicides. We have enough to take care of with the case we're on, right?"

The chief nodded. "We'll meet here for morning coffee and a general briefing, but mostly it will be very short updates."

Louise checked her watch. Eight thirty. She really should plan the day out before calling the hospital. When she got back to her office, she recognized Lars Jørgensen's coat draped over the chair on the other side of the two desks.

I can't handle this, she thought. She closed her eyes and hoped that Suhr decided to call Søren in so she wouldn't be saddled with a new partner. Though she knew that was selfish of her.

She'd just sat down when Jørgensen walked in. "Hi, Lars, I figured it must be your coat." She tried to sound cordial.

"Hi, Rick. Yeah, now it's you and me who have to figure all this out." He smiled and walked over to the other side of the two desks pushed against each other.

"Make yourself at home," she said. "I'm doing several interviews today, so I'll be in and out of the office. What's your day look like?"

"I have to talk to Heilmann. I haven't been briefed on the case yet, so I don't know how far along you are."

"I've been with the parents. But I need to get hold of her colleagues at the hospital."

Louise called the neurosurgery department. Heilmann knocked on the door and walked over to Jørgensen.

"May I speak to Anna Wallentin," Louise said, after introducing herself to the nurse who picked up the phone. She tapped her pen on the desk while waiting on the head nurse.

"We're making rounds right now, could you call in an hour? We'll be done by then."

"I want to speak with Anna Wallentin, now. Please tell her to call Homicide within the next ten minutes."

Louise hoped that sounded dramatic enough.

"Of course," the nurse said, clearly nervous.

Louise hung up and glanced at Heilmann and Jørgensen. She was a bit embarrassed about how much she still enjoyed saying *Homicide*. Just to hear the respect in people's voices.

"I've explained to Lars what you two will be doing," Heilmann said.

"I don't need any help. I can do the interviews myself." Louise heard the rejection in her words.

"You two will be partners until Velin returns." Heilmann started for the door. "And from what I hear, he won't be back for another two and a half months."

Before Heilmann slammed the door, Louise's phone rang. "Department A, Louise Rick."

It was Anna Wallentin. Louise asked her about Karoline's colleagues, if there were any of them in particular she hung out with. Louise took down names and numbers as they spoke. Three girls, one guy. Karoline had been in neurosurgery for only two months, and most of them knew her primarily from short coffee breaks.

When she hung up, she looked over at Jørgensen. "There are only four of them; that shouldn't be too much to take care of."

"I have the feeling you're annoyed at getting a new partner. I get it, 100 percent. I like Velin, too; we're both on the police handball team."

Louise felt herself blushing.

"If it was up to me, I'd still be in Narcotics and Licensing, but that's not how it works. I'm here at Homicide for six months before I can go back, says my rotation schedule. And since your partner is taking comp time off, they've stuck me here. We might as well make the best of it."

He leaned back and studied her.

"You're right. You take anything in your coffee?"

"Sugar, two teaspoons, no milk."

He followed her with his eyes as she walked to the door.

When she came back, Suhr and Willumsen were in the office, talking to Jørgensen about the murder of the journalist. Louise set two cups on the desk. No one looked up. Stay out of it, she told herself. She grabbed her phone and walked out again.

"Camilla Lind."

Louise could hear she'd called at the wrong time. "Hi, should I call back later?"

"No, it's okay. I can't find this damn street, Spurvevej. I've been driving all over goddamn Svogerslev the last twenty minutes."

"Maybe you should stop and ask directions?"

"I did, but then I got cussed out. Someone called me a nosy fucking reporter who ought to keep out of people's business."

"You are a nosy fucking reporter," Louise said, laughing now. "You don't usually let that sort of thing bother you. "

She felt her mood lifting. Camilla often went off on tirades, while Louise tended to keep her problems to herself.

"It doesn't bother me, but it's weird down here; it's like Frank Sørensen is this local hero suddenly, and now everyone thinks they have to protect his legacy."

"Surely not all of Svogerslev?" Louise said, teasing her again.

"It sure as hell feels like it. Drosselvej! What's with all these goddamn streets named for birds, bird after bird after…It must be right around here somewhere."

"Just wanted to hear how things are going. I thought you were doing that interview yesterday."

"The police, that's you, took up the family's entire day. The interview didn't happen. I waited until nine o'clock last night, when they finally told Høyer it was postponed until today. And they also told him, in no uncertain terms, that we needed to respect *your* work and stop elbowing in. What the hell kind of crap is that? We're just doing our job."

This was right up Camilla's alley, Louise could hear. She was more than ready to do battle. No one was going to stop her from getting that interview with the weeping widow.

"Shit, here it is, Spurvevej. Talk to you later."

Camilla hung up before Louise could say that she'd called to see if it was okay to whine about being given a new partner.

At twelve o'clock, the investigation team sat around Heilmann's conference table. Suhr had called the meeting, but he couldn't attend himself; he had to appear on the noon news in connection with the murder of the journalist.

That morning he'd observed the autopsy of Karoline Wissinge. As expected, it had been determined that she died from the wounds on her throat. They also confirmed that she hadn't been raped, but they did discover she was pregnant.

"About eight weeks," Heilmann said, before anyone could ask. "I'm assuming you'd have said something if her boyfriend had mentioned it yesterday?"

Louise nodded, startled by the news. "Of course. Neither one of them, Martin Dahl nor her parents, said anything about her expecting. I don't think they knew."

"Okay, so let's see if they bring it up, otherwise we will."

Several witnesses had confirmed that Karoline left Baren with a man fitting the description of Lasse Møller. They decided to bring him in for questioning again.

"You need to come down hard on him," Heilmann said, turning to Toft.

"All right, but this is nothing new. He says himself they left together. He didn't know her before, and they split up at Silver Square. He stopped by St. Hans Square on the way home and went to bed about two thirty. But we can get him to repeat all that, if that's what you mean."

Toft wasn't being sarcastic. He followed the orders he was given.

"Are there witnesses who can confirm this?"

"He was seen at Pussy Galore; the only question is, when.

Møller claims he used his debit card in the bar, but when I went through the receipts with the manager, there wasn't one with his name on it. And he didn't have a copy."

"How's it going with your interviews?" Heilmann asked, looking at Louise and Jørgensen.

Louise turned to her new partner, but he nodded at her. She said they'd spoken with two of Karoline's colleagues who had known her since nursing school. "I didn't get the impression they're part of Karoline's social life. They only saw her at work, so I don't know how much we can rely on what they say about her. But she had another boyfriend before she met Dahl, a male nursing student."

"We're talking to him and another one later today. They're coming in at three," Jørgensen added.

Louise barely listened as the others spoke about their plans for the day. Two detectives were going to knock on more doors around Silver Square to find witnesses.

"We're working hard on Lasse Møller's circle of friends, looking into his past," Michael Stig said, nodding at the detective beside him who apparently was helping.

"Since you're digging into backgrounds, there's someone you might be able to find," Louise said. She leaned over the table. "Karoline's boyfriend, Martin Dahl, has an old childhood friend from Frederikshavn who's doing some dealing, and occasionally he forgets to pay for his product."

Stig raised an eyebrow. "And what makes you think this childhood friend has something to do with the murder?" He tilted his head and stared at her.

"Dahl loaned him a chunk of money once. The friend paid him back, but I think we should have a look; there could be more to the story." She paused a moment. "Not because it's necessarily relevant to the murder, but it's good to stay on top of things."

"Okay, interesting," Stig said. "Was Karoline involved in that sort of thing, too?"

"Not at all. She blew up at Martin when he loaned his friend the money."

"It's definitely something we need to know, if their friends are involved in that type of crime," Heilmann said. She glanced at Stig. "Take care of that. All right, shall we get on with it?"

She glanced at everyone in the room before gathering her papers and leaving the office.

"Incredible the energy that woman has," Toft said, with respect in his voice. "You'd never think she's taking care of a sick husband at home."

"What? Her husband's sick?" Louise said. She'd met Victor Lau several times. He was a good-looking man, about sixty, sporty and tanned most of the year, as many die-hard sailors are.

"They found a tumor in his brain six months ago, and they operated around Christmas. That's why Heilmann was gone then."

"How's he doing?"

"Okay, I think. It's been a couple weeks since I asked about him, but she said he's recovered from the operation, and they were very optimistic."

Louise nodded thoughtfully. Should she say something to her boss, or act as if nothing was wrong? "I can't understand why I haven't heard about this."

"It's not so strange," Toft said. "No one talks about it around the department. I don't think many people know, and she doesn't want our sympathy." He gathered his papers and walked out.

But he knew, Louise thought.

"I'll try the last two again," Louise said when she and Jørgensen were finally back at their desks. "If we can't get hold of them, we'll have to go over to the hospital."

Neither Signe Jensen nor Jesper Mørk answered, so Louise

skimmed the reports on the two who were questioned that morning before filing them.

Louise had already prepared the three folders Monday morning. The red would be sent to the defense lawyer, the blue containing the originals was for the judge, and the police prosecutor would get the green one. The folders were new and thin, but before the investigation was over, they would most likely be overflowing with paper, their edges torn and creased. Actually, it was a bit chilling but also exciting to her when she slipped the first files into the folders.

Usually she wrote a report before people being questioned left, so they could read and sign it immediately. But she didn't always get the reports copied and filed at the same time. Usually they ended up in a pile on her desk.

Jørgensen had just walked out when Jesper Mørk called.

"Department A, Louise Rick."

"I got your message," he said, after an exchange of hellos. He sounded tired, and Louise guessed he'd had a night shift and had just woken up.

"Thanks for calling. I'd like to speak to you about the murder of Karoline Wissinge. I understand you've known her for some time."

She sensed him stiffening, heard him light a cigarette. "I have to get to work," he said, less tired now.

"That's fine, we'll meet you there."

After a long pause, he said, "My shift starts at three."

"We'll be there a few minutes past three. We also need to talk to Signe Jensen."

"How long will it take?"

"That depends on how much you have to tell us."

"What is it you want to know?"

He sounded surprised. Why couldn't people just accept that

when the police talk to them, they simply want to know what *they* know? "Just tell us a bit about Karoline, and if you know something that might help us in connection with what happened Saturday, I would be very grateful if you'd share it with me."

"See you then." He hung up.

Jørgensen was back. "Which one was that?"

"Jesper Mørk. He'll be at work at three; I told him we'll be there a little after."

"Then we'll be able to talk to her other colleagues in the department, too. Should we try to call Signe Jensen again, so she knows we're coming?"

Louise nodded. Her cell phone rang. Camilla sounded ecstatic.

"I'll call," Jørgensen mouthed, reaching for the paper with Jensen's phone number.

"She was fantastic," Camilla gushed. "You'd love her. She's the kind of person everyone wants to be friends with."

"Who?" Louise's voice radiated indifference, which she hoped Camilla would hear.

"Helle Sørensen, Frank's widow."

Louise had completely forgotten about the interview.

"She's younger than us—that I hadn't imagined. Am I interrupting something?"

"I'm on my way out."

That wasn't enough to stop Camilla. "Unfortunately, the boy wasn't there. The photographer was pissed about that. He wanted a shot of a weeping widow and little Liam."

"I see," Louise said, mostly to show she was still listening.

"But Helle's story is incredible, you don't need to see her crying with her kid on her lap."

That a story wasn't good enough without a photo of a sobbing mother and child sickened Louise. The story was the same, with or without photos.

"And she made it clear, no photos of Liam in the paper. It was hard enough to get her to talk."

"She could have just said no," Louise said.

"Yeah, but she felt she had an obligation to Frank. Apparently, it's something they talked about once."

That was too much for Louise. She couldn't imagine exposing herself to a national paper in a situation like this, a family member in a murder case. "Sick," she managed to get in.

"Frank did a lot of these kinds of stories himself over the years, and he always said if anything ever happened in his home tragic enough to catch the media's attention, he'd damn well speak out, too. He felt he had to, otherwise he couldn't look himself in the mirror."

"Because he'd asked others to tell their stories?" Louise was still acting as if she were a part of the conversation.

"Yeah, and now Helle feels she owes Frank to do the same. She says it's what he would have wanted. I'm not so damn sure I could do it."

"No, and that's why you ought to consider covering something else. Lifestyle, or fashion. Where you don't have to push people into doing things you wouldn't want to do."

Louise knew Camilla was impervious to any objections when she was in this mood, but she tried anyway. *Double standards* was a phrase that popped up in her head when their conversations reached this point. "Anything else you wanted to talk about?"

"No, just wanted to share my good news. Talk to you later."

"Did you get hold of Signe Jensen?"

Jørgensen shook his head. "I left a message. We'll have to track her down at the hospital."

Louise stood up and walked to the door. "I'll see if there's a car available."

"Already done." He fished the key out of his pocket. "If we leave now, we can fill the head nurse in before they show up."

Louise grabbed her jacket and noticed the newspaper on Jørgensen's desk. "Is it okay if I take that along?"

He tossed it over to her, and she stuck it under her arm. They headed down the hall.

She and Velin usually took turns driving, but it made sense somehow for Jørgensen to drive, since he'd picked up the key.

In the car, she opened the newspaper. *Journalist Brutally Murdered* dominated the front page, along with a photo of Frank Sørensen. The murder of Karoline Wissinge was also mentioned. If she'd been raped, too, the photo on the front page would probably have been bigger, Louise thought. She looked further inside the paper and found Camilla's half-page article.

"Maybe we should take a look at any unsolved rape cases," she said. "The ones where the victims have choke marks like what Flemming found on Karoline." She looked over at Jørgensen; she knew it was a shot in the dark.

A moment later, he nodded. "That might be a good idea." He glanced at her. "When we get back, maybe we can check up on cases about internet dates that led to reports of rape."

Department A also handled rape cases. Murder, violent crime, and vice. Or as they usually put it: blood, spit, and semen. Many rape accusations came from women who met a man on the internet. Several gruesome cases had shown up in the past few years. The investigations were extremely difficult; it was a different type of rape than what happened on the street. Often during interrogations, it came out that the sex was consensual—to begin with. The trouble occurred when there was disagreement about when it should stop. Maybe that was the kind of guy who had assaulted Karoline. A guy who wanted to do more than just follow her lead.

Louise remembered a woman who had dated a guy, Kim Jensen, for a month. They'd met on the internet and went out five times before she invited him home. She lived in Rødovre; he came from Hørsholm. In Louise's mind's eye she saw the thin woman, late twenties, a single mother with a young daughter. She'd been so badly abused that the doctors at the National Hospital's Center for Victims of Sexual Assault were deeply shaken when they called the police. When they went to pick the guy up, it turned out that Kim Jensen had disappeared into thin air. His online profile had been deleted. The phone number he'd given her no longer existed, and most likely his name wasn't Kim Jensen. In addition to the violent assault, the woman was filled with shame about having been with a man she hadn't really known. The humiliation was almost as bad as the pain.

Louise shook the memory off. She was glad that Jørgensen was going along with her suggestion, even though it probably wouldn't help. One point for him.

"How's it going?" Terkel Høyer stood in the doorway.

Camilla smiled. "Fine. I'm sending it to you now."

"What about the photos?"

"Christian surely must be about done. He's over on the computer working on them. I've seen the portraits he took; they look good."

"Send me the article; I'll read it while he's finishing."

He ducked out again, and Camilla read what she had written one last time before sending it. Sometimes the words just flowed out, and later she'd be surprised they came from her. Usually it was some of her best writing. The passages difficult to write were often a bit awkward.

She glanced out the window. Earlier, the rain that began the day before had intensified; it had looked as if it could last all day, but now it was clearing up. The King's Garden was dreary and showed no signs of spring. She decided to run up to the cafeteria. She'd skipped lunch, but she had time to catch a bite before writing the captions.

"Looks great," Høyer said when she returned. "Sounds exactly right. You're a star; you sketch them perfectly. She's a dear woman, isn't she?"

Camilla nodded. "Very. It's like I've known her forever."

A door slammed outside, and footsteps marched down the hall. The photo editor burst into the room in a rage. "What the hell is this? We can't get a goddamn photo of the kid?"

At first Camilla didn't know what he was talking about.

"You have no goddamn right to interfere with the photographer." Høyer and Camilla were both astonished; the man looked like he wanted to strangle her.

Camilla was numb. "What are you talking about?"

"What's going on?" Høyer said.

Holck had been the photo editor of the paper longer than anyone could remember. He was brilliant at his job, but his temper was legendary. And it exploded when someone barged in on his territory. "Little Miss Lind here went along with not getting a photo of the widow and the kid together. Unbelievable. But we're printing that shot. Thank God for archives; it'll be an old photo, but we'll just have to live with that."

Camilla gasped. "No, you won't," she yelled. She flew up out of her office chair, which smacked against the wall. "Helle said no to a photo of the boy, and I promised her we wouldn't use one."

Holck sneered at her. "When the hell did you become managing editor? You're not authorized to promise shit. Your job is to scribble some words down, and we'd all appreciate it if you kept to that and let the rest of us do our jobs."

Saliva shot out of his mouth as he turned and marched back to his office.

"Explain," said the managing editor.

"Helle asked us to keep Liam out of the article. That's why he wasn't home when I came. And she doesn't want us to use another photo of him. We have to respect that, damn it."

Høyer eyed her for a long moment. "Stories are always better when you can see who they're about. You know that. Can't you explain that to her?"

Tears came to Camilla's eyes. What were they doing? Here she'd handed them a top-notch interview, and now it sounded as if it wasn't worth shit without a photo of the mother and son. For a moment, she thought about letting herself explode, but she backed off. "What can I say. I don't know what it is you want. She's completely against us using that photo."

"Did you pressure her?"

She couldn't believe this. He wouldn't have had the heart to do it, either. He knew her much better than Camilla, who after all had only met Helle once. "She said no."

After a few moments, she said, "Terkel. Helle is absolutely devastated. She totally doesn't want her son involved, or to see a front-page photo of him torn up about his father. She only agreed to the interview because she felt it was what Frank would want."

"And that's why it shouldn't be so hard to explain we need a photo of her and her son together."

"How can you say that? We can't twist her arm about this."

"We're going to have to figure out something." He walked out of the office.

This couldn't be happening! What about the plain old good, solid story? What the hell were they thinking? She'd done what no one else had been able to do; none of the other papers had even gotten a foot in the door, and now it wasn't good enough because the goddamn photographers thought they needed a photo of someone sobbing. The story was the important thing.

Suddenly, Høyer appeared in the doorway. "We're checking the archives. I'm pretty sure we have a photo of Helle and Frank and Liam together. They were at some reception last year we covered, with a lot of celebrities, remember?"

She didn't.

"Otherwise you're going back to Helle to convince her," he continued.

She thought about that for a moment. "I won't do it." She stared straight ahead.

He stared at her. "Yes, you will. It's your job!"

While she collected herself, Holck appeared around the corner and stood in the doorway. Without so much as a glance at Camilla, he told Høyer all they had was a photo of Frank standing with baby Liam in his arms. "We need a newer photo."

Høyer agreed. "Check stock photos, otherwise we'll have to do it."

"I'll send Christian out to find Helle's parents. You know where they live?"

"I think they live in Viby or Borup, but we can find that out."

Camilla stood up and confronted them. "You can forget about that." She turned to her boss. "I want to talk to you in private."

She walked over and slammed the door on Holck, who barely managed to step back and not get hit. "You're not doing this. I'm pulling my interview if you don't believe it's good enough without that photo."

"Camilla, don't make a scene about this. It doesn't reflect well on you." He sounded cold.

"You can't treat Helle this way. We have to keep our word."

"I didn't promise her anything, and my word goes here at this paper. Whatever deals you've made, that's your problem. You know how things work here. If we can get that photo, we will. We don't give up until we've tried everything. That's how you usually do it."

Camilla had to swallow that. She'd hunted down lots of school photos of kids when the parents or family wouldn't give her one. Danish School Photo worked all over the country, and often they could come up with a photo when classmates or friends wouldn't part with one.

"I promised. She trusted me, and that's why the interview is so good. She'd never have talked to me if I hadn't promised to not push her on that photo."

"I care a lot about Helle and Liam," Høyer said. "But that doesn't stop me from doing my job. Let's see if we can find one, otherwise you'll have to go back to her."

"I won't do that. And just try to print my interview if you use a file photo."

"Oh, come on, Camilla."

She was close to tears, so she stood up, grabbed her bag, and stalked out the door. Out in the hallway she ran into Holck; she nearly punched him in the gut, but she held back at the last second.

When she reached the street, she decided to find a café and drink a cup of hot chocolate with whipped cream. She started down St. Regnesgade and noticed Søren Holm coming her way. She panicked and looked around for a place to hide; she didn't want to talk to a colleague right now. But he was lost in thought, plus he looked like hell. It occurred to her he might need a warm cup of something, too.

He was startled when she grabbed his arm and said, "Hi, how's it going?"

"I'm burned out, haven't been home since yesterday. You headed back to the paper?"

She shook her head and explained that she was going some-where for a cup of hot chocolate because she was royally pissed off.

He thought about that. "I'll go with you."

They sat in a corner, and even before their hot chocolate arrived, Camilla had told him about the photo situation.

He laid his hand over hers. "It's a real shitty situation, but there's not much you can do. The photo editor has the say on pho-tos, and that's that."

She didn't feel like talking about it, but she leaned forward when the waiter came and handed her the cup. The small bowl of whipped cream raised her spirits. Strangely enough, extra calories often cured her bad moods. "So tell me, how are you? I see from the paper you've been busy."

"Yeah, we're trying to cover every angle. Everything they said about Frank at the press briefing has to be followed up. I don't know what the hell's going on. I've been out all night, trying to find somebody who knows something, but I didn't have much luck. I think it's a hit. No one saw anything, no one heard any-thing, and that's a little strange."

Camilla nodded. She didn't know much about that crowd.

"The drug case is coming up day after tomorrow. Frank worked on it a long time, and I got this feeling he dug something up that isn't supposed to come out during the trial. I don't know that, though. Just a guess. I'm meeting one of my sources this evening. Maybe he'll have something for me."

"You need to get something written for tomorrow?"

He shook his head. "They're going with your interview. I'm off the hook until the end of the week. But the police might have something new, so we need to keep in touch with them."

Camilla let that hang in the air. She had a really good idea of who would be in charge of doing that.

6

Signe Jensen had never met Karoline's boyfriend and knew none of her girlfriends, but she had only good things to say about Karoline. She cried throughout the interview.

They sat in a small meeting room for personnel. On the table stood a thermos, a stack of the hospital's small white coffee cups, a sugar bowl, and a creamer.

Every time she asked a new question, Louise said, "I'm sorry, but I have to ask you…" Finally, she realized how annoying that sounded, but focusing on the interview was hard, because the girl was sobbing so intensely. Louise was only trying to soften the blow of Karoline's murder.

Louise stared at the large whiteboard hanging at the back of the room. Two patient names were written under each room number, with the days of the week in a column on the left side. Marie Larsen had physical therapy on Wednesdays and Fridays. Louise's thoughts wandered as she read the many names and schedules.

Signe was still crying. Louise took a deep breath and was about to try again when Jørgensen spoke up.

"Okay, listen. We'll be finished here in just a bit. You'd be doing us a big favor if you could pull yourself together and be an adult for the next five minutes."

The girl straightened up and looked in surprise at Jørgensen. As if she'd only now noticed him. "Of course, I'm sorry." She waited for him to continue.

A hint of irritation rose up in Louise, but she put it aside. She smiled at Lars before finishing up the interview, which didn't give them anything new.

"Sometimes a few sharp words from an outsider helps," Jørgensen said after the nurse left the room.

Louise nodded. "Maybe I should have raised my voice."

"Not at all, then she'd have clammed up on you. You're great at getting people to talk."

Louise looked at him, a bit disoriented now. "She didn't talk, she cried."

"In the last half hour, she told you everything worth knowing about her feelings...yeah, about her entire life."

Louise smiled. "You're right. But I was trying to get her to tell us something about Karoline's life and feelings."

"If she'd known something about Karoline, she would've told you. Now you can say in good conscience that Signe Jensen doesn't know anything useful to us."

"Thanks. I'll take that as a compliment."

Louise had expected Jesper Mørk, the murdered nurse's male colleague, to be the same age as the rest of their nursing school class. But when he entered the office in his white coat, she guessed him to be around thirty.

"Thirty-two," he said when she asked.

His voice was a bit hoarse, and his dull brown hair had been tucked behind his ears.

"Would you like a cup of coffee?" Louise pointed at the cups on the table and pushed the thermos over to him.

Nine years is a big difference at that age, she thought. Karoline had been eighteen when she was with Mørk, so he must have been twenty-seven. She hadn't imagined this ex-boyfriend could have a wife and children.

"When did you and Karoline become a couple?"

Louise checked his eyes for any lingering feelings, but all she saw was a vague mournfulness. No pain, no emotional reaction.

"We were together less than a year. It started right before she turned eighteen."

Louise wrote in her notebook as he spoke. "How did it begin… I mean, there's quite a gap in your ages?"

His laugh was brief and dry. "Yeah, nine years is a lot, especially for girls that age. When you're on the other side of thirty, no one thinks about a man being nine years older than his wife."

"Exactly." She resigned herself to him not volunteering much. Anything would have to be dragged out of him. She leaned back in her chair. "So tell me about it."

"She fell in love, that's about it. We were in the same group at nursing school. I trained to be a metalworker, but after my apprenticeship I knew it wasn't for me, so I moved on."

"Big change in professions," Louise said, hoping he would stick with her.

"Personal development, is how I'd put it."

Louise nodded. She noticed he had trouble concentrating. She leaned toward him and immediately was annoyed at herself; some interviews felt wrong from the very start and were hard to get on track. She spoke sharply. "Would you please tell me how you got together?"

He squirmed in his chair. "She hit on me. I had a girlfriend I was living with."

He paused, inspected his hands. "I guess I was flattered about being seduced." He looked up at her in defiance.

"You didn't fall in love with her?"

"Yeah, but not until later. At first, I was in love with the affair, the game, the flirting."

"With screwing someone on the side?" The words flew out of Louise's mouth; she didn't mean to give him a hard time, but a crude remark would hopefully shake him out of this conceited romantic crap he was feeding her.

Sometimes you just have to yell *pussy* at people to get a reaction. Camilla had taught her that once, and there was some truth to it.

"Okay, yeah, maybe."

"So explain to me. Were you having an affair while you were still living with your girlfriend, or did you drop your girlfriend and start up with Karoline?"

He thought about that for a while. "A little time went by before we became a couple." He reached for his cup and took a sip of coffee.

That didn't fit with Louise's picture of Karoline. A girl from a nice family with a white console table and tasteful furnishings wasn't the type to lose her head and go after someone already taken. But apparently, she'd been wrong. "So, you had an affair, and it ended up with you two together, is that right?"

"Yes."

"The relationship lasted…" She looked at her notebook.

He helped her out. "Eleven and a half months."

"Okay." She had that written down already, but she made a note that he knew exactly how long they'd been together. "How did it end?"

He slumped and stared at his hands again. Finally, he said, "She met someone else."

Louise sighed heavily. Luckily, Jørgensen wasn't sitting there watching all this, though he'd have gotten a lot out of it, and he surely wouldn't have been complimenting her on how well she was doing.

"You must be talking about Martin Dahl," she said, looking away.

"I don't remember his name."

She straightened up and stared at him in surprise. "Are you saying she had a boyfriend after you and before she met the man she moved in with?"

He shrugged.

Louise leaned forward. "Why do you have a problem talking about this?"

"I don't have a problem with it. There's just nothing more to tell."

"Did you kill Karoline Wissinge?"

The question knifed through the air between them. And the reaction came just as she suspected it would—immediately.

"Oh, for God's sake—no, of course I didn't."

He looked like an overgrown puppy and talked like Louise's aunt and her friends searching for things to fuel their outrage. The same aggrieved tone.

"We'll get back to that later. Right now, I want to hear exactly how this relationship that lasted eleven and a half months started and ended. Would you be so kind as to tell me? I'm all ears."

He looked pale now, she was happy to see.

"The girl I was living with saw us together at a café, so there was no reason to deny it when she accused me. I was going to tell her, but just hadn't got around to it."

Louise jotted everything down without looking at him.

"We were planning on living together..."

"Go on."

"Suddenly I just wasn't interesting anymore. She terminated me. Dumped me."

Louise cut him off before he really got going. "That was when she met the other guy?"

He nodded slowly, several times.

"Thanks." Louise stood up. "We might need to speak with you again, but right now this is all we'll need from you."

He stared at the table while she spoke. She began packing up, and he came to life again. He stood expectantly, as if he wasn't aware they were finished.

Louise walked by him and opened the door. "Bye," she said, without shaking his hand. She looked around for the head nurse, Anna Wallentin, who was nowhere in sight. She started down the hall to the large bank of elevators.

Lars Jørgensen was standing by the car when she came out.

"Strange guy," she said as she approached him.

"How's that?"

"I don't know if there was something he didn't want to tell me, but I had to wrestle every word out of him."

"Was he lying?"

"Mmm, I don't think so. He kept going on about how they became a couple, but it really was all about him having another girlfriend when they met, and then Karoline dumped him, she met someone else, who almost has to be Martin Dahl."

"But were they still friends?" They stopped at a red light, and Jørgensen eyed her.

"Yeah, the four girls and Mørk usually ate lunch together. I think Karoline kept to her friends from nursing school. She hadn't been at the hospital that long, though. I guess it makes sense."

"Maybe he still had the hots for her?"

"It didn't seem like that to me. He's probably just a little strange."

The office was cold when they got back. The window stood open, and Louise smelled cigarette smoke. Someone had used the room for an interview while they were gone, she guessed. She left the window open and packed her things. She had to take the bus because Peter had driven her in that morning. It annoyed her now; it would have been nice to bike home.

She walked up to Central Station and waited for bus 15. Suddenly she regretted saying she'd come home for dinner. They wouldn't have much time; Peter played badminton at seven. She could call and hear how far along he was with dinner. Maybe they should meet somewhere to eat.

The phone rang; she was so startled that she almost dropped it.

"It's me, sorry to bother you again," Camilla said. She sounded nothing like the euphoric woman from earlier that day.

"It's okay. What's wrong?"

"I think I'm going to have to quit."

"What do you mean? What happened?"

Louise saw the bus coming, but she stepped back. She had to hear this.

"They're crazy here. I won't be a part of it."

Camilla summed up what had happened, why she was prepared to put her job on the line. "It's a matter of credibility."

Louise had to agree with her. But was it necessary to resign? That sounded extreme.

"There's only so much I'll take. I don't understand Terkel; he's sick in the head."

"Calm down. Getting yourself all worked up won't help."

Dumb thing to say, Louise thought. But she couldn't take it back.

"There's absolutely every reason to get worked up," Camilla snapped.

And in a way, she was right. Louise would hate to be in her shoes. In her experience, though, it was smartest to keep a cool head, otherwise people might call you hysterical. Your words carried less weight when you screamed them out. She'd tried to explain that to Camilla many times.

After a moment, she said, "Are you really prepared to quit if they print the photo?"

"That's what I'm not sure about." Camilla seemed to mull that over a moment. "Like hell I'm not! I'm sure. I can always freelance."

"Okay then, it's settled. If you really feel that way, it'll be easier to stand up for what you believe is right."

The bus approached. Camilla's conviction was back, it sounded like. Louise crossed her fingers for a happy ending.

Camilla took a deep breath and walked back down the hall. She might as well get it over with. Høyer's door was closed. She knocked on the door resolutely and walked in.

"What have you decided?" she said, before he could open his mouth.

He looked at her in annoyance.

"Did you find a photo?"

"Yes, we have one, so you don't need to go back to Helle."

She sat down across from him. "Do you really think you could have made me do that?"

He eyed her for a moment. "No, I wasn't counting on it. But you really need to get rid of these hang-ups of yours."

"I don't have any goddamn hang-ups, I just treat people decently. Funny, but I thought you did the same."

She reminded herself to sound calm; her voice had jumped

an octave at the end. She breathed deeply into her diaphragm, checked her watch, and said, "The time is five fifty-eight p.m. I resign."

He glared at her. "I won't let you." He straightened up in his chair. "I'm a little busy right now, can we do this later? You have a message to call Detective Superintendent Willumsen at Homicide."

He waved her over to the door and turned back to his computer screen.

"I mean it," she said. But all he did was point to the door.

What the hell was going on? She went back to her office and read the message. Let him call that old grouch Willumsen. He was the last thing she needed right now.

Before she could sit down, her phone rang. "Camilla Lind."

"Is this the star reporter from *Morgenavisen*?" a deep voice said. She frowned.

"Willumsen here." Now she was totally confused. The detective wasn't in the habit of calling her.

"Hello, Willumsen. I just saw the message to call you."

"Yeah, but you didn't; that's why I'm calling you."

Camilla was bewildered.

"We're reconstructing the movements of Frank Sørensen on Saturday night, and I thought you might help us by asking your readers if anyone saw him, if I tell you where we think he was."

"I think Søren Holm is covering the story," she said, without sounding too discouraging. There was no reason to go into this, now that she had resigned.

He ignored her. "Your boss just said you're the one. Got something to write with?"

She sighed and found a notepad in the pile on her desk, then she searched her drawer for a pen. "Okay."

"We know he was here at Police Headquarters late Saturday

evening, and we assume he biked to the Royal Hotel. But we don't know if he stopped anywhere on the way."

Camilla was puzzled. "What was he doing there so late Saturday?"

"I'll get to that. The hotel employees didn't see him, but that doesn't mean he wasn't there. We'd love to talk to anyone who recognizes Frank Sørensen from a photo, who saw him biking between Police Headquarters and the hotel around ten Saturday night."

Camilla wrote that down.

"Did you get that? To begin with, it would be a great help to get this going."

"What was he doing at Police Headquarters?" she asked again.

Pause. "He spoke with Birte Jensen. That's between you and me. But give her a call and talk to her."

"Who's Birte Jensen?" Camilla felt like a greenhorn.

"Birte is the head of Narcotics and Licensing; she's running the investigation Sørensen was covering. The drug case."

"Okay. But will she talk to me?" Camilla hoped she didn't sound too surprised. You could hardly pry a word out of the heads of Department A and NL, that much she knew.

"She said she'll contact you. She'll decide what to tell you. It's no secret there's probably a connection between the drug case and Frank Sørensen's death. But call her. She's okay." He hung up.

Camilla was still holding the phone when Høyer knocked and came in. "Are you resigning, right now?" he asked, with a straight face.

"No, I am not resigning right now," she snapped. She thought about what Willumsen had told her.

Høyer was sitting across from her now, and she turned to him. "Yes, I am. I'm not going to stand for this. It can't be right that a story isn't good enough just because you don't squeeze every last drop out of someone. This is her life we're talking about, their lives."

"We're dropping the photo. I've spoken with Holck. He's not happy at all; the only reason he went along with it is because the photos we have aren't good."

Camilla sighed. That was a weak argument, bad photos. What about doing the right thing? Where was that in all this? "So, what will you do?"

"We'll use the photos Christian took; they're good."

"What did Holck say?"

"You're a bitch who should get a warning because you're a conniving little weasel." He winked at her.

She grimaced. "Very funny."

"It might be a good idea for you two to sit down and have a chat."

"Dream on. Or else he'll have to come to me. He's not the one out there in the real world. It's easy for him, sitting on his fat ass, ordering people around in here. He doesn't have to deal with everything." Camilla was just warming up.

"He's been there, been out there, but you're right. It all looks easier from inside here."

She suspected the mother-and-son photo had been dropped only because it had reached the point where Høyer himself would have to twist Helle's arm. Then suddenly it wasn't so important after all. She snorted.

"Did you get anything out of Willumsen?"

"He wants us to print what Frank was doing late Saturday evening. They're hoping someone saw him."

She still felt she'd been pushed around, and she decided not to mention that Willumsen had encouraged her to speak with the person leading the drug investigation. There was no reason to get anyone excited; it might be nothing more than an off-the-record chat. And given what had just happened, Høyer might say to hell with it and pressure her to write about something she'd promised to hold back. No way she'd do that. She'd talk to Birte Jensen first and then decide what to give him.

And was it okay for her not to tell Holm about this? After all, it was his beat. She decided that could also wait until she knew what came out of the conversation. "How big an article are we talking about?"

Suddenly she was tired. Christina was home with Markus; they were going to make crepes. The young girl had been a helper at Markus's day care center his first year there, until she started at the university.

Back then Camilla hadn't realized how lucky she was to nab Christina, but in the past two years she'd almost become part of the family. Or at least a lifeline, as Camilla put it. At first Christina had discreetly asked if it was okay to take Markus to the Naval Museum to see the submarine, or to the fire station. Camilla had been absolutely thrilled. She'd never taken her son to the Naval Museum—in fact, she hadn't even known it existed.

"Write a half screen."

"Have you heard from Søren?" she asked.

"He's resting in his office. He's meeting a few people later. The type you can only find when the rest of us are asleep, it seems. I'm counting on him to find something we can work with. But you're the one in charge of the entertainment in tomorrow's paper." He smiled at her.

She raised her eyebrows. Entertainment! But really, when it came down to it, that's how people looked at it. She flipped the page on her notepad and settled into her chair. She might as well get started. They'd need some computer graphics to show the route Frank had taken, but Layout on the fourth floor would take care of that.

Louise stuffed the last bite in her mouth. Peter was in the bedroom, pulling on a pair of jeans and a sweater. He never wore a suit when he was off work, and that was fine with Louise. They had stopped hauling clothes back and forth between their apartments long ago. He had three shelves in the large wardrobe, and his shirts hung at one end.

"I'm riding with Henning; we have the court between seven and eight," he yelled to her.

"I'm going to take a walk in Østre Anlæg while you're gone."

"Is there anything more to look for? Didn't the forensics people check everything?"

"I just want to have a look around." Louise didn't feel like explaining that sometimes she could think things out better at the crime scene, after all the hectic activity was over.

"You're off work, hon. No one is forcing you to go out there. Why don't you just stay home and relax until I get back?"

Louise sighed. He'll never learn! "No one's forcing me. I might come up with something useful there, that's all. Sometimes things make better sense when you're right there."

"And you're the only one who can do that?"

She didn't answer that. They'd gone there so many times.

"See you when you get back," she said.

"I have to stop by the apartment and pick up some papers to go through for tomorrow. If you take the car, you could pick me up on the way back." He lifted his keys out of his coat pocket.

"Okay, I'll call you at eight thirty and see if you're ready."

She went out in the hall with him and kissed him goodbye. Stood in the doorway, watched him walk down the stairs. Smiled at him.

She wondered if life would be more boring when they finally decided to move in together. Or if it might be more exciting. But something was holding her back. Occasionally, she wondered if it was the expectations and pressures in their lives that kept her from starting a real family.

That's silly, she thought. She went back inside for her coat.

She parked the car in front of Krebs School. She'd brought along an umbrella, just in case. It had stopped raining, but the sky still looked threatening.

She walked to the gate and down the park's gravel path. From a distance, in the twilight, she could just make out the bushes where Karoline had been hidden. Thick bushes under the trees, all leafless, forming a small cave-like space where she'd lain. The red and white police barrier tape stood out sharply against the naked branches. She felt a tiny stab in her chest when she saw the flames flickering—tea lights protected from the rain by small lanterns had been set out.

She stopped and studied the scene. Breathed in deeply, concentrated on etching the surroundings and all the details in her brain. The curve of the path, tall trees, low bushes. The bench where Karoline might have been sitting before she was strangled.

Louise stood on the path and closed her eyes while trying to empty her head of thoughts. The young woman had lost her life here. Something had startled her, and she opened her eyes wide— was someone watching her? Louise had no psychic abilities and no intention of gaining a reputation for having them. She was just trying to sense a mood.

For the hundredth time she wondered if the same person came several times a day and changed the candles, or was it several people, independent of each other, making sure the small flames were burning?

Many people had left behind plastic-covered photos of Karoline. Old schoolmates and friends, she guessed. Several rows of flowers had been dropped off. Letters also covered in plastic lay beside some of the bouquets.

Remembered. Missed. Loved. The same words had been written, over and over. Louise's throat tightened, but she focused on keeping her emotions in check.

She noticed a white card.

Thy will be done had been written with a felt tip, the block letters blurry. It stood out from the other messages.

It couldn't have been there very long, otherwise the letters would have been blurred completely out.

She kneeled to see if the card was attached to a bouquet; it wasn't. She reached in her pocket for a pair of thin plastic gloves, the type used at crime scenes, but of course she didn't have any now that she needed them.

Carefully she picked up the card by its corner, naïvely hoping something on the other side would reveal where it came from. It was blank.

She fished her book-style planner out of her bag and laid the card between two pages. Then she grabbed her phone and called the National Center of Forensic Services on Slotsherrensvej. There was no reason to wait until tomorrow; she could just as well drive out there with it.

"This is Louise Rick from Department A. Is Niels Frandsen or someone working on the Karoline Wissinge murder there?"

Usually the head of Forensic Services was working during the most intense period of an investigation. The techs were undoubtedly busy with evidence from the park and the hotel where Frank Sørensen had been killed.

"Hi, Rick, you're working late, too?"

Louise liked his warm baritone voice. She visualized Frandsen, a man in his late fifties, with an ever-present pipe hanging from the corner of his mouth. It was seldom lit, but that didn't seem to bother him. The first time she met him, she thought he was the easygoing type, *very* easygoing. Like someone who would rather be home with the wife and grandchildren, drinking coffee while he packed his pipe. But she'd quickly realized he had another side.

He was sharp as a knife and worked like a horse, and he was more patient and thorough than anyone she'd met.

"Hi, I figured you'd be around."

She glanced at her watch: eight fifteen. She would have to pick Peter up soon. "I'm in Østre Anlæg, and there's an interesting card someone laid where Karoline Wissinge was found. I'm coming by with it."

"All right then. It must be really interesting to get you to come all the way out here."

"Probably it's just some idiot with a bizarre sense of humor, but it's different from the others."

She read the short message to him, and they agreed it should be checked for fingerprints, plus the writing should be looked at, too.

She called Peter and explained she was going to be delayed, that she was driving out to Forensics but would pick him up on the way back.

He didn't have much to say. He sounded annoyed that she was still working. The mood of the conversation turned gloomy. She suggested that she drive home and pick up some clothes after delivering the card, and then she'd come over to his apartment.

He broke her off. "It would be way too late." Either he would go to bed early or watch a good film. She gave up. When he was in this mood, there was nothing she could do.

"Okay. What about your car?"

They decided she could keep it; he had a meeting in town the next day and wouldn't need it.

"Okay then, have a good night's sleep. Are we still meeting up with Camilla and Markus tomorrow?"

"Of course, yes."

She couldn't read the tone in his voice.

"You use milk?" Frandsen yelled from the reception area, on his way with their coffee.

"Please, if you have any."

The hallway was quiet, but Louise knew people were working behind many of the closed doors. She'd parked behind the gray building and had walked past four of the forensic technicians' blue vans, which were ready to pull out past the low, red buildings housing the small special departments.

So much went on here. Clothes were inspected for blood and semen before being sent to the Department of Forensic Medicine, where the Forensic Genetics department did DNA profiling; the IFIS database with 250,000 fingerprints was searched for matches; castings of footprints were compared; and all the small fibers and hair picked up at crime scenes were studied meticulously. She was fascinated by the evidence Forensics examined, so much so that once she'd even thought about applying to become part of the technician team.

They sat down at the rectangular conference table. "All right, let's take a look at what you have."

Louise brought out her planner and dumped the card on the table. It landed back side up. Frandsen grabbed a pair of tweezers, standard equipment for the department. After turning the card over, he studied the short sentence.

"An idiot, was that what you said?"

She nodded.

"Surely you don't place a card at the crime scene if you killed the girl?" He frowned. "It would be idiotic, yes, to draw attention to yourself."

"You never know. You'd never believe killers would be stupid enough to leave semen behind in a female victim!"

"No, you're right, of course you are. But surely he wouldn't voluntarily leave evidence." He shook his head. "I just can't see that."

Louise rubbed her forehead. Her thoughts were sluggish as her exhaustion began taking over.

"It'll be interesting anyway to see if there are fingerprints on the card," Frandsen said. He lifted it up with the tweezers and held it to the light.

"Did you find any fingerprints on her?" Louise hadn't seen any of the lab results yet.

He shook his head.

"I'm hoping you find something," she said. "But this might turn out to be completely innocent. Someone might have thought this was a good time and place to profess their faith." She stood up and put on her coat. "We'll see, anyway."

He followed her down and gave her a fatherly pat on the shoulder when she thanked him for the coffee. They agreed to talk the next day.

It was close to ten thirty when Louise headed for Frederiksberg. She was fine with Peter not being there. She'd have a glass of the red wine left over from dinner, then go to bed.

7

"What the hell are you spending your time on?" Suhr thundered. "Sitting on your asses drinking coffee instead of getting something done, it looks like. What do you think this place is, some spa for pregnant nuns?"

Louise sighed. The storm blew over. He exploded once in a while, but it never lasted long. It usually happened when they were stuck on a case and it seemed they'd never get anywhere. When all their leads were cold, when no one had seen anything. He probably hadn't gotten much sleep the past two and a half days, and they'd had nothing even close to a breakthrough in the two cases he was responsible for. It was understandable, him blowing his top out of frustration, but it was damn irritating while it lasted. She stole glances at the others around the table. Henny Heilmann's eyes were on her boss; she took the brunt of his outburst. She could take an awful lot, Louise thought.

Back in her office, she leaned over to stick her bag under the desk. The intercom suddenly came to life, and instantly she jerked up and banged her head on the underside of the desk.

"Heilmann here. Meet me in my office in a half hour."

Her voice crackled. Jørgensen stood up to turn the volume down.

Heilmann greeted them, and they all sat down to bring each other up to date, but Suhr burst in before they could start. He was barely inside when he asked when they expected to make an arrest. No one spoke; there was nothing to say.

Louise straightened up automatically, preparing for what was coming. Across the desk, Michael Stig's lips narrowed.

Heilmann seemed completely unaffected. "We have a few leads we hope will pan out later today. Last night Rick found a card at the crime scene; she drove out to Forensic Services with it."

Everyone stared at Louise. She'd been expecting to bring it up herself at this meeting, but she'd informed Heilmann about it right after the morning briefing.

Suhr nodded at her. "Interesting. What about the interviews?" He looked around.

Heilmann opened her files. "CID reports that no one in the area recognized the victim. They went through the nearby apartment buildings twice, also expanded their questioning toward Gammeltoftsgade and the apartments facing Nørre Farimagsgade. Either no one was on the street when Karoline Wissinge walked along there, or else she didn't attract any attention." She looked up from her papers.

CID, Criminal Investigations Department, didn't participate in the regular briefings. They were kept up to date and called to do specific tasks that didn't require their presence at Homicide.

Suhr glared in dissatisfaction at everyone in the room. Louise noticed that Stig slumped when the head of Homicide's eyes passed right by him. Everyone wanted to contribute something that would earn them a nod, Louise thought.

"Lasse Møller," Suhr screamed, seeing that everyone sat silently, waiting for his next outburst. The only one who didn't cringe was Toft, who straightened his glasses and smiled.

"I had him in here most of the day yesterday, and frankly I can't see him hiding something from us. He says he and Karoline left together from Baren. A witness saw him at a café on St. Hans Square. The techs have been through his apartment; there isn't a single piece of evidence on his clothes to connect him with the victim."

Suhr grunted as Toft continued. "We have a report from Forensics on every piece of clothing he was wearing Saturday night, and it checked out with him having walked in the rain for about a half hour. His coat wasn't soaked, and it would have been if he'd been out more than an hour."

Suhr was still dissatisfied. "Witnesses?"

Louise was sitting on a chair against the wall. On the way to the meeting she'd grabbed a notepad and a pen, and now the paper lay balanced on her knee. She wrote *Lasse* with crooked letters and crossed it out with two lines.

"I'll stop by Pussy Galore again this evening," Toft said. "The witness who confirmed the time he was there was absolutely certain, but let's see if we can find some others who saw him. And then there's the missing debit card receipt."

Heilmann smiled at him. Toft never gave up if there was a shred of doubt. He was known for that, and everyone accepted that sometimes he clutched at straws, even though he should move on.

"Good," Suhr said. He'd worked with Toft so many years that he never questioned his priorities. He glared at the rest of them and spoke sternly. "This is day four. It's starting to look like we've got a long, drawn-out affair ahead of us."

It irritated Louise to hear him talking in those terms already.

"Saturday we're doing a week-after canvass. CID will be assisting us; we'll start at nine p.m. by stopping everyone—and I mean everyone—in the area around Silver Square, the victim's home, and Østre Anlæg, the most likely park entrances the murderer used. But we're placing officers along the entire route from Baren to the crime scene."

Louise groaned. This type of canvassing was a killer. The idea was to find people who had been in the same place at the same time a week before, when the crime took place. People might be on the way home from work. If they were lucky, they'd run into witnesses. Karoline was strangled between midnight and seven a.m., so they'd have to be out all night. Louise prepared herself for a lost weekend.

"I know, I know," Suhr said. "But we have to do it."

Everyone nodded. Heilmann took over. "Has anyone asked for her phone records? I'm assuming she had a cell phone."

No one answered.

"Everyone has a cell phone!" Suhr hissed.

Heilmann ignored him and turned to Louise. "Check which carrier she used, and let's get a warrant and light a fire under them."

Louise jotted that down in her notepad.

"Rick suggested we check out Martin Dahl's childhood friend from Frederikshavn." She turned to Lars Jørgensen. "Let's take a good look at how much Karoline's boyfriend is involved in what his friend is selling. I want to know who he hangs out with. If a few officers help, you might be able to find out who he forgot to pay."

After everyone was clear on their assignments for the day, chairs began scraping the office floor.

"You have a moment?" Suhr asked Louise.

She followed him into the small reception, where his secretary sat engrossed in her computer screen. She didn't even look up.

He closed the door behind them and told her to sit down. "How are things going? Are you doing okay here?"

That confused Louise. In the three years she'd been in Homicide, Suhr had never asked her how she was doing. "I'm fine." She cleared her throat, her mind racing to figure out what was coming.

"Are they treating you decently?"

He studied her; it was as if he was storing every facial reaction in his memory, and it alarmed her. What was this? They had two major cases, everyone was swamped, and here he was asking how she was doing! She pulled herself together. "Who do you mean, treating me decently?"

"The others in the department. The men. Is it difficult being a woman among so many men? After all, you and Heilmann are the only females; are you okay with that?"

Louise smiled. "You mean, am I overcome by all the raw masculinity?"

He smiled back. "That's not exactly how I'd put it. I was just wondering if you're being respected as a woman here. The department never has attracted a lot of women."

Wrong, she thought; the department has never *hired* a lot of women.

She still suspected him of bringing her on board as a sign of goodwill; occasionally he was accused of keeping women out of the department, and every time it happened, he held her up to prove there was no discrimination on his watch.

"I really don't think much about it, but if this is about you wanting to hire more women, I'm all for it. An equal number of men and women is always a good idea."

Louise knew that sounded like gender-equality politics, and it dismayed her. She had no quarrel with the women's movement, with female networking and women speaking out for equal rights.

All that was fine as long as nobody forced her to be part of it. She was sick and tired of seeing the same female writers squawk every time women's rights had to be defended.

She sighed. The only person she dared say this to was Camilla.

Her boss interrupted her thoughts. "Do you have any problems with how people talk here?"

"I've always said I'm fine with working with men. I'm not cut out for the henhouse stuff. But what is it you're getting at?"

Suhr tipped his big office chair back and smiled. "You're more of a man than a lot of the others in our department."

Louise wondered whether she was meant to take that as a compliment. She decided to see where this was going.

"I've been asked to write an article for the international police magazine, about how women get along in Homicide here in Copenhagen."

Now she understood. How typical. He could have just said thanks but no thanks, that he didn't have much experience with women in the department. But his vanity wouldn't let him pass up a chance to have his name on the byline of an article in an international magazine.

"Well, you could mention that you recommend separate bathrooms for men and women. It makes working together a lot less annoying."

He nodded and jotted that down.

"Is your angle going to be how a woman gets by in an environment where sometimes it turns into a pissing contest, or is it whether women have a harder time at a crime scene?"

"Probably both. Do you feel your male colleagues have a better handle on the situations that come up?"

"Not really, but it's possible they've had more practice at keeping their emotions in check. I just don't think you should be ashamed of reacting to what's going on."

"No, no, of course not."

"Sure, you run into things that can be hard to take, but if you can't, you shouldn't be working here." Louise didn't know what else to say. It was a job, and you responded to the details because they were important to an investigation.

"But it wouldn't work with young women lacking your experience?" He wouldn't let go of it.

"That's hard to say. Depends on their attitude. Would you say they shouldn't work in an operating room, either?" She let that sink in. "Besides, a lot of what we do is paperwork."

She suspected he was trying to get her to talk about her breakdown, but if he wanted to discuss it, he'd have to bring it up himself.

"It's my impression that you don't feel discriminated against when you work with the pathologists or the forensic people, is that right?"

"I haven't felt that way, no."

He leaned forward; she saw the sparkle in his eye. "In fact, Flemming Larsen from Forensic Medicine and Niels Frandsen from Forensic Services both claim you'll be the first female head of Homicide someday." He winked at her.

She smiled and nodded. "Yeah, you'd better watch out."

Louise sensed he already was thinking about how to start the article. She stood up and left.

Karoline Wissinge's cell phone carrier was TDC. Louise got along well with their head of security, and she hoped he was at work. She didn't know any of the other TDC people who worked with the police, and anyway, in her experience everything went faster if you dealt with the boss.

She punched in his number and thought about how great it was that practically everyone had a phone nowadays. Being able to track a person's movements was an enormous help. Even though they were reasonably certain they already knew where Karoline had been Saturday night, something could show up when they went through her calls and messages. It annoyed her that she hadn't thought about getting a copy of the phone records.

Lars Jørgensen smiled cheerily at her from across the desk; she realized she was making faces as a moronic old pop number played in her ears.

"Hello," she yelled when she heard a click over the phone, but then a new melody kicked in. She was still on hold, and she drummed her fingers on the desk.

Finally. "Louise Rick," she said.

Before she could say another word, the head of security cut her off. "The girl in the park! That's who you're interested in, aren't you? You need a historical search or location or both?"

Louise thought it was funny they called it a historical search; cell phones weren't all that old, but unlike a location search, which could be used to track someone's whereabouts, a historical search went further back. They could look at the records and see who had called a particular cell phone.

She asked him for both, and he agreed to scan and email them to her. Email didn't function well at Copenhagen's Police Headquarters. They had a joint email address, but there were no individual addresses. They seldom used email.

Louise had just enough time to run over to the National Police to eat. The tasteless sandwiches at the top-floor cafeteria at Police Headquarters weren't worth climbing the stairs for except in an emergency. The only thing positive to say about it was the opening hours, which were longer than the big cafeteria across the street.

There was a note on her desk when she got back, telling her to call Forensic Services. She asked for Frandsen.

"Did you find anything?" she asked.

"Zero. Nothing. No trace of fingerprints whatsoever, and it was written with the type of felt tip you can buy everywhere, that's used at most workplaces."

Louise sighed. There had to be some damn detail they could work with, someplace. She thanked him and hung up.

Lars Jørgensen was busy searching for the childhood friend, Anders Hede, but she could see he'd heard enough to know the card hadn't panned out.

"Who lays a card like that at the scene of a young woman's murder?" he said. "If it isn't the murderer?"

"I don't know. But apparently someone who knew we'd probably look for him, since he took care of the fingerprints."

Jørgensen frowned. "He? Are you sure it's a man?"

"I think so. The writing was blocky, not really feminine, but of course you can never be sure."

Louise walked out to give Heilmann her report.

"Nothing but dead ends," she said, after sitting down across from her boss.

"You're right, we haven't got much to go on yet." Heilmann pushed a newspaper across the desk. Louise saw the obituary, framed by a blue fountain pen. Karoline Wissinge. Our beloved girl. The funeral would take place on Saturday.

The day we're doing the week-after canvass, Louise thought. "Nice for them that it's so soon." She was thinking about the parents. With some homicide cases, Forensic Medicine kept the body for quite a while, which she knew was hard on the family.

"Suhr was looking for you a while ago," Heilmann said. "I know he's going to the funeral, and I assume he'll ask you to go along."

At that moment Suhr walked by in the hallway and stopped when he spotted Louise. "How's your Saturday looking?"

"Okay." She sent Peter a mental apology; she'd been looking forward to spending the day with him before the canvassing that evening. But they still could go out for brunch.

"I think it's a good idea if three of us attend the funeral." Obviously, he'd already decided. "Would you tell Michael Stig?" He disappeared down the hallway.

Louise snorted. Errand girl. Maybe she should have pushed him more when they were talking about the article.

The door to Stig and Toft's office was closed. She knocked softly and stuck her head in. They were sitting at their desks, absorbed in reports. A small radio was playing in the background. It was nice in there, Louise noticed. They'd worked together for several years. Even though Toft was a lot older than Stig, she'd often noticed that they respected each other, backed each other up. Cared about each other. Toft was a likable man. His self-assured and calm demeanor was catching; you always felt things were under control with him. Stig wasn't her cup of tea, but she wasn't sure if others felt the same way.

Several sports medals hung from the bulletin board behind them. They bowled in the police league and had won several tournaments. At first, she'd laughed a bit at them—men and gold medals! Bowling made Louise think of friends having fun, enormous mugs of beer, days with sore arms and butts. She couldn't take their enthusiasm all that seriously.

"Am I disturbing you?" She walked over to Stig.

"You can disturb me anytime you want, beautiful." His eyes lingered on her a bit too long. He invited her to sit down, but she declined.

"Karoline is being buried on Saturday, and Suhr wants you and me to go with him."

"Aw, shit. I can't. Tell him he has to find someone else."

"He just went back to his office; I think you can catch him there." She wheeled around before he could say anything more. Who the hell did he think he was?

Louise sat down in her office and gathered her thoughts. She'd focused 100 percent on finding a lead, but it hadn't happened. She'd set aside the big picture, had dug around only in what she was involved in. Sometimes it was helpful to step back and look at the case from a distance. Look up so you don't stare yourself blind at specific leads and statements.

She grabbed a notebook out of her drawer and began drawing blocks. Above them she wrote the elements of the case they'd already been through. Interviews, family, friends, Baren, colleagues at work.

They must have overlooked something. She realized she was angry. Not about anything specific. Or was it Michael Stig? No, she was just mad. Annoyed. Everything was at an impasse, and she felt restless. Everyone was working their asses off, each on their own section of the puzzle. Sometimes when they didn't have any concrete leads, they became so eager to find something new that they weren't thorough enough with what they had.

A young woman couldn't just show up as a corpse in a park without somebody noticing something.

She began writing names in the boxes she'd drawn, but when she got to *friends*, she crumpled the paper and stood up.

Heilmann wasn't in her office. Louise checked if there was a car free. None of them were taken, so she walked back to the office and called Forensic Medicine to hear if Flemming Larsen was around.

"Hi, Rick, when are you and I going out together?" he said when he heard who was calling.

Her mood lightened when she heard his happy voice. A voice that fit his extremely tall frame, six-six or so. And he was both cheerful and competent. You could always laugh with him, but when he had something to say, you listened.

"I was thinking of dropping by, if you have time."

"Always time for you." Louise knew that was an exaggeration. Most of the time he had far too much to do. "Anything special I need to prepare for, before you show up?"

She heard his beeper in the background. "If you have time for a cup of coffee and a chat about Karoline Wissinge, that would be great." She added that she could come later, that there was just something she wanted to bounce off him.

"Come on over. We're always busy, but a man's gotta take his coffee break."

Louise guessed he had no more autopsies that day, since he was making time for her. Once he'd told her that he and the other pathologists each did one or two autopsies a day. Often, she'd wondered how he could handle cutting up so many bodies. He laughed when she asked him about it. He didn't do the cutting, he said, they had assistants for that, or pathologist technicians, as they were now called. As if that changed anything. He didn't see the body in front of him as Mr. Jensen or Mrs. Jørgensen; Louise of course realized that. But not long ago he had confessed something to her; he felt much worse examining a baby victimized by sexual assault than when he opened the chest cavity of a corpse. She could definitely understand that.

Louise had brought a suspect into the examination room at the Department of Forensic Medicine one day. A reconstruction of an extremely violent assault was to be made, and before that the suspect had to be measured, weighed, and examined for special characteristics. She'd never noticed the small examination couch along one wall of the room before, but she felt nauseated when

Flemming explained its purpose. The instrument beside the table was a colposcope, a microscope in a type of binoculars through which he could see if a hymen had been broken. A Disney figure was painted on the ceiling above the couch. Louise had shuddered.

During her first experience with that type of case, she had seriously considered whether she wanted to work at Homicide. She hadn't thought so much about how cases of sexual assault against children were a large part of their job.

Since then she'd handled several more. Even though they were gruesome, she'd managed to distance herself and maintain her professionalism, but it was difficult to leave such cases at work when she got home.

Also, the investigations of some of these cases were challenging. When too much time passed between the assault and the examination, for example. She'd been surprised when Flemming told her that some lesions in a child's hymen healed in a matter of a few weeks, making it difficult to determine if it had been broken. That's why they looked for tiny scars on the hymen with the colposcope.

Louise told Flemming she would be right over. She sat for a while after hanging up. Did she have the right to take up his time, just because she needed a broader view of the case? Maybe the others on the team felt they were making good progress. She doubted that, but she could have checked to make sure her little expedition was okay. What the hell. Surely there was nothing wrong with having a cup of coffee with a colleague.

She walked into Heilmann's office for the keys to the car. "I'll be gone for a while." She grabbed the keys and hurried out.

"See you," Heilmann said to her back.

8

She found a parking space behind the National Hospital and sat for a moment, gazing out at Fælled Park. A class had wheedled their teacher into going out to play soccer, she guessed. There weren't many other people in sight.

What did she really want to ask Flemming about? What didn't she know, or what did she think she could find out? She shook her head; maybe she just needed to get away from Police Headquarters and talk to someone who no doubt had his own ideas about the case.

Louise walked up the four steps and waited for the large sliding glass doors to open. She studied the sign beside the entrance. Institute of Molecular Pathology. Farther down: Lab for Pathological Proficiencies. What the hell was that?

She took the elevator to the floor for the pathologists' offices, where they wrote reports and such when they weren't busy performing autopsies. Flemming came over and said hello, then they walked down the hall to his small office.

"Good to see you," he said, after they sat down. "Coffee's coming in just a moment."

"That's fine." She smiled. The situation felt a bit awkward. She'd never talked with him this way before, to speculate, toss things around. "What do you think about this murder, what kind of a man is he?" She might as well acknowledge it: She was stumped.

He studied her for a moment, then he sighed and ran his fingers through his hair. "I really don't know. There's no doubt about the cause of death. While I was in there with her"—he nodded his head at the door—"I didn't feel she'd reached the stage where she'd been seriously frightened."

Louise nodded. She had her notepad out.

"Of course, you can't see fear on a corpse," he quickly added. "That's only something you see in films. All bodies look peaceful. But she had no lesions or abrasions, no broken nails, no sign that she'd fought for her life. I mentioned that in the report, too."

They eyed each other a moment. He'd finished with the autopsy report that morning, but the pathologist verifying the report had to read it before sending it on to the police.

Louise broke the silence. "I heard she was pregnant."

He nodded and frowned in concern.

"Her boyfriend didn't mention it when I spoke to him, but he might not have known. I'll contact her doctor to hear if she'd gone to him about her pregnancy. And you've ruled out rape?"

Normally the investigator present at an autopsy informs others on the team of what the pathologist said during the examination, but Suhr had only passed on a few details. They would have to read the rest in the report.

"Yes. The severe lesions on her neck are the only signs of the man."

"Is there any material for a DNA analysis?" To her surprise, she realized that in the back of her mind she'd hoped a DNA pro-file analysis would identify Karoline's murderer; she didn't believe some random attacker appeared out of nowhere and strangled a total stranger. She'd hoped there would be a match with someone they had already spoken to.

"It was raining cats and dogs Saturday night and most of Sun-day. Almost everything was washed away; there's nothing there for us." He spread his arms out in apology.

"The murderer must have left behind some evidence!" Louise couldn't accept that the best chance for a breakthrough in the case was eliminated, while nothing else was leading anywhere.

Suddenly he asked, "Would you like to see her?"

She thought for a moment, then she nodded.

She grabbed her things, and they walked out to the elevator. While they waited, Flemming said that Karoline's parents were coming to view her one last time, therefore she'd been taken to the visitation room on the ground floor.

Thankfully they didn't have to go to the basement. Louise had been there several times, and she never refused, but every time she walked down the long, tiled hallway with the glittering lights and incessant humming of the ventilation system, a heavy mood over-whelmed her.

On the ground floor, they walked into a waiting room, with the visitation room and examination room on one side, a row of of-fices on the other. It was deserted, but Louise smelled the cigarette butts. Someone had probably been waiting on the blue sofa a short while ago.

Flemming stuck his head in the office at the back and informed them that Louise Rick from Homicide wanted to see Karoline Wissinge. He was checking to make sure that Karoline was there. "Fine," he said. She guessed that Karoline was behind the door in the back corner.

"When are her parents coming?" She glanced at her watch as they walked to the door. Almost five. She didn't want to run into Hans and Lise.

"Five thirty or six. Her father was at work today and had to go home first."

Yes, he was back at work. Louise hadn't thought about that.

A white sheet covered Karoline. Louise recognized her easily, even though she'd only seen her face in photographs. Her wavy hair was golden blond, and she looked peaceful and calm lying there. Louise understood what Flemming meant. Nothing made her think this young woman had fought for her life. She noted the obvious abrasions on her throat.

Flemming followed her eyes and shrugged. It wasn't true they used makeup to cover wounds and lesions.

"Her mother is bringing some of her clothes."

Louise nodded.

"They're also bringing a few things to put in the casket. Everything has to be taken care of now, because the funeral is Saturday."

"I know. Suhr has ordered me to attend."

She checked her watch again. She had to leave; her presence might remind the parents that the police had nothing new to report. She felt sorry for them. This would be the second time they had buried one of their children.

She smiled at Flemming. "Thanks for letting me see her. I'd better get back."

She heard voices outside and crossed her fingers it wasn't Hans and Lise.

A man stood with his back to them in the waiting room. He turned around when they came out. He looked shabby, yet something about him made Louise think she should know who he was.

Out in the hall she asked Flemming. He smiled. "Søren Holm from *Morgenavisen*. He's spent most of the day arguing with the lab assistants because he wanted to see Frank Sørensen. He finally got it through his thick skull that he had to have permission from the police. Willumsen gave him the green light, and he finally got a look at him."

Louise hadn't thought about Sørensen being here, but of course, yes. "When's his funeral?"

"It might be a while. We're trying to determine what kind of knife he was stabbed with."

Suddenly the thought of all these bodies overwhelmed her. She was light-headed, as if she lacked oxygen. And the place felt claustrophobic, even though it was spacious with a high ceiling. Flemming took her elbow and walked quickly to the exit.

"So, you're waiting until we find the murder weapon that killed Sørensen?" she said as they stood out in the fresh air.

He nodded. "We also have to be certain what he was anesthetized with."

"Yeah, I can see it might be a while before that funeral."

"It's rough on his wife, but she's being incredibly gracious about it. She has this air of calm about her, like she's the type of person who believes in fate."

Louise thanked him again, and they said goodbye before she hurried over to the car.

How can you believe in fate when your husband is knifed to death, and your two-year-old son has lost his father? Sometimes Louise was amazed at people's reactions.

Jørgensen was gone when she returned to the office. She called Martin Dahl and was told that Karoline's personal physician, Dr. Madsen, lived on Østerbrogade. Louise didn't want to mention that Karoline had been pregnant before she talked to the doctor. It was late, but she might get lucky; like her own doctor, he might have evening consultation on Wednesdays.

"She was here last week," Dr. Madsen said when Louise explained why she was calling.

"She knew she was pregnant?"

"Definitely. She'd been pregnant before; she knew the symptoms. It's just terrible what happened to that poor girl," he added, before Louise could break in.

"Excuse me, you believe she'd been pregnant before?"

The doctor groaned a bit, as if he'd suddenly thought of doctor-patient confidentiality, but then he apparently remembered she was dead. And it was the police he was speaking to. "She had an abortion two or three years ago. I don't remember exactly when, but I can find it…just a sec."

Louise grabbed a notepad out of the pile of papers on her desk. She heard the doctor clicking the keys on his computer.

"Hmmm…" Louise could almost hear him reading Karoline's medical records. "It was four years ago. Time flies."

"Is there anything there about who the father was?" Louise asked eagerly.

"No. Father unknown. I remember she felt awful when she came in to me. The pregnancy was an accident, and she was afraid her parents would find out. I felt bad for her. It's always best to have someone to talk to and help deal with the situation, right from the start."

Louise agreed. She wrote everything down; though she wasn't sure the abortion was relevant to the investigation, at least they knew about it. She thanked him several times before hanging up.

The records from Karoline's cell phone had arrived. The same five names and numbers dominated the list. Her parents, Martin, work, and the two girlfriends she'd gone into town with. She laid the list down and went into Heilmann's office to tell her about the pregnancy, but her boss wasn't there. Louise stood in the hall, not sure what to do. Finally, she knocked on Michael Stig's door to hear if he had talked to Suhr about Karoline's funeral.

"Hi," she said.

Stig sat with his legs on his desk, reading. He smiled when he saw her.

"Did you tell Suhr?"

"Tell Suhr what?"

"About Saturday," she said. "That you can't make the funeral. Whoever he picks, it would be nice for them to know in good time."

"I'm going. We agreed to meet here; we'll go together."

Louise groaned inside. He'd griped to her, but apparently, he had no problem kissing the boss's ass. Should she just shrug it off?

"Okay then, it's all settled." She walked out. She realized what irritated her so much about Michael Stig: his fickleness. One minute he said one thing, the next something else. Plus, he was arrogant and chauvinistic as hell.

She decided not to waste any more time and energy on him. And to that end, it was best to keep as far away from him as possible. The terrifying thing was that a man like him could be her boss someday. Showing up for work would be hell.

She stuck her key in the door, and immediately a child's footsteps pattered in the hallway. "Hi, Louise!" Markus shrieked. "Peter gave me a cool skater sweatshirt."

"You look really cool in it."

She admired the much-too-big red sweatshirt, grabbed the hood, and gave him a big hug. Then she walked out to the kitchen and immediately sensed the laid-back, homey atmosphere pulling her in. "Hi."

She hugged Camilla. Peter stood up and put his arms around her, then planted a kiss on her forehead. He poured her a glass of red wine and refilled Camilla's and his own.

She looked at Camilla. "How's everything going?" Peter walked over to the kitchen counter and filled a plate for her.

"Good, really good in fact. Mom just arrived, and we should get home and keep her company, but like I've been telling Peter, it's been a very strange day."

Louise raised her eyebrows at her, then smiled at Peter when he set a plate in front of her. "Have you found a new job?"

"No, no, we cleared all that up. They agreed not to include a photo of the child."

"Fine, so everything's back to perfect."

"I met with Birte Jensen, the head of Narcotics and Licensing," Camilla said, ignoring Louise's irony. "Do you know her?"

Louise shook her head slowly. "Only what I've been told. A real lady, I've heard."

"Yeah, she doesn't look like a policewoman, anyway. More like some rich woman involved in charities and clubs."

Louise tried to remember what she looked like.

"I didn't even react when she met me in the hall. I couldn't imagine someone like her breaking up the big international drug cartels, but I guess you shouldn't let appearances fool you."

"She's married to a lawyer who argues before the Supreme Court, and I think they live up by the Royal Forest. Why did you talk to her?"

"Willumsen asked me to call her."

Louise was puzzled. Police leaders seldom got involved with journalists this way.

"It surprised the hell out of me, too," Camilla said. She tipped her wineglass and drank. "She has a nice office, I'll say that. Diplomas, fancy framed paintings on the wall, plush armchairs."

"Come on, what happened?"

"Now I know what it feels like to be granted an audience with the queen. Very ceremonious, a little bit fake. It annoyed me; *she* was the one who wanted to talk to me."

Louise smiled and looked at Camilla; she was pretty, with her blond hair hanging down on her shoulders, her big deep blue eyes. Like Birte Jensen, her appearance deceived most people when they met her. One thing was that she swore right off the bat. But her mind was sharp as a razor, and she never backed down. If someone avoided a question, she looked them straight in the eye and didn't budge until she got a decent answer. Many times, she'd made Louise's toes curl in such situations, but it was fun to watch people reassessing Camilla. She was no sissy.

"I told her I'd spoken with Willumsen, and I'd heard she met with Frank Sørensen on Saturday evening."

Louise pushed back her plate and took a drink of wine. Again, she was surprised. "At Police Headquarters?"

Camilla nodded. "She wanted to fill me in on some of the stuff she and Frank had talked about. Maybe I should have told her to talk to Søren Holm—he's the one covering the drug case for us. But since I was there, I figured I might as well listen to what she had to say."

Peter and Markus had gone into the living room. Louise noticed how quiet it was, and she assumed the little man had conked out. It wouldn't surprise her if the big man had, too.

"Seems they've had a surveillance going on in the Royal Hotel for quite a while, in connection with the drug case. She said they were expecting a shipment of what for some ridiculous reason they call 'green dust'— like in some comic book. Why don't they just call it heroin or cocaine or whatever the hell it is?"

"Because it has a light green color that makes it recognizable when it's sold."

Camilla raised her eyebrows, as if she was surprised her friend knew about things like that. "She said Frank stopped by Saturday evening, said he'd been told he could come along when the police moved in. He'd sniffed out what was about to happen, and it sounded like he'd been pushy, which annoyed the hell out of her. But they made a deal about where he'd be and who he'd be with when it all came down. The police had access to two hotel rooms. One they used to listen in on three other hotel rooms. And they had plainclothes cops stationed around the hotel, in the restaurant on the top floor, in the bar, down in the lobby."

Louise visualized all that.

"The police used the second room for taking breaks, or if they felt too conspicuous."

Louise was familiar with such operations, but she was glad she seldom took part in them. You could wait for days without anything happening.

"Jensen told Frank to just show up. She would be in the surveillance room, listening in on the rooms being bugged. Is it common to let reporters in on things like this?"

"It depends on the reporter and who's in charge. What you've just told me isn't normal. But he might have known something and was using it to pressure her with."

Louise thought about what she'd just said. She wasn't completely familiar with how Narcotics worked. There might be other advantages to working closely with the press that she didn't know about. She did know that reporters often asked to be at the scene of a homicide and witness the start of an investigation, but she'd never heard of anyone being allowed so close.

"The reason this hasn't come out is that Narcotics wants the places they have under surveillance to be a secret, and of course that's understandable. The plan was that Frank would show up late that evening, hang out for a while in the bar, and if something happened, he would be tipped off. But he was ordered not to talk to any of the police."

"So, did anything happen?" Louise was curious; she hadn't heard about any raid.

"Yeah, it did. But Jensen wouldn't go into that. They made a few arrests and confiscated quite a bit of heroin."

"Was he there during the arrests?"

Camilla shook her head. "No one saw him."

"If Jensen made a deal with him, isn't it odd he didn't show up?"

They thought for a moment. "Her theory is that Frank arrived at the hotel, but then he met a few of the men the police were after, either inside the hotel or outside. Obviously, he had something going on."

Camilla stared into space for a moment. "Something he was holding over Jensen, otherwise she wouldn't have let him be there. But also, something the bad guys didn't want him to reveal. Maybe they decided to stop him. Not that the men who were arrested did it themselves. Things like that can be arranged on short notice."

Louise thought about that. She stood up to put water on for coffee. "Why did she tell you all this? If they know who killed Sørensen, they'd want to round them up without telling anyone about it."

"She wanted to make a deal. She'd scratch my back if I scratched hers."

Louise sat down and leaned her chair up against the wall, then she crossed her arms and stared at her friend in curiosity. "What the hell do you have that she wants?"

"Nothing right now. But she gave me the name of one of their snitches and asked me to pay him a visit and twist his arm a bit."

Louise was incredulous. "She gave you the name of one of their informants?" She poured the boiling water in the French press. "Why would he tell you more than he'd tell the police?"

She grabbed two cups out of the cupboard and set everything on the table.

"Jensen thinks he might hold something back from them that might put him in a bad light. He can't be charged with anything for leaking information to a reporter. And anyway, snitches usually want to tell what they know."

"How much of what you find out can you print?"

"I have free rein. She just wants to know what the talk in the underworld is."

"Be careful. You don't just elbow your way in with these people. You don't belong there."

Louise realized too late that she'd waved another red flag in front of Camilla. "Listen," she implored. "It takes years to develop the right sources. You can't simply stroll into some hole and expect to be accepted as one of the gang. That's not how it works. If anyone suspects you're snooping around, they'll tie rocks around your feet and dump you in the harbor." After a moment she added, "But of course we'll take care of Markus."

"Relax, it's not going to be that way. I'll let Holm deal with all that. But I can ask around and try to find the snitch she's talking about."

"What's his name?"

Louise noted that Camilla hesitated. "The Finn. Do you know him?" Suddenly, Camilla looked tired.

Louise shook her head. "How much are you thinking about getting involved in this?"

She hoped this wasn't a new crusade, but she sensed a spark in Camilla, and when that happened, her friend was off and running.

"I'll talk with this Finn guy, if I can find him, and then I assume Søren will take over. The drug trial starts tomorrow, a Dutchman and the Danish middlemen will be in court, and the ones they arrested Saturday have been charged and are in custody the next four weeks. Looks like they still haven't found the Danish gang leader."

Her phone rang. "Hi, no, no, nothing's happened yet. We're still over at Louise's. We're coming home now."

She laid her phone on the table. "That was Mom. She was getting worried."

Louise checked her watch; it was past eleven. "Better get home then," she said. She walked into the living room, where Markus lay on the sofa, buried deep in Peter's arms. She called for a taxi while Camilla put her coat on and packed Markus's things into a plastic sack.

"How long is your mom staying?"

"Until Sunday."

"It would be nice to see her."

"She's going out in the country on Friday, but otherwise she just wants to spend time with her spiritual friends and Markus."

"I miss her. I'm always in a good mood when she's around. Maybe she's met some new spirits she can tell us about." Louise lifted Markus up and handed him to Camilla. They said goodbye at the door, and Louise watched them walk down the stairs.

Peter was up when she returned to the living room. "Wow, I passed out."

Louise nodded and smiled. "It's almost impossible not to when you lie down and try to put a kid to sleep. That's a really nice sweatshirt you bought him." She felt a bit like an outsider.

"I found it on Skindergade on the way home from my meeting. It caught my eye, and I just had to buy it."

"You'll spoil him to death." She laughed, and he pulled her close, told her this was how it would be as long as he didn't have his own kids to spoil.

"Then you'd better get some," she said. She walked to the bathroom to wash her face and brush her teeth.

"Yeah, but it looks like that will have to wait, if the offer I just got turns out to be as good as it sounds."

She stopped and turned to him, her mouth full of toothpaste. "What offer?" She wiped off the foam running out of the corners of her mouth.

"From our Scottish office."

She realized he was talking about what happened at the dinner with the Finns. "You make it sound like it'll be all work and no play if you accept."

He walked into the bathroom. "If I do, I'll have to move to Aberdeen for six months."

She spat and rinsed her mouth.

"And I hope you'll go with me."

9

Let's get started the old-fashioned way," Suhr said as they sat in Heilmann's office Thursday morning. The report from Forensic Genetics had arrived. As Louise already had heard, there was no usable material on Karoline Wissinge, so a DNA profile of the murderer wasn't going to happen.

Louise told them about Karoline's abortion. Suhr sat quietly as she spoke, then nodded when she finished.

"So, you've spoken with her doctor?"

He seemed to feel she'd gone behind his back, not informing him beforehand about contacting the doctor. She was about to explain, defend herself, but at the last second, she held back. "Yes!"

An awkward silence followed.

"Okay," he said, nodding at her. Louise tried to get her heartbeat under control.

"Let's keep that bit of information to ourselves," the Homicide chief said, looking around the room pointedly. Clearly, he wouldn't tolerate this being leaked to the press. "I'm expecting the autopsy report by noon."

"The boyfriend didn't say anything about it?" Michael Stig said.

She shook her head, annoyed at how he made it sound. Like it was her fault the family hadn't mentioned the pregnancy or the abortion. "But, of course, I'm going to ask him."

"After lunch," Suhr said, "Forensics is coming in. We'll meet in my office, and the rest of the day we'll go through the evidence we have, together with the officers assigned to us."

Several of them nodded. No one looked particularly eager, and Louise noticed that Heilmann was lost in her own thoughts.

"When we meet, I want you all to bring a list of the facts you're certain about, and we'll brainstorm. We'll continue until we have a clear picture of what happened." He looked grim as he stood up and left the office.

"Okay then, we'd better get to it," Toft said, pushing his chair back to stand up.

"If I could have a minute first," Heilmann said, gesturing at him to sit again. "There's something you should all know before this afternoon's meeting."

The next few moments reminded Louise of the phrase *so quiet you could hear a pin drop.*

Heilmann didn't beat around the bush. "I've just been granted an open-ended leave of absence."

"Henny, what…?" Toft said.

Odd, how personal he sounded, Louise thought. Unusual.

"Perhaps you all know that my husband has been ill," she said.

Only Toft nodded.

"He was improving, and we hoped the worst was over. But last Wednesday he was admitted to the hospital again, and on Friday they found a large tumor on the left side of his head." Tears had swelled up as she spoke, and now they fell. After a moment, she dried them off with her index finger.

Louise sighed heavily. "Can it be operated on?"

Heilmann looked at her and shook her head. "Listen, I'm stopping today. Right now, in fact. I won't be at the meeting this afternoon. I don't know if they're planning to promote someone, or if Suhr will be taking over the investigation."

"If there's anything I can do, let me know," Louise said after they all stood up.

"Thanks. If I don't come back to the department, take care of yourself."

Louise was startled. "Why wouldn't you come back?"

"I plan on it, but we don't know how long I'll be gone, and obviously they can't promise to hold the job for me forever."

"They won't get rid of you. At most they'll appoint a temporary DCI until you come back."

Heilmann smiled weakly. "Thanks, but to tell the truth, that's the least of my worries right now. I can't even imagine myself working. Hopefully that will change later on, but right now I just need to let go of everything, concentrate on what's happening at home."

Louise nodded. She thought about Peter. When they went to bed the night before, he had suggested she take a leave of absence and go with him to Aberdeen. Before he could finish, though, she'd cut him off. She wasn't going to leave her job and play housewife in some Scottish city for six months.

She pushed her conversation with Peter out of her mind. Even though Henny Heilmann's situation made an impression on her, there was no way she should feel guilty about not putting her life on standby while Peter's career took off.

Camilla sat in the Metro on the way to work, considering what to tell Høyer about her meeting with the head of Narcotics. She was also anxious to hear if they'd given Søren Holm permission to be in on Wednesday's raid, and if so, what he'd gotten out of it. Maybe she should ask him if he knew anything about the Finn. But first she would make some inquiries.

The hallway outside the editorial offices was quiet, the doors closed. Her monitor crackled when she turned the computer on. She wanted to start by checking Infomedia, a database for articles published in major Danish newspapers. Maybe she could read up on what was happening in the drug underworld and check for names mentioned frequently in the articles.

She typed in *narcotics*—over eight thousand results. She sighed and limited the search to the past year. A little over a thousand. Still too many. She had to be more specific. Drug gangs. Finally, she got it down to thirty-nine, which she could handle.

She scanned the articles and found eleven that looked promising. Then she searched for drug raids; sixteen articles showed up, five of which looked potentially useful. She started reading them, noting in which articles the persons arrested were named. She printed them out. Also, the articles about Copenhagen's drug underworld.

She noticed that many of the articles in front of her were written by Holm and Frank Sørensen. A lump came to her throat when she began highlighting an article called "Prisoners' Families Threatened by Drug Lord."

She was almost finished with the articles when Høyer knocked and came in. He asked her if she'd seen Holm. She shook her head. "I don't even know what he got out of the police raid yesterday. Did they let him go along?"

He shrugged. "I don't know. He promised to let me know, but I haven't heard from him since Tuesday evening."

Camilla stiffened. "He isn't answering his phone." She had a bad feeling about this, but she tried to come up with a plausible explanation. "He might have gone home to sleep. He's been at it almost twenty-four seven. When I saw him Tuesday afternoon, he looked like a walking corpse."

She stopped abruptly, though not before that last word slipped out. Høyer didn't react. Camilla sighed. She knew she was riling herself up, that everything going on around her was getting to be too much for her to think about rationally. She needed to focus and not see ghosts. Maybe handing everything over to Søren when he got back wasn't so stupid after all. Then she could concentrate on Karoline's murder and not have to cross swords with gangsters.

She took a deep breath and leaned back. "Could we call his wife if he still has a home phone?" She breathed deeply until she felt herself relaxing.

"Yeah, I'll do that right now. He doesn't like being disturbed at home, but I want to know where the hell he is. You have to keep track of your people." He smiled a bit bashfully before walking back to his own office.

Camilla could see he was worried, too.

She decided to call Hans Suhr and ask if there was anything new in the Karoline Wissinge case. She would concentrate on that until Søren showed up. The thought of telling her much more experienced colleague about the talk she'd had with Birte Jensen, the deal she'd made with her, eased Camilla's mind. She punched the number for Police Headquarters and asked for the chief of Homicide. While waiting, she realized she hadn't heard if anything had come out of the article written for Willumsen about Frank Sørensen's movements last Saturday. She'd have to check on that later.

"Hans Suhr is currently in a meeting."

"How about Willumsen?"

"Not in."

She hung up. It annoyed her that they always said to call later. You hardly ever got hold of them on the first try.

Louise counted fifteen at the meeting, which had been moved from Suhr's office to the conference room.

"Let's hear from Forensic Services first," Suhr said, gesturing at Frandsen.

Louise was the only woman in the room. Just as in Homicide, few women worked at Forensic Services, and apparently none of them had been assigned to this case.

Frandsen lit his pipe before standing and walking over to the big screen in the corner of the room. "I'll start by showing you what we filmed at the crime scene when we were called in."

Several of them turned their chairs to get a better look. Louise grabbed her notepad, ready to take notes, even though she knew they would go through everything later.

The first thing to appear on the screen was the red and white barrier tape. A few techs were expanding the area initially blocked off by the first officers on the scene.

The camera then showed the entire crime scene. The body wasn't visible, but a few men walked in the background, setting up a tarp to block the view of curious bystanders.

"The rain was definitely a big advantage for the murderer," Frandsen said. He laid down his pipe.

Louise nodded almost imperceptibly. Flemming had already pointed that out.

The next image was a close-up of Karoline Wissinge. The camera zoomed in on the bruises on her throat. Her blond hair was wet and stuck to her pretty face.

She swallowed. Karoline looked so terribly vulnerable lying there. The young woman's life had been taken away, and Louise found it even more difficult when she thought of the embryo inside her.

Small marks had been made in the earth around the bush, and a close-up showed a pair of footprints, a cigarette butt, and a wrapper from a bar of chocolate. Several of the things marked were so small that Louise couldn't see what they were. It was getting dark, and several techs walked around with small, extremely bright spotlights. She was surprised the entire crime scene hadn't been illuminated by then.

Frandsen explained they had focused on searching for footprints. The rain could be useful in one way: There was a chance the murderer had left behind a set of visible impressions. Had it started to rain again, they would have lost many valuable footprints, which is why they had rushed to make castings of the ones they'd found. He explained that they'd also waited for the civil defense to arrive with a large tent to cover the body.

Louise tipped her chair back. She hadn't been asked to pick up shoes from Martin Dahl or Karoline's ex-boyfriend, to be compared with the prints found. Apparently, they didn't have anything useful. But clearly, they'd had to protect every potential clue for later evaluation.

"We found two cigarette butts. Our examinations show they came from two people. One of the butts had disintegrated, but Genetics managed to do a DNA analysis on the other." He looked around the room, as if he expected them to applaud.

"Great," Toft said. Several others nodded. They had so little to go on, and this could prove to be important.

Louise smiled, too. She was impressed by how incredibly little it took to do a DNA profile on a human. Saliva and sweat contained no DNA, but it could be found in the tiny skin cells that sweat carried out of the body, or in the mucous cells in saliva. When you sneeze, the spray can provide enough DNA for a profile.

"If there were any fingerprints on Karoline Wissinge, the rain washed them away."

The faces around the table drooped. He shut the TV off. Hans

Suhr stood up and walked over to Niels Frandsen. "Rain is our enemy," he said as dramatically as he could. They had absolutely nothing.

Louise wrote down what had been said, though not because she couldn't remember. She had to do something.

She'd promised Karoline's parents the police would do everything they could, but right now there were no leads. She was surprised how much her anger bothered her. In her mind she saw Karoline in the park, but immediately she put aside the image and instead saw her lying in the room at Forensic Medicine, cleaned up and looking nice. That helped calm her, though it did nothing to ease the discouragement she'd been feeling the past two days. Not one single breakthrough in the case. Had she been attentive enough to everything she'd discovered, the people she'd met? She could have been sitting across from the murderer, without any sense at all of who he was. She hoped not. But she was having trouble concentrating, and that wasn't like her.

Suhr wanted everyone to briefly tell about whom they'd been in contact with. It took an hour. Louise told about the abortion and stopping by to talk to Flemming, about his observation that Karoline apparently hadn't tried to defend herself. "Presumably she hadn't been afraid. Maybe she didn't have time to react, or maybe she didn't expect to be assaulted."

They took a short break; most of them walked out for a cup of coffee. Louise followed them slowly. After filling her mug, she returned to the room at once. She needed a moment to herself before they started brainstorming.

Suhr stood at the whiteboard, holding Flemming's autopsy report. On the right he had written the pathologist's estimated time of Karoline's death, between midnight and seven a.m. Sunday. On the left he'd written *One a.m.*, the time she'd left Baren. The space between was blank.

Everyone drifted in and sat down. "What happened between one and seven?" He glanced around the room. "What the hell happened from the time she left her friends until she ended up in the park?"

"Her boyfriend came to pick her up. He saw her with Lasse Møller, got jealous, and strangled her!"

"Lasse Møller wanted more than just a walk. She shut him down, and he strangled her!"

Louise had drawn a stick figure of a girl on her notepad, and every time a new idea came up, she drew a line from the figure and wrote the idea down.

"Childhood friend from Frederikshavn confronted her before she got home. Maybe she'd told her boyfriend not to loan him more money."

By the time they finished, Louise's head was spinning. Nothing was too stupid or unwelcome when they brainstormed; they listened to every idea, even though some of them were far-fetched.

"We are going to bring in every person we have named here today for questioning," Suhr said, "whether they've already been questioned or not. As far as other unknown persons possibly involved, we'll have to hope our week-after canvass flushes them out. Like a witness who saw something Saturday night, but maybe didn't connect it to the murder."

Almost everyone in the room responded positively. Enthusiasm had crept in during the afternoon and grown with every idea tossed out. Of course, some of the ideas would lead somewhere; all they had to do was put their noses to the grindstone.

Louise looked around the room. It was incredible how important teamwork could be. Every new idea, no matter how far-out, had been met with cries of approval.

"Are we ready?" Suhr asked. He stood up. "Does everyone know what they'll be doing?"

They nodded.

"Wait!" he yelled, after several of them already were out in the hall. "Come back a second."

They all gathered around the doorway.

"I almost forgot to tell you. There will be some changes in the department leadership."

Everyone pricked up their ears. "Unfortunately, we'll be without Henny Heilmann for the time being."

Several of them mumbled in surprise. "She's applied for and been given an open-ended leave of absence." More mumbling. "We haven't yet decided if a temporary DCI will be appointed, but of course we'll keep you informed. For the present I'm taking over as head of this investigation."

Louise heard several of them talking about Heilmann out in the hallway, posing questions, such as, Why is she leaving? Was she forced out? Louise mentally stuck her fingers in her ears. She didn't want to hear the talk, especially not the gossip about who would replace her. She returned to her office and made a list of the people she was to contact. Jørgensen was responsible for Martin Dahl and the ex-boyfriend. She would be talking to Karoline's three colleagues at work and the two friends she was with on the night of the murder. The three nurses felt like a dead end to her, but they had to be questioned again regarding the theory that Karoline had a secret affair going. She might have confided in them. A long shot, Louise thought. Very long.

Her phone rang. "Department A, Louise Rick."

"Hello, this is Hans Wissinge, Karoline's father." His voice was deep and masculine. "I'm sorry to disturb you."

"You're not disturbing me at all," Louise said. For once she meant it.

"Perhaps I should have called the chief of Homicide directly. But when I've done so, I've been told that he's in a meeting, so now you're stuck with me."

He sounded very apologetic.

Louise sympathized with him. "What can I do for you?"

"I'm not sure if you can do anything. I just need to hear if there's any news. We haven't heard anything, and your chief keeps speaking to the papers about the murder of the journalist. Not that we feel that's completely unfair, but he doesn't seem as interested in finding out who killed our daughter."

His voice broke, and Louise felt a lump in her throat.

"I promise you, we're working around the clock to find who killed her. The meeting he's been in all day long has been with us, with Homicide, and officers from the crime division, several from Forensics. We've gone through the whole case, and we're calling people back in to be questioned."

Louise paused to hear if Karoline's father felt reassured, but he didn't answer.

"Saturday evening we're going out on the streets to talk to everyone in the area at the approximate time of Karoline's murder. We're hoping some of them were there at that time last week. This case has every bit as much of our attention as that of the journalist."

He blew his nose. Louise felt the guilt rising like bile in her throat. Of course, more resources were allocated to the murder cases that hit the front pages every day. No one would ever admit it, but it wasn't hard to figure out. Louise had discussed it several times with her colleagues. And with Heilmann.

"Thank you," he said.

Louise was torn; did they know their daughter had been pregnant? She was afraid she would have to break the news to them. "Actually, I was about to call you to see if I could come by tomorrow and give you an update. Would that be okay?"

She scratched her forehead. She really didn't have time for that, but she felt sorry for them. Her day would just have to be longer.

"That would be fine. The funeral is the day after tomorrow, so we have some preparations to make." His voice was weak, but he did sound a bit lighter.

"I'll call you tomorrow morning, and we'll find a time."

After hanging up, she found the numbers of the people she would be questioning. All of them agreed to come in the next day. Great, she thought as she put a check mark beside the last one.

Louise called Peter to say she was leaving. She didn't know what his plans were, and she felt a bit embarrassed about not having asked.

She was disappointed when he reminded her that he was going out with a few people on business. He'd invited her along, and she had said no. She seldom felt like meeting new people, because they usually weren't shy about prying into her work, which she discussed only with Camilla and Peter.

A bit later she called Camilla. She felt alone. Though that usually wasn't a problem, now she felt the need for company. Suddenly she remembered that Camilla's mother was visiting, but Camilla answered before she could stop the call. "Hi."

Her friend sounded down, and Louise decided not to burden her. "Hi, I just called to hear how you're doing."

"It's like Søren Holm has vanished from the face of the earth; in fact, it's goddamn annoying. The mood in here is strained to say the least."

"I saw him yesterday." Louise told her about spotting him at Forensic Medicine.

Camilla livened up. "I'll be damned! Did he say anything?"

"No, not to us. But I was told he'd been arguing with the guys all day, the techs, I mean. Because they wouldn't let him see Frank Sørensen's body."

"How did he look?" Camilla sounded curious but also relieved.

"Like hell. I remember him as a decent-looking guy, shaved and hair combed, all that, but that wasn't him yesterday. He looked more like a bum."

"A bum! Are you sure it was him? That doesn't sound right at all."

"I asked Flemming Larsen, the pathologist who did the autopsy on Karoline. He said it was Søren Holm. They know each other, so of course it was him. He was really raising hell."

"Okay." Camilla didn't sound 100 percent convinced. "I'd better tell Høyer."

"Yeah, you'd better. Talk to you later."

Before she hung up, Camilla said, "Are you still at work?"

"Yeah, but I'm leaving in a minute."

"You have any plans?"

"Not really. I'd forgotten that Peter was going out, but I'm fine with hanging out at home. I need to do laundry. I have to work all day Saturday." She told her about the week-after canvass.

"Mom took Markus out to eat at McDonald's. I told them I'd join them when I left work; why don't you come along? They'd love it if you did."

Louise thought for a moment. It sounded tempting, but then she'd have to wash her clothes later, and wasn't it a good idea to get that taken care of, now that she had time? "Hmmm."

"Come on. You can always do laundry. If you run out of clothes, you can borrow from me. It might be a long time before Mom makes it over again. Pentecost, something like that."

Camilla knew how to persuade Louise. "Okay, let's do it. Where do you want to meet?" Louise remembered she'd biked to work.

"It's the McDonald's on Falkoner Allé. Let's just meet there, okay? I'll stick my head in and tell Høyer you saw Søren and he was okay. Or alive, anyway."

Louise called Peter and told him about her plans. She looped her bag over her shoulder and started down the hall. Heilmann's office door was open, and after glancing inside she stopped abruptly. The office was bare, her desk cleaned off. The Scotch tape holder and paper clips sat neatly on the green felt, but nothing personal was left. Louise checked her watch. She had said goodbye to Heilmann four hours ago, and now it was as if she'd never been there. It felt so sad. Louise was going to miss her.

10

Louise was in a better mood after devouring a McFeast and several Chicken McNuggets. Markus had eaten two bites of his food and then ran off to the playroom full of balls. It was a battle to get him out of there. After a few pointed remarks from two mothers with toddlers, they realized he was too big to romp around in the ocean of colored plastic balls. Three feet eight inches was the limit, and he was taller. They agreed this would be his last time in the room, and he decided it had to be celebrated. He extracted promises of ice cream and films before consenting to go home. Louise walked her bike with Markus on the seat.

"How are things over in Jutland?" she asked over her shoulder.

"The way they always are, thank God," Camilla's mom answered. "Peace and quiet. I have plenty of time to do as I please, unlike you two."

The only thing they'd talked about all evening was the two

"girls." In her opinion, they both worked way too much and took very little care of themselves. They'd tried in vain to convince her she was wrong.

"Usually I have a lot of time to spend on myself and that little guy." Camilla threw him a look full of love. "But if I didn't work, how much fun do you think we could afford to have?"

Her mother sighed. "I'm thinking more about having time for grown-ups once in a while."

Camilla sneered. "Do you have someone particular in mind, if I may ask?"

"A nice man, for instance, but you've become so independent and picky that you don't even see the possibilities, dear."

"There's nothing wrong with being picky."

"No, certainly not. But we can be open to people."

Louise stayed out of it. This conversation happened every time they were together.

"There must be men at your work," her mother continued. "It's such an exciting place."

Louise admired her for her persistence. It never led to anything, but she kept at it, hoping some of it would rub off on her daughter.

"Strange, but there's no possibilities there. And anyway, it's not very smart to get involved with someone you work with."

Louise laughed. "Since when did that stop you?"

Camilla's mother was all ears. "Is there something I haven't heard about?"

"No." Camilla held her open palm out in frustration. "Listen. If anything happens on that front, I will let you know, and if you run into my future husband, I am open to meeting him. How does that sound?" End of discussion.

"Fine," her mother and Louise said in chorus. Camilla opened the front door.

"You're all crazy," Markus said, his finger circling beside his temple. He darted up the steps.

They all agreed he was right and followed him.

Markus was asleep by nine, and Camilla's mother began yawning.

Louise went out in the kitchen, looking for a pack of sweet biscuits she could do some damage on.

"I'm going into town this evening," Camilla yelled as Louise rummaged through her cupboards.

"You have a date?" Louise was surprised. She found a roll of Marie biscuits behind a box of cornflakes and walked back into the living room.

"No, actually I'm thinking of swinging by a nightclub, no date."

That *really* surprised Louise. "What, you're going in to score?" Camilla usually didn't go into town alone.

"No, I'm not that desperate. I'm going to try to find out who this Finn is."

Louise studied her. "Why are you doing this? What's so important that suddenly you're going to spend Thursday night hanging out with drug dealers? You don't know these people. At all."

"I think it's important to find out who killed Frank." Camilla was indignant.

"And you've decided you're the one to do it?" Things went on in Camilla's brain that Louise simply couldn't figure out.

"The head of Narcotics must not think it's so strange, since she asked me to." Camilla had known this discussion would come up if she let Louise in on her plans, and she'd decided not to tell her. But now it was too late.

"I'm going with you." It would be hell getting up in the morning and going to work, but the thought of Camilla out there alone was worse.

"You don't need to. I can handle this alone. I'm not planning on doing anything risky."

Louise ignored that. "Where are we going?"

Camilla stood a moment. Was it best to be on her own? Maybe having someone along wasn't such a bad idea. "You don't think these people can see you're a cop?" She studied Louise.

Louise raised her voice. "Are you kidding? Do I look like a cop?"

"Well…no," Camilla admitted.

Louise was wearing a tight off-white sweater, worn Diesel jeans, and pointed-toe boots, and her full, wavy dark hair hung down on her shoulders.

"We're going to a nightclub close to King's New Square. It doesn't open until midnight, but there's a bar next door. We might be able to get someone to talk."

"How do you know about these places?"

"Birte Jensen told me about the nightclub. And then I've checked some articles in our archives, and the King's Bar keeps popping up. So, I'm just guessing."

"And we agree this is only about finding the informant, right?"

Camilla nodded.

"Let's do it then. But." Louise looked sternly at her friend. "You will not start asking about anything else. These guys are nasty, and a blue-eyed blonde won't blind them. Not if they suspect you're pumping them for information over a drink, anyway."

"No, I know that." Camilla sighed and put her coat on. "Let's just go."

11

Louise glanced around when they stepped into the King's Bar. She carried her coat over her arm and followed Camilla to a table. The place was nice. It wasn't crowded, not for a Thursday night, when the city center usually was cooking.

Camilla searched her bag for her billfold. "We'll have to buy something to drink, I suppose."

"Coke for me," Louise said when Camilla headed for the bar.

A bored young woman was bartending. She could hardly be bothered, especially when Camilla ordered two colas.

Camilla looked disappointed when she returned. "Nobody here's involved with drugs."

"You don't know that."

"Look around. These are decent people; no one here's dealing anything."

An older man came out from a back room and walked behind the bar. It looked as though he was arranging bottles. He carried out a box of empties and returned with a ring binder. Louise caught herself observing him as if she were working. Did he seem nervous or feel he was being watched? Was there anything out of the ordinary going on? She relaxed; he was just doing his job.

A young man walked in and sat on one of the high bar stools. The older man grabbed a bottle of beer and opened it for him. They began chatting.

The grumpy bartender made the rounds, picking up empty bottles. As she passed by Louise and Camilla, she gave their half-empty colas a frosty look. Her mind was an open book; these women weren't going to leave a tip, so why should she even bother?

Several more people walked in. Some of them sat at the round tables, others at the bar.

"Sometimes I wonder how drug dealers can see if people are interested," Camilla said. They were sitting in plush armchairs, the type that invites quiet talk and an intimate atmosphere, but they weren't particularly good for following what was going on in the place.

"Maybe it's the same as what they say about gay people. They always seem to be sure they can spot other gays in a crowd." Not very PC, that comparison, Louise told herself.

Three men in leather jackets and combed-back hair made a racket as they walked in. "There's a possibility," Camilla said.

Louise nodded. They fit the stereotype. Two of them sat at a nearby table, and the other went up to the bar.

"Now it's a matter of keeping our ears open," Camilla whispered.

Louise felt herself tensing up.

"Damn it," Camilla said when two attractive men in their early fifties sat at the table beside them, blocking their view of the three men in leather jackets—and ruining every chance of overhearing anything they said.

They looked at each other. It was a quarter to eleven, over an hour until the nightclub opened. Now the bar was almost full, with only a few tables unoccupied.

"Maybe we should just ask for him?" Camilla said.

"Ask who?"

"The man up at the bar. He must know him if he ever comes around here."

"Yeah, but let's wait until we're ready to go," Louise said.

She wished that Peter were with them so they didn't look so obvious sitting there. Two women alone always drew attention. Already they had been assessed and discussed by several of the males. Louise felt she was on display. One of the two men at the next table stood up and headed for the bar. When he passed their table, he asked if he could buy them a drink.

Louise just stared, but Camilla smiled at him and said, "Thank you, that sounds great."

"Champagne?" the man asked.

Louise sent her a look. The man back at the table had white hair. He smiled as he stood up and walked over to them. "Hi, my name is Michael."

He pulled his chair over. Out of the corner of her eye, Louise noticed several others watching. She cringed, and things didn't get better when the bartender came over with a bottle of champagne and four flutes. It felt like a spectacle when the cork popped; she was sure everyone had their ideas about what was going on.

"Klaus," the champagne man said, holding out his hand. "What are you two beautiful ladies doing here in town by yourselves?"

Louise bit her tongue; she didn't want to be rude. While Camilla chirped at the man, she tried to smile. He filled all four glasses and they toasted. She was content to sip. She excused herself, and stood up and fled to the bathroom. When the door to the narrow hallway leading to the bathrooms shut behind her, she leaned against the wall.

"So, picked up some company, did you?"

It was one of the three men they'd wanted to eavesdrop on. She felt herself blushing; it wasn't hard to guess what he was thinking. "Excuse me, may I?" She tried to slip past him.

He backed up toward the bathrooms, still blocking the way. "Hey, no need to be so touchy, what with that bubbly you're drinking. No reason at all."

"Would you please move back a bit, so I can get past?"

He sized her up, but instead of moving he squinted and nodded thoughtfully, as if he'd just realized something. "You look like you could stand a little bit of fun. You sure came to the right place. Go on back to your rich boys. I'd watch out if I were you, though. Might not only be champagne in those glasses."

Louise's eyebrows shot up. "What do you mean?" He was the one who looked like he might slip something into their glasses— or in their noses. Yet there was something about him…

"Nothing."

He stepped aside to give her room. She stood her ground. On impulse, she asked, "Do you know a guy they call the Finn?"

She waited, but she'd already seen his reaction when she spoke the name.

He stared at her. "Who's asking?"

She decided to lay her cards on the table. "My friend wants to get in touch with him. But we don't know who he is. Maybe you can help?"

"I don't think so. But the first thing you need to do is get rid of your company. No one's going to feel much like talking to you with them around."

"Why not?"

He sized her up again, as if he didn't know whether she was

playing dumb or really *was* dumb. "You don't know who you're sitting with?" He sounded both startled and sarcastic.

"No," she said, though she had the feeling he would tell her. "What is it you're trying to say?"

"You come in here asking about somebody who knows a few of this town's not-so-nice guys. Since you're interested in that sort of stuff, maybe you heard about a raid yesterday?"

She nodded. Before he could say more, the door opened and a woman walked over to the bathroom. Louise made eye contact with her, as she'd done earlier at the table. She probably thought Louise was a man hunter; first the men at her table, now this hallway liaison. The woman slammed the door behind her.

"The news mentioned the raid," she said, hoping he was still willing to talk.

He nodded. "The guy out there who bought champagne for you and your friend is Klaus West. He owns the apartment that was raided yesterday. He wasn't there, but the police confiscated a whole shitload of green dust, if you know what that is."

Green dust. Louise nodded.

"You're standing here asking about the Finn. He's way below where you're at now; you're with the big boys."

Louise was stunned. She stared at him as what he'd said sank in.

"What's your friend want with him?" he asked.

He sounded different now. Like a normal guy, less like a smart-ass. Louise had to get back to Camilla. She could just see the police storming the bar and arresting her along with the two drug kingpins. At least Louise assumed the other man was involved.

"There's something she wants to ask the Finn about, but I can't tell you what."

"Listen, I think you two little ladies ought to grab your purses and hit the road. You don't know shit about who you're messing with." Before she could answer, he said, "It's a bad idea to snoop around when you're with guys like this. Trust me, you need to get out, now."

The door opened again, and Camilla walked in. "What the hell are you doing? I thought you'd left without your things, without even saying goodbye."

She stopped when she noticed the dark-haired man standing partly hidden behind the doorframe. She looked at Louise.

"Camilla, we have to go."

"Hell no. They just bought another bottle; they're a lot of fun. Where have you been?"

"We're going now. Tell them I'm sick."

Camilla ignored her and turned to the man. "So, who are you?"

He looked her over. "I'm guessing you're the one looking for the Finn. Your friend here"—he pointed at Louise—"is way too classy to hang around guys like them. You're more their type."

Camilla gasped; Louise could see her wondering if it was worth it to slap him, but she held off. "You're one of his friends, maybe?"

He smiled. "I'm not talking about it here. I don't want your two generous hosts to get interested in me. Go grab your stuff and meet me outside."

He walked into the men's bathroom.

"What's going on?" Camilla was confused.

"Go out and get our coats. Tell them I'm sick, and sorry, but we have to go."

Camilla stared at her, but finally she nodded. "They seem really nice. It's stupid not to stay. We can look for the Finn tomorrow."

"Stop it."

"I could stand a dinner date with one of them."

"No, you couldn't. Go on out there, and don't make any dates. Come on."

Louise headed for the door while Camilla made their apologies and pointed at her. She gave them a little smile and wave while concentrating on looking pale and sick.

They waited to put their coats on until they were outside.

"You owe me, big-time," Camilla said as they walked down the sidewalk.

Louise was about to explode. "I don't owe you shit. We go out to find a source for you, and as soon as a couple of men buy us drinks, you drop everything. You seriously need to get your priorities straight."

Camilla's face tightened, and Louise knew how harsh she'd sounded. "Sorry. But the fact is, you've been drinking champagne with two of the biggest drug bosses in town."

"What are you talking about?"

"Klaus West owns the apartment that was raided yesterday, and not so long ago several kilos of heroin were confiscated in another apartment he owns."

At last, Camilla caught on. "You've got to be kidding."

Someone crossing the street approached them, maybe the guy in the bar, but Louise couldn't be sure; his collar was pulled up, his stocking cap pulled down.

"Follow me," he said as he began walking in front of them. They stood for a few moments before following. They walked around the corner, crossed one of the one-way streets, and rounded another corner. He stopped outside a large gateway.

"Give me your number," he said to Camilla. "I'll see if I can get the Finn to call you. But I'm not promising anything. Especially when you don't say who you are or what you want. It's better I do it than you trying to find him and ending up with those two."

Louise watched as Camilla thought for a moment and then opened her pocketbook. She had thought her friend was going to give him her business card, with her work number and home address. Instead she pulled out an old receipt, wrote down her name and number, and handed it to him.

"Tell him that someone he knows said I should talk to him, that he can help me. What's your name?"

He smiled. "Just call me your friend." He nodded at them and disappeared down the dark street.

"That was weird," Camilla said.

They headed back to the King's New Square. It wasn't midnight yet, but they decided to drop the nightclub. More than enough had happened, and anyway, they might have already found a connection to the Finn. The best thing they could do was wait.

"I've read that the bikers control the drug market in Copenhagen," Camilla said as they rode the Metro. "And there was also something about bikers and what's just been confiscated."

Louise nodded. "You're right. But there are Eastern Europeans involved somewhere, too; they're an evil bunch. I can't remember which country they come from. I don't know so much about it."

"These guys were Danish."

"Yeah." Louise leaned forward. The nearby seats were mostly empty, but she lowered her voice anyway. "When our new friend said the name, I remembered I'd heard it before. I'm pretty sure Klaus West, the one who bought the champagne, was president of one of the big biker clubs in the early eighties. Or maybe even earlier than that."

"He wasn't any biker!" At first Camilla sounded indignant, then she laughed.

"No, he's not, not anymore. I didn't recognize him, either. It's been a long time since he's been heard from."

"Isn't it cocky of him to show his face in town, the day after his apartment was raided? Surely the police are after him?"

"Yeah, but did you notice the couple sitting across from us?"

Camilla shook her head.

"I'd be surprised if they weren't plainclothes. I noticed them when they walked in."

"Wow. And they might think I know these guys," Camilla said.

"Right. That wouldn't be all that great for you, would it?"

Louise stared blankly out the window; green emergency exit signs flashed by at regular intervals.

After thinking about it, Camilla said, "If he's really a hard-core drug boss, surely he can spot a few plainclothes cops. He can't be naïve."

"I would think he did notice. That's why we were a great excuse for them to be at that bar."

Camilla shook her head. "It all sounds so ridiculous. I've been out on the town a million times without running into any drug bosses; why should it happen now? That friend of yours is imagining all this."

Louise hesitated before shaking her head. "I don't think so. Besides, you haven't been in places like this before, have you?"

They reached Frederiksberg and got out. On the way up the steps, Camilla turned and said, "Whatever they were up to, it's not something dangerous for us."

"No, of course not. It's just not the best company to be seen in, and I'm certain the police were there. Maybe they're just keeping an eye on what goes on."

"They must be after both of those guys."

Louise nodded. "There could definitely have been more police in there." She thought about it for a moment. "And they might be waiting for Klaus and his buddy to lead them to someone higher up. This green dust seems to keep appearing."

Louise unlocked her bike outside Camilla's apartment building. "Your cell phone, the paper gave it to you, right? For work?"

"Yeah."

"If someone looks up the number, will they get the paper's address?"

Camilla nodded, then stopped. "Why do you ask?"

"Because you gave the number to someone you didn't know. It's not going to be pleasant if they suddenly ring your doorbell."

"Why the hell would they do that?"

"Camilla, listen. This is why you should stay the hell away from it all. You don't realize what goes on. If they want to talk to you, they'll look you up. And they'll come in, even if you don't want them to. The rules in their world are different. But as long as they don't know where you live, nothing's going to happen. You only gave him your phone number, right?"

"Yeah, and they can't find me through my phone carrier. I've had a secret number and address since some idiot kept calling me about something I'd written."

"Great. The Finn might hold back if he checks you out and sees the *Morgenavisen* address pop up. We have to hope he can be trusted, like Birte Jensen says. That he'll just call, and that will be it."

"Do you really have to be so bleak about all this?"

"As long as it's not the champagne boys you gave your number to, it's probably okay. It wouldn't be good if they found out the police sent you." Louise smiled as she pushed off on her bike, but stopped when she noticed her friend's face. "You didn't, did you?"

She held Camilla's eyes, but she'd already seen it. "You did."

Camilla nodded slowly.

12

Louise concentrated on not spilling the two cups of coffee she carried. By now she knew that Jørgensen took his black with two teaspoons of sugar. She pushed the office door open with her foot.

At the morning meeting, Suhr had said that everyone in the department would take part in the week-after canvass. A little late to be telling us that, she thought; colleagues working on other cases might have been counting on some time off.

She set Jørgensen's coffee in front of him.

"Thanks."

She sat down at her desk. "Was it Narcotics or the old riot squad you were with?"

"I did time in both departments."

"Did you ever meet a guy called Klaus West?"

He looked surprised as he shook his head. "No, I never met him, but I know who he is. They think he calls the shots on who gets which district. He's a major player, but we've never managed to bring him down."

"I met him in town yesterday when I was out with a friend."

He looked startled, then he laughed. "Okay. So now he's one of your friends?"

Now it was Louise's turn to laugh. "I don't actually know him. We were at a bar, and suddenly he and his sidekick sat down with us and bought a bottle."

Jørgensen gazed at her wordlessly. "Where was it?"

"The King's Bar. Close to the King's New Square."

He thought for a moment. "That makes sense."

She frowned in puzzlement.

"I think he owns the place. We've been in there, I don't know how many times. Didn't find one single gram, even though we were pretty sure he had it stowed away somewhere. He's the careful type, and he's way ahead of anyone who's a threat to him."

"That must be why he bought us champagne. He probably wanted to know what we were up to." Louise regretted not talking Camilla out of going there.

"It wouldn't surprise me if he already knew you were with the police."

Her jaw dropped. "How could he know that?"

"He just knows that kind of stuff."

"There are two thousand cops in Copenhagen; I seriously doubt he'd know I'm one of them."

"Hmmm. I promise you he knows every one of the three hundred eighty plus people working in Criminal Investigations. He keeps up on these things. That's one of the reasons we haven't nailed him yet. Like I said, he's always a step ahead, and he never makes a move when there's somebody close he's suspicious of."

"You've got to be kidding me!"

"No, he knows everybody. At one point we suspected we had

a leak, someone feeding him information, and that's not unlikely. He could afford it. But it's damn uncomfortable thinking a colleague is leaking information. Not to mention others suspecting you."

"Did they find a leak?"

"I don't think so. No one heard about it, anyway." He returned to his reading.

She leaned back. What happened at Narcotics wasn't any of her business.

Her phone rang. "Department A, Louise Rick."

"It *was* him," Camilla said. "And the other one with the white hair, his name is Michael Danielsen; they call him Snow."

Probably for several reasons, Louise thought. "You've been doing your homework."

"Yeah, but I had to go a long way back for it. Nothing's been written about him the last five years, so I think maybe we overreacted."

"I don't think so. I've just been told it's likely they knew who we were when they came over and sat down. They were probably just trying to find out what we wanted. I'd say we underreacted."

"Oh, come on now. You're getting paranoid from all these murderers and criminals you track down. They couldn't have known shit about who we were."

Louise realized her words were falling on deaf ears, and stopped. She also had to prepare for the interviews she had lined up, but when she tried to wind up the conversation, Camilla said, "I'm covering the funeral tomorrow."

"I'll see you there then."

"Høyer is pressuring me for an interview with Karoline Wissinge's parents. Could you put a word in for me?"

"You know I can't do that. And I don't think it's a good idea to look them up. Give them some time."

"But I don't have time. We need it for the front page tomorrow, and Sunday, too, if possible. Her funeral will sell a lot of papers."

Louise frowned; she didn't like that side of Camilla. "Leave them alone. I don't know if they'll make themselves available, but no matter what, I'm not getting mixed up in it."

"What the hell is all this!" Camilla said, off to the side.

"What's going on?" Louise said, still annoyed, but also curious.

"Someone just delivered an entire flower shop to my office."

"Who from?" Louise had a bad feeling.

"I don't know. And don't make it sound like it's some big shock that someone sends me flowers. It happens occasionally. Let's see…there's a card here…'To *Morgenavisen*'s most beautiful reporter—worth keeping an eye on.'"

A long pause followed. "Who are they from?" Louise said.

"There's no name."

"What's on the envelope?"

"'Camilla Lind,' printed from a computer, I think. The card, too."

"Can you see where the flowers came from? A sticker on a ribbon, something on the envelope?"

"Nope, just a white envelope, and the flowers are packed in cellophane, no logo or anything."

"Toss the shit out."

"No way. The flowers are beautiful, and anyway, I've gotten anonymous bouquets before."

"I don't have time for this; I've got a lot to do. Please promise me you'll be careful, but keep me out of it. I can't do anything more for you if you can't see what's going on."

"So don't," Camilla snapped. "You're the one who insisted on going along yesterday."

"I'll talk to you later." Louise hung up and stared straight ahead at nothing.

Jørgensen looked up. "Problems?"

"That was my friend. The woman I was with last night. She just got an enormous bouquet of flowers, no name on the card. I have this feeling it's from the champagne man."

Jørgensen thought for a moment. "You could be right. Good idea to keep a low profile."

"Tell her that!"

Louise tried to concentrate, but she was too rattled. The guard called and informed her that her first interview had arrived.

Her brain was fried after interviewing the two friends Karoline had been with last Saturday evening. She'd gotten nothing more out of them than what Toft had already written down, but they had to do this; everyone had to be interviewed again. Maybe one of the others would get lucky and something new would come up.

She drove out to Karoline's parents. She'd thought it would be a break from work, but it wasn't easy telling them about Karoline's pregnancy.

"I see," Lise said. She stood up to put water on. Hans sat staring off into space. Neither of them reacted particularly strongly to the news.

"A grandchild," Lise said quietly as she set the coffee on the table.

Louise saw no reason to tell them about the abortion, since their daughter had chosen to keep it to herself. Learning about Karoline's pregnancy had left them numb as it was.

Back at the office, Louise had a message from Peter, telling her to call.

She ached to go home. Things had been a bit tense between them since he proposed she go with him to Aberdeen. But she had one more interview to do, and she knew she wouldn't be home until eight at the earliest.

"Hi, hon."

She could hear he was driving. Before she could say anything more, he said, "I'm on the way in to buy tickets for a movie tonight, and you're not going to say you can't make it."

That made her very happy. And very annoyed. "Is this something we talked about doing?"

He snorted. "No, this is a surprise."

"Okay, that's…bold." An honest answer, though she tried to sound cheery. "Did you talk to Suhr about letting me off early?"

Pause. She could hear him turning serious. "No, I didn't."

Louise felt the pressure in her chest again. It showed up during investigations, when leading a normal life proved to be difficult.

"We need to talk, and I just thought seeing a movie would be a nice way to start out," Peter said.

She ran her hand through her hair. "Eight is the earliest I can leave."

"I'll pick up the tickets, and we'll see what happens." Peter sounded blue.

Louise felt the same way. He had ambitions of building an international career, and she respected him greatly for that, but it wounded her deeply that he'd even suggest she give up her job to follow him. Even though it was only for six months.

Some girls are nice, decent young women, but some are just so incredibly boring, Louise thought as she closed the door after interviewing the last of Karoline's colleagues. Signe Jensen couldn't understand at all how Karoline could go into town with her boyfriend sitting at home.

Maybe that's why you don't have a boyfriend, Louise had thought.

She put on her sweater and walked out in the hall to look for Jørgensen. She didn't know how the other interviews had gone, but she'd learned nothing new.

She ran into Toft in the lunchroom. "How did it go?"

He looked up with a start. "It's a damn good thing we're not young anymore. All they think about are parties and women; they can't tell one night from the next."

She guessed that either he'd spent the day with witnesses from Baren, the bar Karoline had been in with her friends, or from Pussy Galore, where Lasse Møller claimed he'd gone after leaving Karoline. She smiled at him and asked if they needed help, because she was finished and could lend them a hand.

"The last person just showed up. But thanks anyway."

He walked down to the kitchen for more coffee.

Peter met Louise at the door. They had decided to drop the movie. He gave her a big hug, and she noticed the candles and red wine on the table. She hung up her coat and kicked her boots off before hurrying out to the bathroom. She needed some time. She sat on the toilet and peed with her head in her hands. Finally, Peter yelled out, "Did you fall asleep?"

"I'm coming."

She soaped her hands and rinsed them under hot water three times before drying them off. Mostly she wanted to crawl into bed, escape from the demands he was going to make of her. Three years ago, she'd finally gotten the job she'd been working toward for years, and it wasn't particularly family friendly. But Peter was thirty-eight, his biological clock was ticking faster than hers, and having a family meant more to him.

She flushed and walked into the living room. She joined him on the sofa, and he put his arm around her and squeezed tightly for a few moments. He leaned forward and poured wine into their glasses.

"Just half a glass for me," she said, holding her hand out to stop him.

He handed her the glass half-full. She always felt a bit awkward toasting with someone in this situation; she was more comfortable at dinner parties, where you could lower your gaze after dutifully looking everyone at the table in the eye, glasses raised.

Peter smiled at her. "*Skaal*, hon."

"*Skaal*." She blushed a bit.

"I miss you."

"I really think you should go to Scotland—"

"I'm not going if you don't want to go with me."

She felt dizzy; so now she was going to be responsible for his decision? "Come on, there must be cheap airline tickets. We can fly back and forth and see as much of each other as we want."

"You know that's not what this is about. It's about you and me, our lives together."

He was just getting warmed up.

"This is about making sacrifices for each other. I'd be willing to step back for a while, to put you and your job first—in fact, I feel I'm already doing that. Now I'm the one with the chance to take a step up."

Louise caught herself holding her breath.

"You're not willing to give anything up for me?" he asked.

"Of course, of course I am. I just can't see why you can't take this big step in your career without me taking a leave of absence. You can do it, we can see each other a few times a month, take vacations together, and in six months you'll be back."

"I don't see enough of you as it is. I want to wake up with you. Every day."

"But that's what we do already."

He stared straight ahead for a moment. "It's so easy to run away. There aren't any obligations here. I realized it the other day, when I got annoyed about you not being able to come home. I stayed at my place, didn't want to see you. And I don't want it to be that way between us. I don't want to have that option. We belong together, and I don't want any escape routes in our relationship."

Louise frowned but held her tongue.

"I need a family, a real one," he said.

She felt herself stiffen. Was that what this was about? "I'm not having children now, if that's what you mean."

"I know that." His finger slid through her hair. "Mainly I want my family to be you."

"So, what, are you proposing to me?" She laughed.

That threw him off for a second, but then he smiled. "I hadn't been thinking that far ahead, but I'll gladly put that on the table if you'll come with me."

"No, no," she quickly replied.

"What will it take to talk you into it?"

"I don't want to be talked into it, and right now I'm just way too tired to talk about it."

She walked out. The discussion was over for now.

13

Camilla felt guilty, but she enjoyed the weekends Markus spent with his father. After another run-in with Høyer, she'd dropped everything when several sportswriters asked if she wanted to go along for a Friday afternoon beer. She hadn't drunk so much, but it had been past eleven before she left.

At the front door she reached in her pocket for her key. She hesitated; someone was close behind her. Trying not to tense up, she stuck the key in the lock without looking back. Maybe she was imagining it. She hadn't heard any steps.

She pushed the door open and hurried inside. As she started up the steps, before the door closed, someone slipped in. After one more step, she turned around and found herself standing face-to-face with a man in a black leather jacket and black pants.

"I hear you want to talk to me. Let's go upstairs."

Immediately he grabbed her arm and began pulling her up. She hadn't at all expected to meet this way. He was hurting her arm, and she didn't want him in her apartment, but how could she avoid it? "So, you're the Finn?"

"We'll talk about it when we're inside." He pushed her forward.

Her heart was pounding, which puzzled her; she wasn't scared, not really. What could he do? She tried to hide her shaking hands as she unlocked her apartment door. Thank God her mother was visiting a friend and didn't have to see this. Inside she noticed how messy everything was, but who cared; she wasn't out to impress him. He slammed the door.

"Please, come in," she said as sweetly as she could. She hoped he'd catch the irony.

"Thanks." He pushed her farther down the hall, and she turned in anger.

"That's enough of that. You force your way in here, try to frighten me, but don't fucking push me around in my own apartment. If we're going to have a talk, you're going to behave."

She studied the man as she unloaded on him. About her age, she estimated, mid-thirties, maybe a bit older. Blond hair, blue eyes, good-looking. She took special note of the friendly look in his eyes, which didn't jibe with his behavior. A rush of adrenaline hit her; she had to keep control of the situation. "Now that you're here, would you like a beer?"

He nodded, and she walked into the kitchen. While grabbing two glasses, she wondered how smart it was to be alone with him. But if he insisted on meeting this way, that's how it had to be. She still didn't feel frightened.

"I want to talk to you about the murder of Frank Sørensen."

He was surprised. "First, I figured you were one of my sister's friends, then I found out you're a reporter. Made me curious."

They sat for a moment as he drank his beer. "Who knows we're in contact?" he asked.

"No one."

She hoped his question meant he was going to talk to her.

He poured more beer into his glass. "What's happened to Søren Holm? I thought he'd be digging around in this."

"He is, definitely. We didn't see him for several days, then he showed up out of the blue this afternoon. He spent the last two days talking with everybody who might have heard something. He'd also been down around Næstved," she added, to prove he was serious about his search.

"Ha. He must be shaking every tree, if he's trying to get something out of the Billing brothers." He nodded. "Did he find anything out?"

He stared—bored—into Camilla's eyes.

"I don't know." She looked down, broke off his stare. "I had a few problems with my boss today, and I didn't really pay attention. But when I left he was writing like crazy."

That seemed to amuse the Finn. He leaned back and smiled. "What do you want to know?"

The adrenaline started pumping again. "Do you know who did it?"

That made him laugh. "Hell no. And you think you'd be the first one I'd tell if I did?"

She shook her head. Maybe not.

"What *do* you know?"

"Nothing."

She held her arms out, palms up, thinking she might as well be honest. "I don't know much about the drug underworld. But I get the impression people are linking Sørensen's murder to something he was writing."

"That's probably not far off, thinking it has something to do with his articles."

"Articles about the drug case, you mean."

He nodded. "I don't know exactly what's going on, but he sure never held back. When he dug some dirt up, he wrote about it."

That was the Frank Sørensen she knew, too. "But did he write something that might make someone want to kill him?"

Camilla had read most of Sørensen's articles about the drug case, and nothing seemed particularly revealing. Mostly they covered police raids, and there was straight-up reporting, too. Several times at work he'd mentioned who he thought was involved, and who he thought was behind it all. But he'd never named them in the articles, and anyway, everyone had the same idea of who the criminals probably were.

"Let me put it this way. A lot of people in the drug world didn't like him, and…" He paused for a moment. "They say he sometimes threatened to publish certain stories if people didn't talk to him."

Camilla thought that sounded plausible. "Is anyone talking about who might be behind it?"

He nodded thoughtfully. "The police are. That's probably why they arrested someone this evening." He let that hang in the air.

Camilla frowned. "What?"

He drank the rest of his beer and carefully set his glass on the table.

She tried again. "Who'd they arrest?"

"You ought to know, he's a friend of yours." He smiled wryly.

At first, she was puzzled, then it hit her who he meant. "Okay. Do you think it's him?"

After a moment, he said, "That's what they say. The cops have been trying to pin this on Klaus West a long time. But they don't have enough on him. They know a bunch of stuff, but they can't prove anything."

She was a bit confused. "Weren't we talking about murder?"

"Yeah, and it's also in connection with Frank Sørensen that he's been arrested."

"What are they charging him with?"

"Murder, I suppose. That's all I know," he added, to block off her avalanche of questions.

Camilla relaxed when she realized she was holding her breath. Had she been sitting here sucking up to this guy for no reason? "Why the hell didn't you say at the start he'd been arrested?"

He smiled. "Because I thought you wanted to talk to me."

She stood up and began pacing the floor. "Do you really think he did it?"

In her mind she saw Klaus West's face, toasting with the long-stemmed flutes. Had she been flirting with him four days after he'd murdered Frank? She felt nauseated.

"You can't put it past him," the Finn said. "Everything in Copenhagen that has to do with drugs, you can trace back to him some way or other—at least for now." He paused a moment. "If Sørensen had something on West and his people, that might let someone else get their foot in the door, West is pretty damn likely to put a stop to it. He's done it before."

Camilla sat back down. She sensed that the Finn was happy to see West gone for a while. But where did he stand in all this?

She lowered her head into her hands. Odd, she felt relieved and yet still uneasy. Should she call Høyer? But it was past midnight, and anyway, he might already have heard about the arrest. She decided to call the graveyard shift at the paper when the Finn left. "Is the news out?"

"I doubt the cops are going to hold anything back that shows the world how effective they are," he said, his voice full of scorn.

She stood up to follow him out.

He gazed at her for a few moments. "Don't go around asking for me. My buddy stepped in because he saw who you girls were with; he wanted to know who you were. And like I said, he thought you knew my sister. There's lots of stuff going on right now. People are nervous. They notice when a new reporter snoops around asking about me, and I'm not so crazy about that."

New reporter! Camilla wasn't so crazy about that, either. "Got it."

After showing him out and listening to his footsteps fade, she walked back into the living room and called the paper. While the phone rang, she considered what to say if they hadn't heard about the arrest yet. How could she explain suddenly finding out about it at half past midnight? She hung up. If they didn't know now, they'd know tomorrow.

14

Louise and Peter slept late Saturday morning. Karoline's funeral was at two o'clock, so they had plenty of time to go out for brunch and shop before she left. They had an unspoken agreement to give Aberdeen a rest for the time being.

After sitting down and ordering coffee, Peter headed for the bathroom. Louise noticed the Saturday edition of *Morgenavisen* in a nearby rack. A large photo of Karoline dominated the front page, along with a slightly smaller photo of a young man with longish hair. The caption stood in boldface print: *Younger brother also killed.* Her knees felt weak when she walked over and grabbed the paper. She didn't need to see the byline to know who had written the article. When Peter returned, she was reading intently, her face drained of color.

"Hon, what's happened?"

"She's gone too fucking far this time." Her chest tightened; Camilla had written about Karoline's brother and his traffic accident after all. She leaned back and looked up at Peter. "I'm fed up with her."

He sat for a moment before speaking. "It's her job."

She stared at him and shook her head. "I told her this in confidence, and she's used it. I even told her specifically not to write about it. Everyone's going to know it came from me."

The waiter arrived with a large plate of food, but she'd lost her appetite.

"Come on, who's going to figure it out?" Peter said, trying to soothe her.

"Everyone. The parents, my colleagues, Suhr. They know damn good and well I know her."

"They also know she's a good reporter, and that story was going to come out at some point. Someone would have written it."

"And today of all days! This is not what her parents need now."

She folded the paper and threw it onto the sofa next to them. She cursed herself for telling Camilla too much. Never again! She'd have to completely stop talking to her about cases.

She picked at her scrambled eggs, but then she stuck a fork in a slice of melon instead.

Michael Stig drove with Suhr beside him in the front seat, Louise in the back. The Danish flag hung at half-mast as they approached the church. The red and white colors stood out against the blue spring sky. It was chilly, but the sun was shining.

Stig parked at the curb, and they walked up the gravel path together. They'd arrived at the last minute as planned, so they wouldn't attract too much attention. The parents had gone inside, but a few young people were still standing around. Friends, Louise guessed. As they approached, she noticed Camilla beside the church porch, along with a photographer and a few other journalists.

Camilla saw her and smiled, but Louise stared stiffly down at the path in front of her. She walked between Stig and Suhr, ignoring everyone as they reached the back pew and sat down. The church was nearly filled up.

"Let's keep our eyes open," Suhr said. He suggested that Stig sit farther in front, to watch for anyone reacting strangely and conspicuously.

"You just want the lovely Rick all to yourself," Stig half whispered. He walked farther down and found an empty chair off to the side.

Louise could have murdered him, but fortunately Suhr simply ignored the remark.

"Right before they carry the coffin out, step outside and watch everyone passing by," he whispered to her. The organ began, drowning out all other sounds. Louise nodded.

During the service, she thought about how to react if Camilla walked over and spoke to her outside. She tried to concentrate, to not let the mood in the church affect her, but it was hard to ignore people in front of her blowing their noses, weeping quietly.

She took in fragments of the pastor's remarks. When he said that Karoline had been called home to God, she shut him out; she couldn't hold back her tears if she listened. And it felt wrong for her to take part in their sorrow. She hadn't known Karoline, and it wouldn't be right to cry over her.

Just before the family and close friends rose to follow the coffin out, Louise edged past the others sitting on the pew, tiptoed to the heavy door, and opened it just enough to quickly squeeze outside.

The photographers stood ready. That week the murder of Karoline Wissinge hadn't been the biggest story in most of the media, but Louise guessed that linking it to the death of her little brother had whetted their interest. Now it was front-page material. Camilla stood in the background against a tall hedge along the gravel path leading to the church's graveyard. Without looking around, Louise found a spot right behind the photographers and turned to face the church. She knew someone might take her for a member of the press. She hoped not. Church bells began ringing, and a moment later the coffin and pallbearers appeared.

Hans and Lise Wissinge held the front of the coffin; the mother's face was puffy from crying, while he remained expressionless. Martin Dahl was right behind them, but she didn't recognize the other pallbearers.

The grandparents supported each other as they followed the coffin. The rest of the mourners followed in a thin stream. Louise sensed the bleak, overwhelming mood emerging from the church.

No one spoke; the only sound was the crunch of gravel as the coffin was borne to the hearse. When it had been pushed inside, people gathered around and began singing a Kim Larsen song, "Soon." It gave her goose bumps. Again, she was moved by all the crying and sobbing.

She stood farther back now, alert to anyone who stuck out or in some way didn't belong. She walked over to a man leaning against the church wall. A few others weren't singing, but Suhr stood beside them. An elderly man sat on a bench off to the side, following what was going on. She signaled to Stig that she would talk to the man later. Out of the corner of her eye, she saw Camilla approaching, but before she reached her, Louise said, "I'm working, I don't have time to talk to you. And I don't want to talk to you." But Camilla had already retreated so far that she didn't catch the last sentence.

After the song was over, people spread out in small groups. Karoline's mother came up to her. "Thank you for coming."

Instead of saying she was just doing her job, Louise smiled.

"Would all of you like to come with us for coffee?"

Would it be rude for them to say no? "I'm sorry, but we'll be on the streets around the park this evening."

Lise nodded. "Of course. Please, please find him."

She took Louise's elbow and leaned close to her. "The worst is knowing he's out there, that he might live his life without being caught. It's driving me crazy. I feel like I'm falling apart inside. And now the papers are talking about Mikkel, too."

Louise turned to face her. "I understand, and I promise you we'll do absolutely everything we can."

Lise nodded. "I know."

She walked back to her family. The mourners stood around chatting. Then Karoline's father raised his voice, cleared his throat a few times, and said everyone was invited to their home for coffee.

A half hour later, they were headed back to Police Headquarters.

"Did either of you get anything?" Suhr asked. But before they could answer, he said, "I found one man we need to talk to, and two others had trouble remembering how they knew Karoline."

It was Louise's turn. "The man over by the church wall said he taught Karoline in grammar school. I have his name and address. The old man on the bench had no idea whose funeral it was."

Essentially, they'd got nothing. And Louise was afraid it would be the same that evening.

The mood was sober, very un-weekend-like, on the second floor at Homicide. Most offices were occupied. Jørgensen nodded at her when she walked over and sat down.

A stack of messages lay on her desk, and she looked up at her partner.

"Camilla Lind called seven times this morning."

She took the messages, crumpled them up, and threw them in the wastebasket. She already had deleted four messages on her phone before shutting it off.

She sat for a while, thinking of Camilla. Of course, they would talk this out. Just not right now. The door opened and Willumsen stuck his head in. "Want some lunch? There's food in the lunch-room in fifteen minutes." He stood in the doorway.

Louise didn't react, but Jørgensen said okay, they'd be there.

The lunchroom was buzzing when they came in. Louise was nearly bowled over by the euphoric mood.

A few moments later she realized she hadn't kept up on the de-partment's other cases. Someone had been arrested for the murder of Frank Sørensen. She sat down beside a member of Willumsen's team and filled her plate. "Congratulations. What happened?"

He filled her in on the arrest. One of the big shots. A pre-liminary hearing had been held that morning, and he had been remanded into custody for a week. "We're not a hundred percent sure he killed Frank himself, but he was seen at the hotel Saturday evening."

Louise listened intently, forgetting to eat. "Who is it?" She could almost guess the answer.

"Klaus West."

She nodded. "What do you have?"

He sighed and let his silverware rest on his plate. "Not very damn much. Narcotics thinks they can connect him to the three rooms raided in the Royal Hotel on Saturday, and they're working to make him part of the ongoing case."

"But surely there's more, otherwise you won't be able to hold him."

"Right now, we're holding him on probable cause."

"It's not enough that someone says they saw him," she said, as-tonished that he couldn't see this himself.

"A strong witness put him at the crime scene, very strong. Ap-parently, Frank Sørensen publicly suggested that Klaus West is behind all the big drug transactions, and Birte Jensen from Nar-cotics and Licensing is certain West flew into a rage."

"Still, that's thin, isn't it?"

"We're hoping the murder weapon shows up, of course. We're searching for where West hangs his hat. Narcotics has raided several of his properties, but he wasn't living in any of them."

Louise nodded; she'd heard that. She told him she'd seen West in town Thursday night. He laughed, which embarrassed her.

"So, you're the looker!"

She felt herself blushing. What was going on? How did he…? She stared down at her plate. "More likely it was my friend."

He kept laughing. "The report says you both were most likely bought and paid for." He tried to control himself. Very funny, she thought.

"Well, you can just rewrite that report because we weren't!" She hoped Camilla hadn't made too big a spectacle of herself while Louise had been gone. "So, is he saying anything?"

"Nothing, zero. His attorney is John Bro, and as usual he's advised his client to not say a word."

"Too bad. You've got a rough road ahead of you." Louise pushed her plate away and sighed.

Camilla tried again, but Louise still didn't answer. She'd finished the article about the funeral and was thinking about leaving before something else came up.

She thought about her job. She'd lain awake most of the night, thinking about whether she was cut out to be a crime reporter. Two very unpleasant episodes with her boss in one week—not okay, she decided. She mulled over everything that had happened. The Finn's visit was still on her mind, too.

Friday afternoon the photo editor had marched into Camilla's office brandishing several sheets of paper. He demanded to know why she hadn't said that Karoline's younger brother had been killed in a traffic accident.

Before she could defend herself, Holck pounded his fist on her desk and yelled that he wouldn't stand for this, that he'd first learned about it because a competitor had wanted to buy a photo from their archives.

He slapped the sheets of paper on the desk: prints of articles Camilla had written about the accident. He stared at her in rage. "What the hell are you thinking?"

She thought about taking him on, but instead she sighed and pursed her lips. "Obviously I wasn't. Thinking."

Høyer had joined them. He knew what was going on.

"It didn't occur to me there was a connection." She looked back and forth between them. She fought off her tears; she wouldn't give them the satisfaction. To hell with them.

"God damn it, Lind, Wissinge isn't exactly a common name."

"No," she agreed, but then she looked up in defiance. "This is not what these parents need right now."

She knew what was coming.

"And maybe someone asked you to form an opinion on that?" He turned to Høyer. "I didn't know we had a new boss here!"

He walked out the door without even glancing at Camilla, but she heard him say it was incredible what this girl was sticking her nose in.

Høyer closed the door and sat down. "We have to have that story. It needs to be on the front page tomorrow, the day of her funeral."

"It's not right to do this. At the very least we should let the parents know the story's coming."

Høyer insisted that the article be based on the earlier articles she'd written about the accident, and she should refer to the fact they had covered the tragedy back then. "We're not going to disturb the parents the day before they bury their daughter, when the story's already in the archives."

Camilla was experienced enough to know he didn't want to risk the parents opposing the story. She felt like leaving, but the look on the managing editor's face told her that wouldn't be smart. "Can't you put someone else on it? I have my foot in the door for an interview with the parents; I can't just ambush them with this story."

He shook his head. "I want you to write it. You do this type of thing the right way. We want our readers to be moved; they have to feel the loss, the sorrow. Our thoughts will be with them; we'll share their pain when she's buried. It's right up your alley."

She almost felt sick; she'd never imagined that what she felt was her strength would work against her. "I don't want to write this article."

He stood up and walked to the door. "You have to."

She wasn't sure she could hold back the tears.

"I'm expecting it in an hour," he said, and walked out.

She stared at the door. Asshole! She considered making another scene and putting her job on the line. But instead she decided to take her time, think about looking for another job. It would mean more in the long run.

She began reading the articles about the accident.

She knew the moment she saw Louise in front of the church. She should have called and prepared her for it, but then she'd gone out with the sportswriters, and then the Finn had shown up. Saturday morning she'd tried to get hold of her friend, but Louise hadn't answered at Police Headquarters, and her cell phone was off. It was too late anyway.

At eight p.m., between thirty and forty police officers were gathered in the lunchroom. Suhr had made a sketch of the area they would cover.

"I want four of you in Baren and four in Pussy Galore. We need to find the people who were there last Saturday night. And we need to stop the people walking through or otherwise in the area during the hours when Karoline Wissinge left Baren and later was killed. They're the ones we really need to talk to; they might have seen something. The most important time is after midnight. Everyone will be checking in regularly. We have three men in the bus handling communications. Two of them will be keeping track of what happens on the streets; the other will take care of the officers in the park."

He scratched his forehead. "Obviously, I don't count on there being many people in the park after midnight, but it's open all night, and who knows? Maybe there are people who get up to give the dog a late walk." He shrugged.

Louise was part of the team Suhr placed on Stockholmsgade, which ran all the way along the park. The other teams covered the stretch from Silver Square to where Karoline lived. Everyone in the adjoining side streets would also be stopped.

They left Police Headquarters in one of the green police buses and parked on Stockholmsgade. That would be their base, where they could duck in for a break and a cup of coffee.

Louise made sure she had both her notepads. She was glad she'd brought along gloves and a stocking cap; it would get cold standing around most of the night.

"Okay then, looks like we're about ready," Jørgensen said. He was assigned to stand with Louise where Stockholmsgade ended at Silver Square. She noticed several windows open in the buildings along the street. The arrival of so many police had attracted attention, and people would no doubt come down to ask what was going on.

Their orders were to stop everyone and ask if they'd been in the same place at the same time one week ago. If so, the officers were to ask the person if they'd noticed anything. If they hadn't been close to the park, they were free to go.

Louise expected that many of the people she'd be talking to that night had already been interviewed by officers knocking on doors. Most people who'd be walking by most likely lived in an apartment on the street. But others might be there on weekends, and they might have something of interest to tell. Weekend boyfriends or girlfriends, children of divorced parents. People returning from being away during the week.

She straightened up when their first pedestrian approached.

Louise yawned and crawled in under her comforter. It was ten to eight, and the first thing she'd done when she got home was turn her phone off.

Her feet were sore from walking in small circles. She'd guessed that she had spoken with around twenty people, though she hadn't looked through her notepad and counted. Only five of them were people living in the neighborhood, and they already had been interviewed. The others she'd stopped weren't in the area regularly. None of them had been there last Saturday. Louise's enthusiasm had slowly waned as the cold crept in under her heavy police coat.

It had been quiet on Stockholmsgade in comparison to Silver Square, where cars and bicycles streamed through all night. The concentration of blood alcohol increased as the night wore on. Suhr believed they'd talked to about two hundred people.

Just before her thoughts blurred and sleep took over, she allowed herself to take Sunday off, completely. If she wanted to lie in bed all day, she would.

15

When Louise walked into her office Monday morning, she had a message from Camilla, asking her to call. She ignored it and turned on her computer.

Suhr had spent Sunday going through the results of the canvass Saturday night. It had yielded far less than he had hoped.

Louise hadn't been in touch with Camilla since Friday afternoon, when she'd told her friend to toss out the mountain of flowers delivered to her. If asked, she would have sworn all weekend that it would be a long time before she felt like talking to Camilla again. But it was no use. Anyway, she wanted to hear what Camilla had to say about Klaus West being arrested. She punched in her friend's number.

"I'm glad you called," Camilla said. "So much has happened, and I want to explain why I wrote the article about Karoline's brother."

She started to apologize, but then she broke off and asked if they could meet.

Louise hesitated a moment before answering. "I'm still mad about that article; it was a rotten thing to do. It just means I need to keep my mouth shut. And, of course, that's what I should be doing anyway, but once in a while I need to talk. And I thought I could trust you."

Camilla didn't answer immediately; apparently, she was waiting for Louise to get it all out. But Louise was finished.

"Can we meet?" Camilla said, instead of defending herself.

"I can't, we have a lot of paperwork to go through." She sensed her friend's disappointment.

"I had a visit from the Finn on Friday."

Louise perked up. "What do you mean 'visit'?"

"He caught up to me when I came home. Markus is at his father's until the day after tomorrow, and I was late getting home, a little past eleven. We drank a beer and talked. He told me that Klaus West had been arrested."

Louise's heart began pounding. "You let him in your apartment, you drink a beer with him like he's some old friend—are you crazy? Don't you understand who these people are?"

"I really didn't have much choice," Camilla said.

"What did he say?"

"He said it was common knowledge that Klaus West was tired of Frank. It had to do with Frank threatening to write something."

She had Louise's attention. "Have you spoken to the police?"

"I called Birte Jensen. We're going to meet in an hour."

"Good. Did you ever find out who sent you the flowers?"

"Never did, but they're still looking good." Camilla wants to lighten the mood, Louise thought.

"There's that. It might be a long time before Mr. Anonymous sends you more!"

"Can you stop by this evening, so I can tell you how it went with Jensen? And I want to explain about the article."

"All right. I'll call when I know when I can get out of here."

Camilla pulled on her raincoat and unlocked her bike. She'd thought about taking a cab to Police Headquarters before deciding to tough it out and bike over. She had twenty minutes before meeting with Jensen. It was pouring, and she tied the hood of her raincoat tight and took off.

She parked her bike in the bicycle rack outside the building, walked over to the guard, and told him Jensen was expecting her.

"No answer at Birte Jensen's office," he said. "I'll try one of the others."

She smiled at him and loosened her hood.

He wrote down her name and time of arrival, and he handed her a visitor card. "Someone else will meet you. Go on up."

Camilla thanked him and entered the round courtyard. Her steps echoed on the stairs. Outside Narcotics and Licensing, she took off her raincoat, smoothed her skirt, and fussed a second with her hair. A young man with an outstretched hand met her, and after introducing himself, he led her into the Narcotics chief's reception.

"Birte Jensen is in the basement for a minute," he said.

"That's fine, I'll wait."

Camilla sat down in the chair he pulled out for her. She accepted his offer of coffee and resigned herself to having to wait.

Fifteen minutes later, Jensen walked in with a large black briefcase under her arm. She glanced at her watch when she noticed Camilla and apologized for the delay. "I'll be with you in a minute," she said.

Camilla finished her coffee. Another five minutes passed before the door opened, and Camilla was waved in.

"Would you like more coffee, or perhaps some water?" Jensen asked.

"I wouldn't mind another cup," Camilla said, regretting that she'd thrown her plastic cup away.

Jensen opened the door and asked the young man to bring a pot of coffee in.

"Now," she said, after sitting down at the massive table across from Camilla. "You had a visit, you say?"

"Yes." Camilla filled her in on what the Finn had told her about Klaus West. "It seems that it's common knowledge he's behind the murder, that he even might have done it himself."

Jensen nodded as Camilla spoke. "Did he say anything about where West lived?"

Camilla shook her head.

"He owns a few places; we've searched them. Not in connection with the murder, but during narcotics raids. There was no sign of him living in any of them. He was at the Royal Hotel, but he wasn't registered."

Camilla told about meeting Klaus West and the white-haired man, emphasizing that she didn't realize who they were when she was with them.

"Snow," Jensen said. She wrote the name on her notepad. "It doesn't surprise me. He has no permanent address, either. It would be a great help if you could find out from the Finn where the two of them live. They must have an apartment we don't know about."

The Narcotics leader looked grim.

"Don't you normally wiretap people's cell phones?"

"No doubt he uses burners, a type of prepaid phone."

"How did you find him Friday?"

"He was seen at the King's New Square by an officer on patrol. It's not as if he's trying to hide." Jensen leaned toward Camilla. "But he's only seen when he doesn't mind being seen."

Camilla nodded.

"Try to find out if he uses some apartment as a base. Of course, we're working on that, too, but there's no doubt it's easier for you to sniff around. And I have something for you. Quid pro quo."

Camilla brought out her notepad and bit the cap off her pen.

"We're certain that Klaus West is behind the murder of Frank Sørensen."

Camilla felt a metallic taste in her mouth; she'd bitten the inside of her cheek as Jensen spoke.

"He was at the hotel, and we know he was down in the court-yard."

Camilla looked up from her notepad. "Do you have witnesses?"

Jensen studied her a moment. "I saw him."

"Can I write that?" Camilla asked, excited now.

Jensen nodded.

"Has he been charged with murder?"

"Yes, but we're working against the clock, because we can't hold him much longer without more concrete evidence."

Camilla frowned in concentration. Here was a man who moved around in the center of town with the police on his heels, yet they couldn't keep track of him. Clearly, he knew what he was doing. And it wouldn't make things easier if he were set free and could cover up where he'd been lately. If he already hadn't done so. "What about a custody extension?"

"Our prosecutor isn't optimistic. West's lawyer is John Bro, and he's good at what he does. We know that from experience."

Pause. "Will you try?" Jensen asked, her eyes pleading.

Camilla nodded, though she wasn't wild about meeting the Finn again. She didn't want to owe him anything.

They shook hands, and Jensen followed her out and down the hall. "Call me when you get hold of him," she said, and walked back to her office.

Camilla handed the visitor card to the guard. Her head was swimming as she biked back to the paper. It sickened her that she'd drunk champagne with the man who had killed Frank. Unfuckingbelievable, she thought as she locked her bike.

Back in her office, Camilla read Søren Holm's article in the day's paper about Klaus West's arrest. Because there was a publication ban on his name, Holm had simply written that the police had arrested a man well-known in the drug underworld. The article didn't mention anything about evidence. Should she tell Holm about her meeting with Birte Jensen?

Someone pounded on the door; she stood, but before she could say a word, it opened. For a split second she thought it was the photo editor. It was a relief to see Holm appear. "Hi," she said. Then she got a good look at his face.

"Sit," he ordered, nodding at her chair as he walked in. She sat down stiffly, awkwardly.

He leaned across her desk. "I just talked to a guy who tells me you've been asking around for a police snitch." He leaned farther forward. "You need to stop."

She gaped at him.

"I also heard you were out drinking with Klaus West last Thursday. What the hell's going on? Is there something we should know?"

Her skin tingled as she sank deeper in her chair. Holm stared at her in anger as she thought about explaining herself, but it didn't look like he was finished.

He sighed and sat down. "And I heard you just got back from a meeting with Birte Jensen."

He picked up a pen off her desk and tossed it from one hand to the other. "Camilla, things are hectic right now. Believe me, this is no time to get involved with these people."

She had trouble breathing, but she managed to hold back her own rage.

"I get it, you want to develop your own sources, working in a place like this, but leave Birte Jensen to me. Things aren't as simple as they seem."

Again, she was about to lash back at him. He made her feel like some intern. Something told her, though, that his anger came from her knowing more about the case than him. Of course that annoys him, she thought. Her self-confidence returned, and she straightened up and tried to look unaffected by his tongue-lashing.

"The police are sure Klaus West is the murderer," she said, without blinking. "They have a witness placing him at the crime scene, and Jensen wants me to help find the apartment he's staying in."

She knew that sounded arrogant, and she was sorry for it. He peered at her but held his tongue. She lowered her voice. "I haven't written a word about this, so I can't see that I'm stepping on your toes here."

"Camilla, you have to pull out of this. Give me a little time and I'll tell you why—just let me look around for the apartment."

Before she could protest, he said, "It's no coincidence that Frank was killed." After a few moments, he added, "It's too dangerous. I've talked to Høyer; you're off this story."

She was boiling; why didn't they just fire her? It was incredible how everything was turning to shit. She could see in his eyes that he knew she was about to explode.

"Camilla, I'm not saying all this to make you feel bad," he said, milder now. "Some really shitty stuff is going on, and it's best you don't get involved until it's all settled."

She sat stone-faced as he stood up to go. He turned to her with his hand on the doorknob. "If you promised Jensen anything, just drop it," he said, his tone sharp again. "Tell her you've been taken off the story, and if she wants something, she should call me."

He left. "Fuck you," she said. She stood up and paced, took several deep breaths.

Louise walked into Camilla's apartment just past seven. It seemed empty without Markus, and things were a bit tense until Louise was convinced that her friend had hated having to write the article about Karoline's little brother. They sat down on the couch, a pot of tea on the coffee table, and Camilla talked about her latest meeting with Jensen and being bawled out by Søren Holm.

"I just can't see what the hell he's up to," Camilla said.

Louise thought for a moment. "Why do you think he's necessarily up to something? What he told you makes perfect sense to me."

Camilla gazed at her. Louise knew what she'd said had gone in one ear and out the other. "It's like he's pissed at me for being in contact with Jensen. I'll be the one who's pissed off if it turns out he's trying to ruin that for me."

"I saw him at headquarters when I left; don't you think he has his own sources? He looked a lot better than the other day, too, outside Forensic Medicine."

Camilla pulled a heavy blanket up over her, leaving only her head visible. "Maybe I should just do what he says, leave everything to him and focus on writing about Karoline's murder. I take it from what Suhr said that you got some good leads from the canvassing."

Louise was startled; the canvassing had been a total washout, but she did her best to not reveal Suhr's bullshit. She nodded.

"He didn't elaborate," Camilla continued, obviously struggling to not pump her for information. Then she closed her eyes and rested her head on the back of the sofa.

"I don't even feel like going to work with all those idiots cussing me out all the time."

"Oh, come on." Louise leaned closer to her. "You're taking it way too personally."

Camilla blinked a few times and breathed deeply. "Maybe you're right."

Louise changed the subject. "It's odd that Holm looks like a respectable family man one day, and a bum the next. A big contrast."

"Most of the time he's a family man." She straightened up and flung the blanket to the floor. Her crisis had blown over. "But he didn't even make it home until several days after Frank was murdered. Usually he's the distinguished type. His wife is a schoolteacher, and when you see him with his family, it's hard to imagine he's as hard-core as he is."

Louise nodded as Camilla talked about a Christmas party at the paper that he, his wife, and his two daughters attended. The oldest daughter was a tall, beautiful girl of eighteen; the youngest girl's confirmation was in a few months.

"Why does Jensen want you to talk to the Finn again?" Louise said.

"To find out where Klaus West lives. He won't tell them, and they can't find it."

Louise frowned. "And it'll be easier for you than for all the rest of her people?" Her question hung in the air as she headed for the bathroom.

The teapot was full again, and their legs were pulled up under them on the sofa. Louise told her friend about the job offer Peter had in Scotland.

"Sounds exciting. Scotland is fantastic, and surely there are plenty of pubs to go to?"

Louise set her teacup down and gaped at her friend. "Pubs?" Maybe she shouldn't have started in on this with Camilla. "Of course there are pubs, just like here in Copenhagen! But Peter wants me to take a leave of absence and go to Aberdeen with him for six months. And I can't do that."

"Why not? The police give leaves of absence. Heilmann just got one."

"Yeah, but I can't just go over there and do nothing that long."

"You can't, or you won't?"

Louise scowled. "I don't want to. I can't see myself puttering around while Peter's at work."

"Then he'll just have to go without you."

"He won't. He'll only take the job if I go along."

Camilla slammed her cup on the table. "So go, God damn it! You have to; you have a man who's fantastic at what he does. Somebody found out they need what he can do, and here Little Miss I'm Only Interested in Myself won't give him his chance. Great, Louise!"

If they didn't know each other so well, Louise would have slapped her. But this was what happened when she discussed family matters with her friend.

Camilla leaned back on the sofa. "Life is also about appreciating what you care about," she said, calmer now.

Heilmann's words played in Camilla's voice. She leaned her head back, too. "Peter's important to me. I love him, and that's why it's fine for him to be gone for six months. I won't love him any less."

"For the last three years he's been there for you, like when he backed you up before you got the job at Homicide, when you had doubts about ever getting your dream job."

Louise listened now without arguing.

"You could lose him."

An hour later, as she walked down the steps, her doubts were tearing her apart. She didn't want to lose Peter, and she forced herself to think about taking a leave of absence. At the same time, she felt a noose around her neck. It wasn't going to work.

16

"At five fifty-two a.m., the body of a journalist, Søren Holm, was found in a courtyard on Vestergade close to the Town Hall," Suhr said as he began the Tuesday morning briefing in the lunchroom. "He was found in a basement stairway, and he was murdered the same way as Frank Sørensen. At least this is what we're assuming now."

Louise had arrived late. She and Peter had lain in bed, talking late into the night. She'd tried to convince him that her not wanting to go to Scotland wasn't because she didn't love him enough. She wasn't sure she'd succeeded, but when she said she had over three weeks' comp time due, three weeks she would spend in Aberdeen, he'd finally decided to take the job, even though she was staying home.

She'd barely sat down when the briefing started. Immediately she'd noticed there weren't as many people there as usual, and seconds later her blood froze at hearing whose body had been found.

Suhr looked tired as he leaned on the edge of the table. "The garbage collectors found him. I got a call at six fifteen. The doctor was already there; he pronounced the victim dead. I arrived just after the techs, and we all agree they were killed the same way. The pathologist examined the puncture wound on his neck, but she wouldn't comment on it. She hadn't seen Sørensen's wound; she could only state that they were similar. Two of the techs there had observed Sørensen's autopsy, and they were sure the wound was in the same place."

He surveyed the detectives at the two tables. He was stone-faced. "Ten days have gone by since the first murder. We have the killer, and yet another body shows up."

He began to pace the floor. "We'll release the name of the victim later this morning. It's to our advantage to keep his identity secret as long as possible, but that'll be difficult."

He looked up at the two rows of fluorescents illuminating the entire lunchroom. "It wouldn't surprise me one damn bit if the reporters already know. Several photographers were out on the street where the body was found while I was there."

Toft raised his hand. "Was he killed there?"

Suhr looked at him and swiped his forehead. "We think so, but it's too early to say. He could've been killed in an apartment and dragged down to the courtyard. Frandsen from Forensics is coming in at ten, and we'll go through what we have."

Louise raised her hand, and he nodded at her. She suggested that Holm might have been looking for the apartment Klaus West was staying in. The others stared at her.

"Is this something you know, or are you guessing?" Suhr asked.

"I know he was aware that such a place existed, and he wanted to find it. I'm guessing he might have succeeded."

He nodded. "We're already knocking on doors in the buildings surrounding the courtyard, but we haven't checked if Klaus West lives there. Right now, we're looking for people who might have seen or heard something."

He stopped for a moment and stared at the wall. "We'll have to show all of them a photo of West." He snorted and peered at Louise, as if she were the one piling more on his shoulders. He told Willumsen to make sure all the officers knocking on doors had a copy of the picture.

"I need more personnel for these two murders, so we're going to have to do some shuffling," Suhr said, to no one in particular. "Willumsen's detectives will stay on, of course, and I've decided to move Rick and Jørgensen over as reinforcements."

He continued before checking their reactions. "Toft and Stig will stick with the Karoline Wissinge case. It looks like it's going to drag on. Everyone else is going to work their asses off on the murders of these reporters. We might as well get ready for a lot more media attention. God forbid," he added.

Louise seethed at the unfairness of downgrading Karoline's murder, but she kept herself from showing it because she felt Stig's eyes on her. Most likely he was angry, too, about not being moved over to the new case. Every available resource and all their focus the next several days would be on the murders of the two reporters.

"I've asked everyone who possibly can to attend the briefing with the techs at ten. I want you two there." He nodded at Louise and Jørgensen and stood up. The room emptied out quickly.

Louise put water on for tea. She looked for a thermos that didn't smell of coffee, but finally she gave up and grabbed the clay teapot in the back of the cupboard. The bitter taste from two cups of morning coffee lingered in her mouth. She called Peter from her office to fill him in on the new situation, which meant he wouldn't be seeing much of her the next several days.

Suhr was standing in the doorway when she hung up. "Can I have a word?" He beckoned her to follow him down the hallway to his office.

After they sat down, he said, "Is the move okay with you?"

Usually he didn't ask things like this.

Before she could answer, he said, "I need someone who can get people to talk."

"You already know I think it's unfair to downgrade Karoline's murder, just because another case has more media focus."

"That's my decision to make."

"I know that, and I'd absolutely like to work on the other case," she said, aware that she might as well accept the reassignment. "It's just the principle of the thing."

Of course she would switch teams. She was already involved in the case, and she would love to help put the champagne man behind bars. She flashed on the bouquet sent to Camilla.

"Good! So, we agree."

She decided to tell him about meeting Klaus West. Suhr jotted down a few words as she spoke, looking up occasionally to judge how far along she was in her story.

"Do we know his real name?" he asked, after she told him about Camilla talking to the Finn in her apartment.

She shook her head, but then she realized that Birte Jensen might.

"We need to bring your friend in for an interview, but Jørgensen can do it."

Louise nodded gratefully. It would be way too awkward for her.

"I can see you and Jørgensen as partners on a more permanent basis. It's my impression that you work well together."

He thought for a moment. "I may call Velin back in; you could hook up with him again if you want. No matter what, we're going to need a lot of personnel on these cases. We can't afford to let anything get by us here at the start."

Louise hadn't thought much about her old partner this past week. She was already used to Lars Jørgensen.

"I'd like for you to handle the family," Suhr said. "We'll have to get the wife in for questioning. And the children. Do you know how many he has, their ages?"

"The oldest is eighteen, and the youngest is about to have her confirmation."

He made a note of that. "I appreciate the observations you and Flemming Larsen made about Karoline Wissinge. Holm's autopsy is scheduled sometime between eleven and twelve; I want you there. Jørgensen can take another officer along to speak to the wife and kids. When they come in to give their statements, you'll join them."

She nodded in agreement. Fine. It was rare for her to be sent to observe an autopsy, but she took it as a pat on the back. Almost everyone had their strengths; some were good at crime scenes, for example. Usually she was assigned to families and those closest to victims, while others were sent to the autopsy. Apparently, her skill set was being broadened. "Who informed his wife?"

"Glostrup police," he said. "They were out there early this morning. I haven't spoken to her myself, but I'm assuming she'll call for more details. If the briefing with the techs lasts too long, take off. It's important for you to be at that autopsy."

She checked her watch; the briefing would start in an hour. They stood up and headed for the door. "Do we know what Holm was doing yesterday?"

"We don't know anything really, not yet. The local officers only informed his wife, they didn't ask any questions."

Before she reached her office, Michael Stig walked up and stopped directly in front of her.

"So, you're moving on to the next case." She could hear him trying to hide his irritation.

"Yeah, that's the way it goes. We just do what we're told." Again, she kept her face blank; it wasn't her problem he felt slighted.

"Right," he said, studying her. "Maybe it's for the best, too. We must move on. Solving this case will take more than talk; we've got to put the pieces of the puzzle together."

She took a step back. "And you don't think I'm any good at that?"

He smiled and held his palm up in front of her. "It's not that, but the first phase of an investigation—isn't that more your strong suit? The boss has to use his resources the best way possible."

He was so full of himself. Her stomach began roiling, but she did her best to smile sweetly. "Then it's good he has someone like you."

She tried to slide by him, but he was still blocking her. "It's more that he sees me in another context; that's why he lets me do the heavy lifting." He clicked his tongue.

"Well then, you'll probably be the new DCI." Suddenly she understood that's what he'd been hinting at. She felt light-headed.

"So, you caught that. Yeah, I guess it's pretty evident." He crossed his arms.

"I didn't know you'd taken a leadership course."

At one point, Louise had thought about applying for leadership training, which would qualify her for a promotion to DCI, but she'd decided she was most comfortable with what she was doing. She had no leadership ambitions.

"I haven't yet," he said, "but they're putting a new class together, and I'm meeting with Suhr later today, so I'm just putting two and two together."

"I'm expecting Heilmann to come back."

She squeezed past him and strode directly to her office, fuming all the way. She slammed the door behind her, and Jørgensen jumped. He couldn't help smiling when he saw the grim look on her face.

"What the hell happened?"

"Just had the pleasure of Stig's company out in the hall. He's pushing hard to be our new DCI. If it happens, I'm putting in for a transfer. Traffic cop." She plopped down on her chair and sighed deeply.

Jørgensen wasn't laughing now. It pleased her to see he wasn't thrilled with the idea of DCI Stig, either.

"I thought you two got along okay," he said. "He hardly dares to open his mouth after you've had your say about something."

She couldn't believe what she'd just heard. "Why do you think that?"

"He seems to have a lot of respect for you; you always put him in his place."

"Him, respect for me? I don't think so, but he can be absolutely aggravating." She poured a cup of tea.

"He's applied for the next leadership course." Jørgensen looked out the window. "I did, too. I really hope I get in."

After a moment, she nodded. She could see it, Lars Jørgensen, a quiet man. He'd be good at coordinating investigations. "I'm keeping my fingers and toes crossed that you make it and he doesn't."

He smiled at her. "Thanks."

"Suhr wants me over at the hospital to observe the autopsy when the briefing's over. Has anyone told you anything?" She hoped he knew what they'd be doing, but he shook his head. She explained what Suhr wanted them to do.

"Sounds good," he said. "I'll find out who's going with me to talk to the family. And I'll call and let you know when to meet me back here for the questioning."

She nodded, happy that he had no problem with their assignments. "Sounds like a plan." A good plan, she thought.

Louise called Forensic Medicine and asked to speak to Flemming Larsen. She hoped he would be doing the autopsy, even though he hadn't examined the body on Vestergade that morning. Tuesday was the busiest day of the week for autopsies. Inquests were held on Mondays for those who died from Friday to Sunday. Some of the autopsies would be done later in the week, but a case beginning to look like a serial killer had top priority.

"Flemming Larsen."

"Hi, it's Rick. Are you doing Søren Holm?"

"Yeah, that was my plan, anyway." He almost sounded cheery.

"Good. You're the one best able to determine if he was killed the same way as Frank Sørensen, or if it's a copycat."

He chewed on that for a moment. "That's a possibility. I hadn't thought about it, but of course you can't rule out some psycho joining the party."

She hadn't thought about it, either, until then. Either someone had to be horribly angry with Holm, if there was no connection to the other case, or else someone was out of his mind.

She wrote these thoughts down on her notepad, then she asked when he would start.

"We'll head down at eleven thirty. That's when the techs are coming in."

"Okay, see you then."

The briefing was in five minutes. Louise and Jørgensen grabbed their notepads and walked over to the lunchroom. Frandsen from Forensics was setting up to show a video. Louise smiled at him and sat down. Slowly the room filled up with detectives returning from Vestergade. They sat in groups, speaking quietly with each other. Everyone except Louise and Jørgensen had been working intensely the past several hours, and soon they would be back at it.

"We don't have much for you yet," Frandsen said when everyone had arrived. "But I can show you where we're at."

He started the video. About a dozen techs in white bodysuits appeared on the screen. The basement stairway was in back to the left. Spotlights had been set up in several places along the walls; the blazing light transformed the courtyard into a scene, a fictional, unreal setting. Several techs walked around with eyes glued to the ground. Each carried a small apparatus connected to a laser flashlight, which illuminated traces of blood. Chalk circles had been drawn in several places on the asphalt. The camera zoomed in on two techs leaning over something on the ground; they each held a paper strip that determined if a stain was blood or semen.

Every time Louise watched the techs working with the long paper strips, she thought of all the hours she'd sweat through chemistry classes. The strips worked like the litmus paper her teacher had handed out to test for acid and alkaline. Violet revealed blood, green revealed semen.

Louise watched the paper slowly turn violet. There was definitely more blood there than in the bicycle shed behind the Royal Hotel. The killer had moved his victim, she guessed.

There were seven entrances to the courtyard from the surrounding apartment buildings, and a bicycle shed stood just inside the main entrance. Three techs were sealing it off to protect any evidence, but it appeared they hadn't found anything yet.

Frandsen turned off the video, then he quickly went through the trace evidence they had secured. "As I'm sure you noticed, this time we've found blood from the victim. We did the last time, too, but not nearly as much. We're working from the assumption that he was killed somewhere else in the courtyard and dragged over to the basement stairway."

The sound of pens scratching on notepads filled the room.

"Right now, we don't believe the killings took place in an apartment, but we're searching the back stairs of every apartment building."

He took a moment to catch his breath. "It looks like the same murder weapon, or at least the same type of weapon—likely a butterfly knife. We haven't found it yet, but the puncture wound is similar."

Suhr waved his hand. "The pathologist there this morning is certain that Holm wasn't dead more than six hours when he was found. That means he was still alive around midnight."

Frandsen sat down on a chair against the wall, and Suhr took over. "We haven't spoken to anyone who can tell us when Holm was last seen alive, but hopefully we'll know that by the end of the day. Station City is assisting us; several of their officers will help question residents in the surrounding apartment buildings. We talked to most of them this morning." He took a deep breath. "None of them saw or heard anything, except for a young couple who came home around two a.m. They were parking their bikes, and they noticed a couple who seemed very involved in each other. They didn't want to disturb them, so they hurried up to their apartment. They didn't sense anything at all wrong—on the contrary. The couple seemed to be very affectionate, is how they put it. Apparently, everyone else was sleeping soundly. None of them knew any Søren Holm, or knew of anyone with that name living in the neighborhood. Which is true, there isn't."

Louise glanced at her watch: ten forty-five. She carefully pushed her chair back, stood up, and walked to the door.

They began streaming out of the lunchroom when she was on her way down to her bike. She stopped Jørgensen and reminded him that three o'clock was the earliest she could be back, and she hoped that would be okay for the interview with Holm's wife and two daughters. Jørgensen nodded.

"I talked to Suhr; he's going to call them. He's the one keeping them up to date anyway. He'll ask them if we can come over now and search the house; maybe Holm has an office there. It would be nice to find something he was working on that could possibly explain the murder."

"Don't get your hopes too high," Louise said. She explained that Holm was the kind of guy who left his job behind when he got home.

"Well, anyway, we'll have to go through his things. And then his wife and kids can either drive in themselves, or we can bring them back with us. They might want to get away for a while. I can imagine reporters are flocking around their house, unfortunately."

Louise nodded. That could very well be. She thought about Camilla. "By the way, Suhr wants you to question Camilla Lind."

He glanced at his notepad and nodded.

"I would be forever grateful if I wasn't involved in that interview," she added.

"Of course. In fact, I was going to call her right away, but it'll have to wait until we're back with the family."

Louise nodded. "I'm outta here." She flung her bag over her shoulder. He waved goodbye.

17

Outside the Department of Forensic Medicine, Louise recognized a man from Forensic Services, standing alongside a slender, pale young woman carrying a large bag. She couldn't think of his name, but she walked over and introduced herself. The man greeted her enthusiastically; they must know each other better than she remembered, she thought.

"Åse," the woman said, and shook Louise's hand.

She looked to be in her mid-twenties, and since she was with an experienced tech, Louise thought she must be a trainee. She felt sorry for her; the first few autopsies were tough. Louise asked if she was new there.

"I've worked for the department in Ålborg for three years, but I've only been in Copenhagen for a month."

The strength and conviction in her voice surprised Louise. She didn't seem the slightest bit frail once she opened her mouth. They chatted until the glass door opened and Flemming appeared.

"Okay, he's ready," the pathologist said. He greeted all three of them, and they followed him up the steps to the hallway outside the autopsy rooms. In the dressing room just inside the door, they donned plastic gowns, shoe covers, and masks. Louise also pulled a net over her dark hair before entering the autopsy room with her notepad.

The moment she walked in the long hall with the open stations, the smell hit her. Sterile, clinical. And the smell of death. Intestines also. She took a few deep breaths before following the others to the farthest room, which was twice as big as the others. They called it the murder room.

Søren Holm lay on the steel table in the middle of the room, ready for all the necessary examinations, after which he would be opened. Louise avoided looking at his face.

Åse unpacked the camera and began photographing the body. During the procedure, Flemming described in short sentences his actions and his evaluations.

The front of the body was unmarked, with no abrasions, no sign of a fight or violence or self-defense. Samples were taken with swabs; his fingernails were cut. When the lab assistants turned him over, the puncture wound came into sight. Louise thought it stood out more than the one on Frank Sørensen's neck. She stepped closer for a better look. After the entire body had been thoroughly examined, it was washed with water and a sponge.

"Time for a break," Flemming said when he finished. He walked over to the lab assistants' office to tell them the body was ready to be opened.

Louise followed him. She hadn't noticed how Åse was handling the autopsy, but the young woman looked unaffected.

"Now it's going to get interesting," Flemming said. "We were fooled last time, at least in a way."

Louise didn't understand. "What do you mean?"

"Several things went wrong when we found Frank Sørensen." He poured coffee for all of them. "At first we thought it was a natural death. We assumed he'd suffered fall-related injuries, abrasions like those often found on alcoholics when they fall down drunk. His injuries weren't very serious, but he stank from booze and he'd bit his tongue. That's common in those cases. It wasn't until we found the puncture wound and got the results back from our tests that we discovered he didn't have a drop of alcohol in his blood."

"So why did he stink of booze?" Louise said.

Flemming shrugged. "It was only his coat; someone apparently poured a bottle of whiskey over him to trick us. The samples did show, though, that he'd been sedated with GHB—fantasy, or easy lay, it's also called. It makes people more open and susceptible. Some men put it in drinks to get a girl to come home with them. You lose your defense mechanisms."

All this was new to Louise. She'd heard that Sørensen had been doped, but she hadn't known it was this kind of drug.

"We took similar samples this morning, and the results are on the way," Flemming said. "There's no question the drug made it easier to handle Frank Sørensen. He was no lightweight, and neither was Søren Holm."

Louise wondered how Flemming could keep a distance from these people he was talking about. Less than a week ago they had met Søren just outside, where he'd insisted on seeing his friend. And now he was the one laid out on the table. She felt bile rising. Quickly she took a drink of coffee and forced herself to think of other things.

They sat in silence. She studied the only decoration in the room, a large framed reproduction of a wild ocean. She couldn't see who had painted it, but clearly it had been picked out to match the curtains alongside the broad window.

Back on the second floor, the body had been opened with a single long, straight incision. Åse brought out her camera again, and Louise pulled an office chair on wheels to the wall and sat down. Flemming slowly lifted the organs that had been freed. The neck area had been opened, and from the side the wound was visible and could be measured.

"A transverse, upward, slightly gaping puncture wound is visible in the neck, two by zero point five centimeters," Flemming told the forensic technologist.

Louise jotted that down.

After studying the wound closely, he said, "I'm certain the perpetrator used the same sharp knife, or one identical to it. It's the same type of wound, resulting in a severe lesion on the backbone." He and the tech described in detail the puncture wound. Everything was photographed and recorded.

Louise guessed that the killer's height could be estimated by an examination of the path and angle of the wound. She was also curious to hear about the force of the wound, which would give her an idea of the killer's physique.

"The wound is just under the cranium, between the base of the skull and C1. That's difficult if the perpetrator is shorter than the victim." Flemming looked around at them. "I had the same impression with Frank Sørensen, but at the time I thought it was because he'd been stabbed on the ground."

Again, that was news to Louise, but she assumed it was simply because she hadn't been updated.

An hour later they were finished. Flemming needed to start writing the autopsy report so it would be ready when his boss showed up.

They threw their gowns into a large sack. "The cause of death is presumably the puncture wound in the neck, which severed the spinal cord."

Louise was about to leave, when a woman in a lab coat walked in and handed Flemming a sheet of paper. After leaning back against the wall and skimming it, he looked up for a moment, lost in thought.

"We'll have to go back in."

The two techs exchanged glances, then they followed him.

"What's going on?" Louise said as she fished her gown up out of the sack and grabbed a new mask.

"He's been jabbed," Flemming said. He seemed frustrated.

Louise frowned. Jabbed? Yeah, of course, that was what they'd already concluded. She waited for an explanation, but he ignored her and walked over to the body. The two lab assistants were nearly finished sewing him up.

"Let's turn him over," Flemming said.

A click echoed through the room when he turned on the blinding light above the steel table and pulled it down to the back of Holm's head. He leaned over and examined the wound. Everyone else stepped in closer for a better look, though far enough away to not disturb him.

"I'll be damned if I can see it," he said, straightening up. He turned to them. "The perpetrator took the time to inject him with an overdose."

Louise shivered. "Can he have been injected without putting up a fight?" She couldn't quite see that.

Fleming weighed her question. "Maybe. If he was totally unprepared for it, he wouldn't have reacted instinctively. But if he was alert, and you have to imagine Holm *was* alert, maybe not expecting to be shot up with something but aware of what was going on…yeah, it's hard to see it."

The others nodded.

Louise walked over to the table. "Surely he was lying down, too, when his spinal cord was cut?"

"Probably." Flemming stood beside her at the table. "The drug could also have been injected somewhere else. It's a possibility. But it's logical to think the perpetrator camouflaged the injection with the stab wound, since we didn't find a needle mark anywhere on his body."

Louise walked around; she needed to get some fresh air.

"Let's have them look for a needle mark in his clothes," Flemming said to the techs. They nodded. The clothes he'd been wearing were to be examined at Forensic Services, and they were already packed singly in paper bags, ready to be taken.

Åse agreed to call Louise when they'd finished with the clothes. Louise wanted to know the results before the official report was done.

The sun was shining as Louise unlocked her bike and rode along Fælled Park. She regretted not bringing sunglasses along; the glare of the spring sunlight blinded her after the many hours spent in the intense artificial light. She leaned the bike against the back wall of Police Headquarters and hurried up the steps. It was just past three when she entered the department's bathroom and glanced in the mirror; it wouldn't be good to look windblown and out of breath. Then she prepared herself to talk to a grieving, sobbing family the rest of the day.

She rapped on the door to her office and walked in. No one there. That suited her just fine. She'd be on top of things when they arrived. She checked her phone—no messages—then laid her bag and coat down and went to find something to drink.

Out in the kitchen, she almost ran into Suhr's secretary. "The wife and two daughters are in his office," the secretary said as Louise poured herself a glass of water.

"Will they be long?" Louise said.

"I don't think so. They arrived fifteen minutes ago."

Jørgensen was there when she got back to the office. "New orders."

She stared at him.

"We're going in to *Morgenavisen*."

"What? But the family's here."

"Yeah, but Willumsen just dropped in. He wants to oversee the questioning, and he was in no mood to argue about it."

"So, what's the plan?" Louise gulped down her water.

"I just spoke to the managing editor, Terkel Høyer. He'll make sure everyone working the crime beat is there when we arrive."

She nodded. She wouldn't be able to avoid Camilla after all. The situation was going to be awkward.

"They'll provide a room for us to question everyone. A few techs are coming in, too; they'll go through Holm's office."

She nodded again.

"They might already be there," he added.

"How did Høyer sound when you talked to him?" She remembered what Camilla had told her about his reaction when he found out Frank Sørensen had been killed. Now it had happened again.

"He wasn't happy, but he seemed clearheaded enough."

"It must be pretty damn tense in there," she said. "Two reporters killed; it can't be a coincidence."

"No, probably not. Well. Shall we go? We have a car."

She stood up, grabbed her bag, and laid the folder with notes from the autopsy on the table. It would be late before she got home. First, she'd have to type the notes up, then she'd have to write a report about the interviews they were about to conduct. She sighed and grabbed her coat.

On the way down the hall, Louise said, "How many will be there?"

"Two reporters, Camilla Lind and Ole Kvist, then there's an intern, Jakob, and the crime editor. And there's the photo editor and the three photographers, but only two of them are full-time, the

other is a freelancer. I don't know if we'll be talking to him." Jørgensen held the front door open for her.

"We'll only need to talk to him if he's been working with Holm
since the murder of Frank Sørensen."

They parked on Gothersgade and walked along the King's Garden. She realized she hadn't been thinking about food since the
autopsy, but now she was hungry. Though she didn't know how
anyone could be hungry after witnessing an autopsy.

"You want to do the talking, or would you rather write?" Jørgensen asked while they waited for the elevator.

Louise shrugged. "We can trade off. It's hard to write for hours
at a time."

He nodded.

Høyer met them on the second floor. His face was ashen and
pinched as he held out his hand and introduced himself.

"We cleared out a room for you, last door to the left." He
pointed, and they thanked him. On the way, Louise noticed the
door to Camilla's office was closed. She'd been there a few times,
but she'd never met any of her colleagues.

There was a case of cola on the floor in the room, cups and
glasses on a small buffet.

"Our secretary is bringing coffee and tea. Let us know if there's
anything else you'd like. We've ordered sandwiches for everyone;
they'll be here at five."

He sat down at the white oval table and slumped in his chair.
"This is goddamn tough. We have a lot of pages to fill, and no one
wants to do it; it's impossible to care about writing when you're
covering the death of a colleague."

They nodded and sat down across from him.

"We spent most of the day sitting around talking; we only
started to work an hour ago. And now you're here."

He spread his arms out in resignation.

"We need to send flowers to his wife," he said, into the air.

They let him talk.

He smiled in apology. "Of course, I want everyone to take their time in here with you, it's just that we're under pressure. One of the news journalists on the fifth floor is coming down to help until we're back on our feet. The entire newspaper assembled after lunch, our editor in chief told everyone about the murder, and of course we needed to talk afterward. We don't know many of the details yet."

Louise wondered for a moment if they'd start interviewing each other, but she cut off that thought. This wasn't the time for sarcasm. "Clearly you're all shocked by this."

"Are you the one who knows Camilla Lind?" he asked.

She nodded.

"She's not doing so well. We offered to bring in a crisis counselor for her." They'd offered the same to everyone at the paper, he added.

Louise brought out paper and a pen from her bag and laid them on the table, hoping it would signal that she was here to work, not to talk about her friend. She felt a pang of guilt, though. Shouldn't she go in and give Camilla a hug? She had to be suffering, in the middle of all this, especially after the episode with Holm the previous day. And what the hell, everyone knew they were friends anyway. But they needed to start interviewing people. Everything else would have to wait.

"Who do you want to start with?" Høyer said.

"How about you?" Jørgensen said.

They hadn't discussed that before they arrived, but Louise quickly nodded.

"Okay, I'll just tell the others." Which he did. He came back in, sat down, and looked at them expectantly.

18

Camilla deleted the first paragraph and started the article again, her third attempt. Her face was puffy from crying. She was supposed to do a portrait of Søren Holm, but every time she started, it sounded like a section of *Who's Who*. She wanted to give it more life, but how? She had all the facts in front of her: when he'd graduated from the School of Media and Journalism, places of employment, date of marriage, first child born. And yet she couldn't see him in what she wrote.

She rested her head in her hands and tried in vain to picture him. She'd found an article from the staff publication, and she'd planned to use some of it, but she couldn't sense him. It just wasn't working, and every time she tried, she thought about the squabble they'd had. Which gave her a guilty conscience. Tears began welling again. She'd been so angry with him, so certain that his warning about the danger she could be in came from wanting the story for himself. That was the first thing she'd thought when she heard about his death: that he'd meant what he said.

She took another stab at it. *For over seventeen years, Søren Holm was a journalist at* Morgenavisen. She stopped, looked at what she'd written. Rubbed her eyes, shook her head. She couldn't do this, couldn't even make a last attempt. She closed the document and went out to find Høyer, to tell him someone else would have to write this. An article about what had happened would be better for her. She could handle that.

His office door was closed. She knocked and waited, but when there was no answer, she opened the door and saw he wasn't there.

Ole Kvist walked by. "He's in with the police," he said.

How could he be so unaffected? When the editor in chief had told them the news earlier, he'd also seemed a bit remote. Camilla guessed that he and Holm might have been rivals at some point, competing to be the star reporter at the paper. And Holm had won. Maybe the loss wasn't so tough for Kvist.

"What are you working on?" she asked, before he walked into his office.

"I'm trying to find someone who saw Søren yesterday evening. The police aren't saying much, and it's not very goddamn easy when we all have to stick around here. I need to get out and talk to people who live on Vestergade."

He was absolutely right. She walked back to the office to see if she had ten kroner for a cola. Then she checked Ritzau for something more about the killing. They'd assumed the head of Homicide would hold a press conference, but when Høyer spoke with him early that afternoon, he said he didn't have time. They would have to keep an eye on the news bureau, and he would be sending out press releases when there were new developments.

She was in her chair, staring out the window, when someone

knocked. Her thoughts were on everything Holm had said to her the day before. She'd tried to get hold of Birte Jensen, she needed to talk to her, ask what the hell was going on, if Holm had called her. But Jensen hadn't called back.

Another knock. She glanced at the door. "Come in." A tall man stuck his head in and introduced himself. Lars Jørgensen, Homicide.

He smiled. "We'd like to speak with you now."

Butterflies fluttered in her stomach when she stood up. She'd never been questioned by the police before. She'd written about it many times, but now it was her turn. She followed him to the meeting room and then stopped abruptly when she saw Louise.

"Hi," she said, faltering a bit. She nodded at her friend; it felt normal yet strange to see her.

"Hi." Louise smiled and gestured for her to sit down.

"May I tell my boss something before we start?" Camilla blushed when she sensed that it was an odd thing to say. Deep down she felt insecure, which surprised her. There was no reason at all to feel uncomfortable with the situation so far, but she did.

"That's fine," Jørgensen said.

She thought he might follow her, but he didn't.

"Good Lord," Louise said when Camilla left. "She's falling apart."

He nodded thoughtfully, as if he was imprinting on his brain how Camilla Lind looked.

"She had a run-in with Holm yesterday, just so you know, if she doesn't mention it," Louise said. "I mean, not that she killed him or anything," she hastened to add. "But it's probably why she's so crushed."

Camilla returned and sat down across from them. "Søren Holm gave me one hell of a cussing out yesterday," she said, before Jørgensen could even ask her name and personal ID number.

Louise smiled at her. She couldn't help but enjoy her friend's way of barging right in. And it was also nice that she spoke directly to Jørgensen.

After relating what Holm had told her, Camilla started crying. She dried her tears off and apologized. "It's just so damn strange. Yesterday I was mad as hell at him because I thought he was over-reacting. You know that." She glanced at Louise.

"And I woke up in the middle of the night, still furious with him, how goddamn unfair he was, acting out of self-interest, and there I was, there in bed cussing him out, while he was being stabbed to death."

She broke down, began sobbing deeply.

Louise went over and found a pack of Kleenex in her bag. She laid it in front of Camilla and squeezed her shoulder.

"He was right," Camilla stammered, struggling to stop crying, her eyes already red. She looked up at them. "What the hell is going on, anyway?"

She blew her nose, and Jørgensen and Louise waited for her to compose herself.

"It sounds like a line from a bad B movie, but it could have been my spinal cord they cut." She couldn't stop her tears.

Louise had thought the same thing. Her chest ached.

"That's not how you should look at it," Jørgensen said, trying to comfort her. Then he asked her to repeat everything Holm had said to her. She couldn't remember so much other than he felt it was too dangerous for her to snoop around.

"He just wanted me to keep my nose out of it," she said.

Louise looked away. This was getting too close to home.

Jørgensen spoke slowly, as if he was afraid she couldn't follow. "Your boss also said that Holm had reliable sources in the police department, including leadership, but it seems like you suspected him of being annoyed that you had a new source, a department head. But she was already one of his own sources, so why would that bother him?"

"I don't understand it, either," Camilla said, shaking her head.

"Did he say anything about what was too dangerous for you to get involved in?"

"Not really. Just that things were happening that no one knew much about."

She thought for a moment. "It's related to the drug case he was covering…"

Jørgensen waited patiently as she tried to remember.

"When I heard what happened, it's like someone clicked delete. I just don't feel at all like I can remember exactly what he said. And it had been banging around in my head, but suddenly it all feels so strange and distant."

"What did Jensen say to you yesterday when you met her?" Jørgensen asked.

"She wanted me to help find out where Klaus West lived."

Jørgensen and Louise glanced at each other.

"Do you have any idea how Holm knew you'd been at Police Headquarters?" he asked.

Camilla shook her head. "I don't, no. It was a terrible situation. I felt like I'd been spied on, like it was a rap on the knuckles for horning in on his territory."

Louise could understand that, but she also knew Camilla could blow up when the same thing was done to her. She wrote everything down as her friend described their evening at the King's Bar and meeting Klaus West and Snow. She also mentioned the flowers, and her episode with the Finn.

Jørgensen held up his hand for her to stop. "Why did he want to see you in person? You'd already given your number; wouldn't it have been easier for him to call?"

They sat for a moment. "Yeah," Camilla said, "but I didn't ask.

Maybe he wanted to threaten me. He didn't like me going around asking for him, he said."

She shrugged and shook her head slowly.

"Maybe," Jørgensen said, then told her to continue.

After going through everything with Holm again, Camilla agreed to stop by Police Headquarters the next day and sign the report.

No one spoke for a moment after they'd finished. "Who's writing about the new murder?" Louise asked.

"All of us, a little bit. But I'm just completely empty." She ran her fingers through her hair; she looked exhausted, unhappy.

"I'm thinking more along the lines of later on," Louise said. "I hope you're all sensible enough to take this as a warning."

Camilla shrugged again. "We haven't really talked about it." Now she straightened up. "But we're not going to be intimidated into silence. We're not going to tolerate people getting killed for reporting what happens."

She looked defiant. "That would be pitiful."

"It's already—"

"We're not living in a banana republic here, where people get their heads cut off when they fight censorship. If someone has that much at stake, where they'll kill just to keep something from coming out, then it would be pretty damn interesting to find out what that something is."

Out of the corner of her eye, Louise saw Jørgensen about to speak up, possibly say something that would provoke Camilla into making these two murders her crusade. She cut him off. "Okay, I guess that's about it." She stood up and gave Jørgensen a look to do the same. At the doorway, she put her arm around Camilla's shoulder and promised to call later that evening.

"We won't be done until late," she said when Camilla asked if she could stop by instead.

"All right, but stop by my office and say goodbye when you leave. And if I'm gone, just give me a call."

She left, and Louise closed the door and then poured herself some water.

"Sorry I stopped you. I was just afraid she was going to take it on herself to solve these two murders." She smiled. "It's hell when she first gets started on something. She never lets go."

"I can imagine. You two are just alike."

That caught her off guard; she'd never thought of the two of them as being similar, at least in that way.

They took a break and chatted a few moments. "The question is if this is going to continue," he said. "I mean, there's only so many reporters you can kill to keep a lid on a story."

She shrugged. "The drug case is at the center of this, definitely. Usually these people don't care what's written about them, so I guess anything could happen. But West couldn't have killed Holm while sitting in jail. They must have found out Holm had something on them. What the hell did these two reporters know? Other reporters are covering the trial, and they haven't been threatened. These two definitely had something."

He nodded. "It sounds likely."

"Maybe we should bring in all the reporters covering this, both the case in general and the trial itself. They might have an idea what Holm and Sørensen found out that's so vitally important to someone."

He nodded again, but she could see he wasn't sold on the idea. "Surely someone else has already spoken to them?"

"Maybe."

Louise considered whether it could wait until the late briefing, but she wasn't sure they would make it back in time. And if they didn't already have a list of reporters, maybe Høyer could help them. No doubt he knew the competition, at least those writing for the major papers.

She called Police Headquarters and asked for Detective Superintendent Willumsen, then she turned to Jørgensen and told him she was going to ask about the journalists.

Willumsen answered. "Yes."

"It's Louise Rick."

"Yes."

"Lars Jørgensen and I are over at *Morgenavisen*."

"I'm aware of that."

"We were wondering if you have a list of journalists writing about the drug case that Holm and Sørensen covered."

She knew that might anger him. It was so easy for people on the outside to tell others what they should have done.

"We've spoken with a few of them. It's a good idea to make a list of everyone involved, though. We've assumed the motive had something to do with what Sørensen was working on, but now two men are dead, so obviously it's not personal against Sørensen. It's more likely the motive is connected to what they were both writing about, the drug case."

They agreed she should ask Terkel Høyer to make a list of names, and Willumsen would assign someone to call all the newspapers—maybe even all the TV stations, too, he added. They covered so much crime these days.

They finished with the interviews at eight thirty. Høyer had given them the list, though it wasn't long; few reporters covered crime exclusively, the way Holm and Sørensen had. Of course, many smaller papers sent out reporters on local cases, Høyer explained when he handed them the list. But a lot of papers simply cited Ritzau, the Scandinavian news service.

"What will you do now?" Louise said as they sat in the managing editor's office.

"Right now, we're focusing on the fact that one of our own people was killed."

Louise caught herself wondering if he felt the same way about a story as she did when leaning over a dead body. That it was work. Was it still a good lead story, even though it was about a colleague? But she saw in his expression that it wasn't the same for him. At all.

"I met with the newspaper brass a few hours ago; we discussed not covering this case out of respect for Frank and Søren. But we all agreed it would show more respect to continue. They would never have stopped, and we won't, either. But God knows it's hard to ask people to do this."

Louise felt for him.

"It was hard enough with Frank Sørensen. And now we have to write about a popular colleague who's been with the paper for seventeen years." He rubbed his face hard, until finally his cheeks reddened.

"Who's going to be reporting on the case now?" Jørgensen asked.

Louise tensed up.

"I'm doing it myself," Høyer said. "I can't put anyone else on it. Frank and Søren were personal friends of mine, and I can't afford to lose any more reporters." He forced a smile.

Louise smiled with him to lighten the mood.

Serious again, Høyer looked at her pleadingly. "You've got to help me keep Camilla out of this. She follows her instincts, and when she sees a good story, she goes for it."

Louise knew he was right, but anyway, she felt she had to defend her friend. "It looks to me like she's genuinely scared."

Høyer nodded. "In a way, I hope you're right."

"Do you happen to know Birte Jensen, the head of Narcotics?" Louise asked.

"A bit. Not well."

"She's the one who asked Camilla to get involved in this. Maybe you should tell her that Camilla is off the story. Just so everyone is on the same page."

"You're right," he said. "I'll have a word with her."

Back at the car, Louise messaged Camilla, telling her she'd call when she got back to the office. She didn't want to talk in front of Jørgensen.

"So, do you have children?" she asked as they drove back. She'd noticed that he wore a wedding ring, but she'd never asked about his family.

He smiled. "Two boys, three-year-old twins."

She was surprised; she hadn't pictured him as a father to young kids. Hadn't actually pictured anything about him. She studied his profile. "How do you keep things together with these work hours?"

"My wife stays home." For a moment he seemed to consider whether to tell her more. "Our boys are from Bolivia. She quit her job when we went over to get them, and since then she's been taking care of them."

Louise stopped herself from making a big fuss about that. Having children from South America sounded exotic to her, and she was surprised to hear he was an adoptive father, though she couldn't say why she felt that way. "Hmmm." She wondered how a family of four could live on a policeman's salary, but she was tactful enough to not ask. "Fantastic."

He nodded and smiled. "Let's stop and stock up on some supplies for later. We can't sit and write all this down without something to keep us going."

He parked in front of a kiosk and went inside. Louise's mind went blank, and she jerked when her phone rang. "Louise Rick," she said, without even checking to see who was calling.

Camilla didn't beat around the bush. "I had a message when I got home."

"From who?"

Louise leaned over and searched her bag for a notepad. Pure reflex.

"The Finn. He wants me to meet him at eleven at Cafe Svejk." She sounded excited. Svejk was their favorite bar when they felt like drinking a beer. Over the years they'd become friends with the owner; the atmosphere was refreshingly informal, and his Czech beer tasted heavenly.

"How the hell does he know I like the place?" Camilla said.

"He doesn't; it's logical to suggest Svejk when you're living in Frederiksberg," she said, though she knew the argument was weak. "How did you get the message?" That's what interested her most.

Jørgensen slid back into the driver's seat. He sensed something was going on and waited to start the car.

"Someone slipped it through the mail slot in my door."

"You're not thinking about meeting him, are you?"

Silence.

"Are you?" Louise said, louder this time.

"People are dropping like flies, and here's a guy who might know what's going on. I've got to hear what he has to say."

Louise moaned. Just as she'd feared. When Camilla first latched on to a good story, she got excited and let her emotions get the best of her, but after digging into it and seeing where it was leading, her mind took over and focused on it like a laser.

"Two reporters have dropped; maybe it's a good idea to keep a low profile," Louise said.

Jørgensen looked curious now.

"Just a minute," she told Camilla.

She let Jørgensen in on what was going on. At first, he fiercely shook his head and ran his finger across his throat—no, no! But then he sat and thought for a moment. Louise could see he was changing his mind. The hairs on the back of her neck rose.

"Hello!" Camilla shouted.

"Just a second."

"Maybe we should talk this over within the department?" Jørgensen said. "It might be smart to hear what the Finn has to say."

Louise looked daggers at him—Camilla had heard every word he said.

"I've got to find out what he wants," Camilla said, before Louise could speak. "Nothing's going to happen just from listening to him."

"We'll talk about it later," Louise said. "I'll call back when we have time to discuss this, and don't go until we agree on what to do."

She hoped Camilla had gotten that through her thick skull.

19

Everyone was busy back at the department when they returned at nine thirty. They had many reports to write. Three officers from City had taken over their office, but they stood up when Louise and Jørgensen walked in. The department simply didn't have enough room for everyone. Or enough computers.

"Sandwiches in the lunchroom," one of them said as they packed their folders.

Louise smiled and thanked him. She felt too exhausted to eat, but she decided to grab a bite anyway. She wouldn't be home for several hours, and food might help with her energy.

She picked up a sandwich for herself and Jørgensen and set his on a plate in front of him. "Where's Willumsen?" she asked a tall officer.

"He'll be here in a minute. They've questioned Klaus West again."

"What did he say?" Louise took a bite and listened eagerly.

"He denies any knowledge of the two killings. His lawyer still won't let him talk, and we don't have anything more on him. Only that we're almost sure he has something to do with the drug case. Nothing to connect him to the killings, though, except the witness statement that confirms he was at the hotel."

"One witness statement is about as thin as it gets." Louise felt discouraged.

"I don't know, though. When the statement comes from one of us, it's stronger in court than if it were a civilian."

"But he couldn't have committed the last murder, and if both killings were done by the same person, presumably he's innocent of both."

"That's exactly the argument his lawyer used on Suhr, and it looks like he's probably going to let West go."

Louise unzipped her boots and kicked them off, then sat on her office chair with her legs pulled up under her. "There must be something. What about his partner, Snow—Michael Danielsen, is that his name? Could it be him?"

"He's been sitting in here most of the day. He has an alibi, but of course he could have paid to have it done."

"There has to be somebody willing to talk."

The Finn! They needed to bring him in for questioning. If he really knew so much, they had to know what it was.

Louise tried to concentrate. Suddenly she noticed Willumsen standing in the doorway, and she nodded at him. "What does West have to say about being seen at the hotel?"

Willumsen walked in and leaned back against the low shelf just inside the door. "He says he wasn't there. He claims he wasn't even in the country, that he first came back Monday. Otherwise he's not speaking. John Bro is scared he'll blurt something out and start changing his story, and then we'd have him."

He sounded bitter. Clearly, he was annoyed by being up

against Bro. Murder cases were complicated enough to begin with.

She was puzzled. "How do we know it's true he was out of the country?"

"He has a plane ticket from London. We checked with SAS, and they confirm a passenger by that name checked in. No one can remember what he looked like, but it wasn't someone who stood out in a crowd."

That eliminates Snow, Louise thought as she recalled his chalk-white hair.

"It sounds like his alibi is airtight," Willumsen said. "He also has a taxi receipt from the airport to the King's New Square."

"Or else it was planned out perfectly," Jørgensen said from the other side of the table. "If he had someone to cover for him, to confirm his alibi."

The others agreed.

"Jensen says it wasn't until that evening that she gave the okay for Sørensen to tag along at the Royal Hotel."

"Is it possible West set up an alibi because he was involved in the delivery of the drugs to the hotel?" Louise said.

Willumsen nodded in acknowledgment. "It's entirely possible. Birte Jensen saw him at the hotel Saturday night. She was in charge of the raid. They didn't speak, but they almost ran into each other on the ground floor, near the courtyard exit."

They all sat and thought for a moment. Louise decided she'd better tell him about Camilla and the message from the Finn. The meeting was to take place in less than an hour.

"I'll go get Suhr," Willumsen immediately said.

It was out of her hands now. She regretted further involving her friend in this mess, but really, there was nothing she could do. And if they stayed out of it, Camilla would meet him anyway, and that was too risky.

Suhr's face was red when he walked in. He quickly greeted everyone in the office, then he walked over behind Louise, who had to turn to see him.

"What's this all about?" He stared at her forehead.

He grumbled while she explained it all again.

"We have to be there," he said. He began swaying from side to side. Anyone who didn't know him would have thought he was about to fall, but it was a habit, what he did when he was thinking.

Louise tried to catch his eye. "We can't let him know that Camilla has talked to the police."

"But she has." He kept staring at her forehead.

She turned away from him. "No, she told me because I'm her friend."

"Hmmm. We'll go in and grab him when they sit down."

She swung back around in anger. "No, are you out of your mind!"

Finally, he looked her in the eye. "It's also too dangerous if we do nothing."

Louise knew he was right.

"Birte Jensen knows him, if I've heard right," Jørgensen said. "Why can't we get her to talk to him?"

Louise knew that Suhr wouldn't wait to get that arranged. "What about if we listen in and wait to pick him up until he's away from Camilla?" She offered to take care of the microphone.

Suhr laid a hand on her shoulder. "That's what we'll do."

That was easy, Louise thought. Maybe too easy, maybe that had been his idea, too. He'd just been waiting for her to suggest it so he'd have her support. Smart. Though she didn't like being sucked in. She also wanted to hear what the Finn had to say.

"Let's get going," Suhr said. "Call Camilla Lind; we need to get the mike on her quick."

After the others left, Jørgensen said, "What if she doesn't go along with this?"

"She will." Louise picked up the phone. "She's not going to like it, but she doesn't want to miss out on anything, either."

He smiled and shook his head. "Strange woman!"

"Hi, Camilla, it's me. I'm going to be there, too."

"What do you mean? You can't come along!"

"I don't mean physically. You're going to wear a mike, and we'll be listening." She hoped Camilla would be so relieved about Louise not insisting on holding her hand that she'd go along with the plan.

Her friend thought it over. "So where exactly will you be?"

"I don't know, maybe in back, or outside in a car."

"He'll see right through that," Camilla said.

Louise could hear she was getting nervous. She had to convince her that people didn't discover these things. "How could he do that?"

"When the shitty little mike makes noises or something."

"That only happens in the movies. He's not going to find out; he won't hear or see the mike. Look, we don't have much time. I'm coming over right now to put it on you."

Say as little as possible, she thought; that's the best way to calm down Camilla.

"What if he sees you? You never know. Maybe he's down on the street."

"I'm coming alone. I'll bring a few papers along, like I'm just delivering something to you, then I'll get out of there. See you in a bit." She hung up.

"Good," Jørgensen said. "Take the car." He threw her the keys. "Suhr sent two men over to Cafe Svejk to find a place for you. Call them when you leave Camilla's."

Louise stopped on the way and bought two women's magazines, then she parked in front of Camilla's apartment building. She grabbed the magazines and held them so they were conspicuous. Without looking up and down the street, she strode over to the door; the second her finger hit the buzzer, the door unlocked. The small box with the mike rattled in her pocket as she ran up the stairs.

Camilla stood outside her door. "Hi!"

"Hi, get inside. We don't have much time."

She was out of breath when she entered the apartment, from running as well as the adrenaline kicking in.

Quickly she peeled off the protective tape from the small mike and pressed it onto Camilla's chest. It was the size of a button, and no thicker. Then she clipped the small transmitter on the inside of the waistband of her skirt.

"That's it?" Camilla said. "No cords or anything?"

"Nope." Louise shook her head and guaranteed her the mike wouldn't fall off. She got ready to go. "Remember to ask him."

Camilla rolled her eyes and nodded toward Louise. "What the hell are you thinking? I'm not brain-dead yet."

"Great." Louise hugged her, then she left and ran downstairs. She glanced around after starting the car and backing out, but she saw no sign of the Finn. It would have surprised her if she had, but he could be lurking around anyway. As she drove down Falkoner Allé, she grabbed her phone and called the two men assigned to help, to say she was on the way. She turned down Smallegade and into the large parking lot behind Frederiksberg Town Hall. The officers would pick her up and then drive behind Cafe Svejk and park.

Louise stayed in the car. There weren't many vehicles there this time of day, and she would draw attention if she waited outside.

She spotted them at once when they drove up. It couldn't be seen that they were police. The generic van had tinted windows, but that wasn't unusual. She hopped in back when they parked beside her.

"We've got ten minutes," said the tech in charge of the bugging equipment.

She nodded and got settled in. "Are you getting sound from her?"

"Yeah, but she's not saying anything."

Louise had forgotten to ask Camilla to speak so they could adjust the sound.

"We're picking her up; I can hear her walking." He held out a pair of headphones. She reached over for them and was startled at the sight of Suhr stretched out in the seat behind her, his eyes closed. She hadn't noticed him when she got in.

She pointed at him and mouthed, "What's he doing here?"

"Sleeping," the tech mouthed back.

That much she had figured out. Why was he there?

The driver left the parking lot, then he turned in behind the bar and parked. Suhr sat up the second the driver turned off the engine.

"We're ready then," he said, looking at the others. He was like a kid waiting for the circus to begin.

"Almost." Louise smiled at him. "The only thing missing are the stars of the show."

He looked puzzled.

"Camilla and the Finn haven't arrived yet," she added.

He was still half-asleep, which no one could blame him for. He'd had little time off lately. "Do we know what he looks like?"

Two men came walking toward the door.

"Light hair, good-looking, mid-thirties," Louise said.

"In other words, neither one of those guys," he said.

The driver picked up a thermos and offered everyone coffee. They chatted for a while, everyone was in good spirits, but they kept their focus on the door.

"There she is," Louise said, pointing to the crosswalk.

Camilla was wearing a heavy coat, with a thick scarf around her neck. Louise had the feeling she was looking over at the van, wondering if that was where Louise would be listening. The light changed, and she disappeared when she crossed the street. While they'd been talking, Louise had listened with one ear free, but now she took a sip of coffee and slipped the headphones on both ears, shutting everything out except what came over the mike.

She waited for Camilla to reach the door. Was there live music tonight? She'd forgotten to ask. Usually on weekdays they played CDs. She heard a bicycle stop, and Camilla made some sort of sound, muffled from her heavy coat and scarf.

"Walk," a voice said.

Louise turned and saw Camilla and a man with a bicycle walking behind the van. His arm was around her, and if she hadn't known better, she would have thought they were a couple.

"Shit," Suhr said. "What the hell's going on?" He leaned forward until he was almost touching the rear window, but they were parked in a way that blocked him from seeing them. "Back out," he ordered.

"Wait!" Louise said. "He's only walking away because he's afraid we're here. If we back out now, he'll know."

After a moment, Suhr said, "Okay, but where the hell are they going?"

Louise had one ear free of the headphones again. "There's another café across the street. Should I follow them?" Instantly she knew her idea was just as stupid as backing up the van.

"No, you shouldn't follow them!"

Suddenly she heard a sound, a whisper. Camilla's voice was strange and distant; she seemed to be saying, "Sokke."

"Wow, it's still cold, huh?" Camilla's voice blasted into the headphones, and the tech hurriedly turned down the volume. He, Suhr, and Louise were wearing headphones. Louise pointed far-

ther down Smallegade and said, "Sokkelund." A café. Suhr un-
tangled himself from the cords and glanced at the tech. They took
off their headphones and discussed something with the driver—
whether to drive closer, Louise guessed. Then she heard Camilla
and the Finn talking. They were about to sit down, and she told
the others.

The driver backed out and drove slowly over to the café,
about a hundred meters away. He parked in front of a produce
market. Both voices were clear. Apparently, the bar was having
a slow evening, because all they could hear besides their talking
was music.

"What do you want to drink?" the Finn asked.

"Coffee."

"Anything in it?"

"No thanks."

Camilla sounded nervous. The Finn was more relaxed.

"We're sitting at a corner table in Sokkelund," Camilla whispered. Louise could imagine how she looked.

"There you are," the Finn said. They heard something being set
on the table.

"What is it you want?"

Damn! Louise had hoped that Camilla would take it nice and
easy and avoid provoking him at all costs. But she wasn't surprised. They should have talked about how to handle him.

After a few moments of silence, Camilla added, "What do we
need to talk about?"

Louise straightened up, as did Suhr and the tech. Camilla
would have enjoyed seeing her audience in the palm of her hand.

"I got some news, might be useful to you." Again, he sounded
calm. A nice voice, Louise noted.

"Let's get it all down," Suhr told the tech, who stuck his thumb
up in the air—he was already recording.

"Interesting," Camilla said. "Is this about the murders or the drug case?"

"That's up to you to decide. But first we're going to make a little deal."

"What sort of deal?" Camilla sounded as if she did things like this every day.

The Finn hesitated; the four of them in the van were all ears.

"You have to promise to write about what I tell you—"

"I can't promise you that."

Louise winced and cursed under her breath at her friend's lack of experience; he might take that as a rejection. But then Camilla continued.

"I can't promise anything before I know what you have to say. Surely you understand that."

"Before I go on, I have to know if you're going to use my tip. Otherwise I'll give it to somebody else."

Louise could practically hear Camilla thinking that over. The others in the van were nervous.

"I can't promise."

"Suit yourself." The Finn's voice was cold as ice. It sounded in the headphones like he stood up.

Suhr and Louise exchanged glances. The driver sat up, ready to start the car. Thoughts raced through Louise's head. Suhr had to decide what to do if the Finn left.

"Take it easy," Camilla said. "If it's not something completely crazy, and you're sure it's something I can use, of course I'll write it."

Louise could just see Høyer's face. She hoped he was okay with Camilla's promise.

The Finn sighed and spoke hurriedly but softly. "Klaus West had Holm taken out, just like he did Frank Sørensen."

"But why?"

Several moments passed before he spoke again. "West has been shoveling in the money for years. Lately he's been flooding the center of town with green dust. People not already hooked get hooked. It's some of the best product to ever hit the streets. He wasn't going to let two crazies ruin his business."

Camilla kept her mouth shut.

"Maybe you haven't heard about the drug trial going on lately?" Now he was being ironic.

"I have. So why is he not on trial like the others, if it's so obvious what he's doing?"

Louise smiled at Suhr. Camilla was doing what she could to get him to talk.

"So you think Sørensen and Holm had something on Klaus West, something that could prove he was running the whole show, and the ones on trial are taking the blame?"

She sensed the thoughts of everyone in the van: It would be tough for Camilla to get anything out of the Finn he hadn't already decided to tell.

"You really don't know shit about this, do you?" the Finn said, avoiding her questions.

Before Camilla could answer, he said, "There's no reason to know anything more, either. All you have to understand is that Klaus West is damn good at covering his tracks. He's got an apartment here in town, the cops haven't found it yet, but I know where it is."

All the oxygen, all sense of time and space were sucked out of the van; the three of them listening in on their headphones stared at the floor, completely frozen.

He spoke slowly. "Before I tell you, I want you to promise your paper will publish a photo of Klaus West, and that you're looking for people who might know where he lives."

"Why?" she asked, almost in a whisper.

"I don't want it to look like the cops were tipped off about the apartment. It has to look like the neighbors contacted them after seeing his photo in the paper. Understand?"

Louise imagined Camilla nodding.

"For all I care you can call and tell the cops about the apartment right after I leave. It's fine with me if they look at it. I just don't want to be connected with the tip."

"Okay." It was still difficult to hear Camilla's voice.

"We have a deal?"

"Yes," she said, a bit louder now.

"Vestergade 26. The name on the door is Sanne Hansen."

Suddenly, the sound of chairs scraping against the floor filled their headphones. A few moments later they saw the Finn walk out the door and hop on his bike.

Louise watched him until he was out of sight. "Okay, he's gone."

The driver pulled up to the curb just outside Sokkelund Cafe. Louise slid the door open for Camilla to step inside.

"Fantastic!" she said to Camilla. She squeezed her arm. "We were about to go in and get him."

That frightened Camilla. "Yeah, you'd have loved to do that, wouldn't you? Are you crazy!"

Louise noticed she was starting to tremble. Maybe because she could let go, now that she didn't have to concentrate. "We'll take you home." She leaned over and plucked the microphone off her friend. The driver hung a U and headed back to Falkoner Allé.

"Very well done, Ms. Lind," Suhr said. He held his hand out. "I don't believe we've met."

She shook his hand. Now she sounded tired. "I didn't understand all of it. I hope you got more out of all that about the drug case."

"We got an address, and that's what we'd lacked." Suhr

sounded unusually satisfied. "We've already got people on the way to check it out."

"You heard what I promised," Camilla said, a bit nervous now. "I hope it doesn't come out that you found the apartment before we write about it."

Suhr laid his hand on her arm, leaned forward, and spoke quietly. "In this world you have to act. When you've been doing this long enough, you learn how valuable information and knowledge are."

She listened with interest, but said nothing. The mentor was instructing the student.

"The police deal with informers like the Finn. He might get caught with drugs on him, but we let him go if he has something interesting to tell us. That's probably how Birte Jensen got to know him. The police deal with the press. You help us. Quid pro quo. You get your story."

Louise watched her friend lap all this up.

"But again, what happens if all this about the apartment comes out before we get it in the paper?"

"Then the story is that we got the information from routine questioning. The apartment is in the building next to the courtyard where we found Søren Holm. It's logical that we'd talk to people in the surrounding apartments."

Camilla nodded, but Louise saw that she wasn't totally convinced. "What does he get out of this? That you find the apartment?"

"Hard to say, but I'm guessing he's involved somehow with Klaus West. And for whatever reason, he'd like to see West behind bars for a long time. Maybe he wants in on the drug market and needs some elbow room."

He gazed at the traffic outside for a few moments before turning back to Camilla. "Why was it you two didn't go into Cafe Svejk?"

Louise leaned in to listen.

"He just said he'd changed his mind. He'd rather have a cup of coffee."

"I'm not so sure he's as small-time as I thought he was," Suhr said, more to Louise than to Camilla. "I'll get hold of Jensen in the morning; we'll find out just who this guy is. I'm sure she wants a good look at the apartment, too. If he's not lying about it."

The driver parked in front of Camilla's building.

"What about the recording?" Louise said. "Do we need to transcribe it now?" It was half past midnight.

"I'll have somebody else do it. Go with your friend. You can pick the car up later and keep it until tomorrow."

Before Louise got out of the van, she remembered they needed to talk to Camilla about how to tackle the situation at work the next day. Suhr scratched his chin for a moment.

"Maybe we should just meet tomorrow, say, nine thirty, if it turns out the tip about the apartment is real. Then we can decide what to say and what not to say."

"I can come by before going in to the paper," Camilla said. "So I can hear what you decide."

"That sounds fine," Suhr said. He waved goodbye.

Camilla brought two bottles of beer into the living room, and she and Louise plopped down on the sofa.

"I really thought he was going to leave when I wouldn't promise to write what he wanted," Camilla said as she poured beer in her glass. The foam overflowed before she could set the glass down. "Shit."

Camilla held it while Louise went into the kitchen for a rag.

"I was nervous as hell when you walked by Svejk," she said when she came back. "Weren't you?"

"Not really. He was friendly; he just suggested we have a cup of coffee instead of a beer."

Louise sat back down.

"I don't think he did it because he thought someone was listening in," Camilla said.

"I was getting seriously worried, anyway," Louise admitted. She took a drink of beer.

"I thought maybe you would be, but I couldn't really say anything before I took my coat off and he left for a moment."

"You did the right thing, but I was just sure he'd spotted us. And you never know what people will do under pressure."

They sat for a while, absorbed in their thoughts.

"It surprised me when your boss started in on that quid pro quo stuff. I feel like a total greenhorn when I hear things like that. I know it happens; I just haven't been a part of it before."

"Yeah, but you made a great impression; now you're one of the people the police can trust. That's good for you, isn't it? Or what?"

"Yeah, sure. You just make it sound like I joined some intelligence service." Camilla laughed, but Louise knew she was proud of the confidence the head of Homicide had in her. "I wonder if the apartment really exists."

"Yeah, and if it does, it's going to be very interesting to see what they find. We really need a break in this case." Louise glanced at her watch. "I've got to get home."

Camilla jumped up. "I'll call a taxi."

"I've got to pick the car up at the parking lot."

"You shouldn't be running around out there alone now. The taxi can take you to the car."

Louise was fine with that. She'd put in a long, full day. An eventful day. While Camilla called, she went out and put on her coat, yawning as she buttoned it up. Suddenly, she felt completely exhausted.

20

Peter shook her gently. Louise had vaguely heard the alarm clock ringing and him getting up. Her body felt heavy as lead. She crawled further under the comforter and buried her face in her pillow.

"Up we go." His words sounded like someone calling from afar.

Silence. Heavy, tired. She counted…eight, nine, ten. Without opening her eyes, she threw her comforter aside and cringed when the cold air slapped her warm skin.

"Come on, get up." Peter stood beside the bed. "It's past seven; you have to be out the door in a half hour."

She forced her eyes open. "Coming."

She sounded raspy and dull. She rubbed her face, pushed her skin around with both hands.

"Hon, don't squash your nose all over your face. It makes you *not* look like your charming self!"

She looked up in surprise; she hadn't noticed him standing there.

"I've got to be at the airport in an hour." He swept her hair out of her face. Now she remembered: He was flying to Aberdeen; he'd been invited for a look at where he'd be working.

"I'll see you Friday afternoon," he said.

She nodded and let him pull her to her feet, then she wobbled out into the bathroom to brush her teeth. That much she owed him before kissing him goodbye.

"The car key's on the kitchen counter," he yelled on the way down the stairs.

Louise found a clean pair of jeans in the closet, and while she put them on she thought of the conversation between the Finn and Camilla. The apartment might be another dead end. She finished up and walked out to the hall without checking herself in the mirror. She had mascara in her bag; she'd deal with it at headquarters. Camilla never left her apartment without makeup on.

Louise parked on Otto Mønsteds Gade. Jørgensen hadn't shown up yet when she reached the office, though it was five to eight. She turned on her computer; the chances were decent that the startup would be finished by the time she got back from the morning briefing.

She entered the lunchroom and sat down at one of the long tables. After a moment, Suhr walked in. He had deep, dark circles under his eyes, and he looked like death warmed over. Twice.

Louise guessed that they'd found the apartment.

"Good morning. It finally looks like we caught a break." He sounded surprisingly fresh.

Several in the room greeted him back. Louise glanced around. Everybody looked beat, and yet she sensed the energy behind the weary eyes. Most of them had been working practically around the clock, but now they were all ears.

Occasionally, Peter accused her of being an adrenaline junkie, during the periods when work filled about 80 percent of her day, sleep the rest. You get a rush, and lack of sleep is just a minor detail—that's how she usually ended the discussion.

Suhr was going over the main points of Flemming's autopsy report.

"Jesus!" said the officer across from Louise when Suhr explained about the overdose Holm had been given before being stabbed.

"Yeah, it's safe to say it wasn't voluntary on his part," Suhr said.

He stood in front of the whiteboard that filled most of the wall. The courtyard behind Vestergade 28 had been sketched with a blue marker, and every spot where something linked to the corpse had been found was marked in red.

Suhr said the techs were now certain that Holm had been killed in the courtyard. He also said that even though Forensic Medicine wouldn't finish the final autopsy report until later that day, Flemming Larsen was convinced that the same type of weapon had been used in both murders, possibly a long, narrow butterfly knife.

Suhr didn't say a word about the apartment, and several times during the briefing she felt he was avoiding her eyes. After he finished, she sat for a few moments before standing up. Immediately he called her name.

"Could we have a word in my office?"

She nodded. "Of course." There was a distance between them that hadn't been there last night when she'd left. "How about a cup of coffee?" she added, hoping to lighten things up.

"That sounds good, I might need it. Let me just send a message to Willumsen."

Holding on to two cups of coffee, she walked a tightrope to his office.

"Need a hand?" Jørgensen said when he met her in the hall. He grabbed one of the cups and followed her.

"Thanks. Where were you?" They reached Suhr's office and set the coffee down.

He stifled a yawn. If anything, he looked even worse than their boss, Louise thought as she caught herself staring. "What the hell have you been up to all night?"

He sighed dramatically and leaned against the conference table. "First I wrote out all the interviews from the paper."

She'd forgotten all about them.

"When I *finally* got through all of them, Suhr came back from your little adventure and asked me to go out with him to look for an apartment in Vestergade."

"Good Lord, you were in here that late?" Now she felt sorry for him.

He nodded. "Unfortunately!"

"Too bad you didn't find anything."

He looked surprised. "What do you mean?"

Suhr walked in and gestured for her to sit down. Jørgensen left without explaining.

"Good work last night," Suhr said, after sitting down and reaching for his coffee.

Louise was puzzled, but she waited for him to explain what happened after she'd gone home.

"We found the apartment." Suddenly he smiled broadly. "Did you think I was going to keep you in the dark about it?"

She shrugged; what did he expect her to say? He was acting oddly, she felt.

"We were in there most of the night. I decided not to announce it this morning so the news doesn't come out until we're ready. With regards to Camilla Lind, I mean."

She smiled at him. He knew that sounded like he didn't trust the others in the department, and he added that of course no one would let the cat out of the bag. But anyway. So, the only ones who knew about the apartment were those who had been with him.

"That's fine." She nodded to show that she got it, she agreed with him.

"It was 26C. And we knew what we were looking for, so it wasn't difficult."

She leaned across the table, eager to know. "Did you find anything?"

For a moment he considered what to say. "Maybe. We found a small plastic pot with WS5 powder in the kitchen."

She didn't understand.

He smiled. "It's a green coloring agent; it gives things a greenish tint!"

Louise laughed. "You don't mean to tell me that Klaus West stood in his kitchen and poured green coloring over uncut heroin." Louise visualized that and laughed even harder. "It sounds totally insane."

"It's almost certainly the source of the green in the heroin. Jørgensen was sharp enough to make the connection."

Louise shook her head. It sounded too crazy. "Was there anything else?"

"Not much, except for some papers that could be records of his sales. We'll have to look through them, of course."

"What about Sanne Hansen? Where was she?" The name the Finn had said was on the door.

"We haven't got that far yet."

"I can't understand why they hadn't already found the apartment."

Her boss looked at her and slowly shook his head. "We don't understand, either. But he's a sharp guy, no doubt about that. That's how he's survived up to now, by his wits. That probably explains it."

Louise chewed on that for a second. "Probably so."

She'd been hoping for more, much more, and now she was disappointed. "No drugs?"

"They hadn't found any when I left. That doesn't mean there

aren't any. Jensen has her people going through the apartment with a fine-tooth comb, together with the techs. We called her early this morning."

Of course, Louise thought. Since no murder weapon or anything to connect Klaus West with the murders of the two reporters had been found, the apartment was more interesting for Narcotics.

"When Jensen heard we bugged the Finn yesterday, she said he'd run into serious trouble with Klaus West about four years ago."

Louise perked up.

"He was selling for West. Not just on the street, but bigger deals, in discotheques around town, places like that. After a year or so he wanted out, but West said no."

Suhr looked grim. "We're talking about broken bones, and worse. When the Finn didn't do what he was told, West got his little sister hooked on heroin, and last year she died of an overdose. Twenty-seven years old. West denied knowing her."

Fucking shithead, Louise thought.

"The Finn wants him in prison, and he wants him there yesterday."

She nodded. "You can hardly blame him."

"That explains his motive, anyway."

"It also explains why he needed Camilla," Louise said, after a moment's pause. She'd wondered why the Finn hadn't simply told Birte Jensen what he knew, but now she understood. "By going through her, he wouldn't be suspected of snitching. At least not so easily. Maybe Klaus West was suspicious, but this way he could never be sure it was the Finn."

"Yeah, you have to be sneaky to survive."

"But how does all this help us?"

"Jensen is still sure that West is our man. We just need to keep looking; she's convinced we can find something. The techs are going through the basement and attic rooms; another team is tearing the apartment up. I spoke with her just before the briefing, and she said she'd try to be here when Camilla shows up."

He glanced at his watch. "Which won't be long."

Louise tried to make sense of all this for several moments. Someone knocked on the door; Suhr's secretary stuck her head in and said Camilla Lind and Birte Jensen were waiting outside. He walked out to greet them.

Louise shook Jensen's hand when she came in, then she quickly said hi to Camilla.

Jensen's cheeks were splotched, her eyes glittering. They sat down at the conference table. "We've got him," she said.

Suhr raised his eyebrows. "'Got him'?"

"We found a small butterfly knife with traces of blood. Forensics has it. It's almost certain they can prove the knife is the type the killer used; the blade matches the puncture wound." Jensen paused dramatically. "And in the bottom of a closet we found a little box that happened to hold six hundred grams of pure heroin. So..." She turned to Louise and Camilla. "Your little excursion yesterday was a great help to us!"

Louise stared at Jensen as her words soaked in. "And the coloring agent?" Suddenly she recalled the absurd image in her brain when Suhr had told her what they'd found in the kitchen.

Camilla frowned at her in confusion.

Birte Jensen nodded. "That's right. His trademark. A chemist from Forensics called me up this morning. He said that Vegex Chlorophyll WS5 is a food colorant. He tried mixing it with some talcum powder and pure heroin, and he's pretty sure that's how Klaus West made his green dust."

Camilla could hardly believe it. "Talcum powder!"

Jensen explained. "Pure heroin is cut with lactose or talcum powder. Heroin sold on the street is thirty to 40 percent pure. Before it's cut, it's 80 to 90 percent. Take that and you'll die, your respiratory organs will be paralyzed, and your heart will stop. So, heroin doubles in weight when it gets cut."

After a few moments of thoughtful silence, Jensen excused herself. "I have a meeting with the prosecutor in ten minutes. We have enough to charge him with this new evidence."

"You're also pressing charges?"

Suhr hadn't said a word since she told them about finding the presumed murder weapon, but now he was alert. Before Jensen could answer, he leaned over the table. "When will the results on the knife come in?" he said, his voice stern.

Louise leaned back in her chair and eyed them. She glanced at Camilla; her friend looked tense as she listened.

Jensen's voice, in contrast to Suhr's, was silky. "Of course, we'll let you know. I'll call just as soon as I find out."

"I'll call them myself. I'm sure you have plenty to do."

His words were cold, which made Louise cringe. She didn't at all enjoy being in the middle of this power struggle.

Jensen held her hands up in surrender and smiled. "All right, he's all yours. I'll take over when you're through with him."

Suhr nodded, satisfied now.

"Before I leave, I think we should plan on how to handle the press," Jensen said, looking back and forth between him and Camilla.

"I promised the Finn that we'd publish a photo of Klaus West, and ask people to contact us if they think he's living in their apartment building. We're doing that tomorrow."

"We can't wait to charge him until tomorrow," Jensen said, leaning down to pick up her bag under the table. "We have to go public with what we have." She raised an eyebrow at Suhr. "Don't you think?"

"We made a deal yesterday, but I can see it's going to be hard to keep our promise."

Camilla stood up. "What do you mean 'hard to keep'? You have to keep it. Please!"

In the awkward silence that followed, she stared pleadingly at the head of Homicide, who looked sheepish.

"No one could have known this would happen. The evidence has been filed, the charges are being made now. But under no circumstances will we say anything about finding the apartment through a tip."

The end of Camilla's nose was pure white. "Come on—you can't do this."

Louise could see her friend was struggling to speak calmly.

"The Finn will find out, and then he'll think I'm screwing him around. I don't dare do that!"

"I'll have a word with him," Jensen said as if it were no problem at all. "Clearly, we can't have you seeming to be someone who doesn't keep their word."

She walked over to Camilla. "I'll tell him what we found. He'll understand we must proceed with this. And I'll make sure he gets something in return later on."

Camilla nodded resignedly and shrugged, as if they were talking about something that no longer concerned her.

Jensen quickly circled the table and shook everyone's hand before leaving. Suhr stood up and pulled a chair over to Camilla.

"I understand your reaction, but sometimes things happen, and we have to act. We really have no choice in this situation; we have a killer we've worked hard to find."

Camilla slumped in her chair, her eyes glued to the table in front of her, her face expressionless as he spoke. Louise felt sorry for her.

"You have to nail him!" Camilla straightened up and turned in her chair to Suhr, leaning toward him until their faces were inches apart. "It's okay; I understand. But what do I get?"

Louise breathed easy now, her stomach unclenched. She pressed her lips together to suppress a smile. If you mess around with Camilla, you're going to pay.

"What?" Suhr was startled for a moment, then he began to laugh. "Of course you'll get your piece of the cake." He laid a hand on her shoulder and stood up. "Give me time to find out about all this; right now I don't know any more than you do."

He walked over to his desk. "I'm sure we'll put out a press release, and I promise, you'll hear from me. The next few hours are probably going to be hectic, though."

Camilla stood up and put on her coat. "Can I print what we've talked about here?"

He rubbed his chin. "Right now, you can write that we found what we presume to be the murder weapon. But I'd like to hear from the techs before you quote me."

"What about the six hundred grams of heroin and the food coloring?"

"Go ahead and write that."

Camilla seemed satisfied. Louise followed her out the door and watched as she finally found her bike key. "So, you got something after all." She smiled.

"I didn't get a damn thing more than they're giving everyone else. They still owe me."

"Your witness statement from yesterday is finished. You have time to read it before you leave?"

They walked over to her office, and ten minutes later Louise watched Camilla walk to the revolving door. Her heels echoed against the arched walls.

21

The loud voices out in the hall annoyed Louise. She thought about walking over and slamming the door shut, but instead she tried to block out the racket.

Her eyes stung; she'd had the office to herself all day and had spent it writing reports on the events of the previous night. The recording of the conversation between the Finn and Camilla had been transcribed. She'd read through it and marked the places of special interest for the prosecutor.

After lunch they'd discussed whether they should try to find the Finn, but it turned out that Birte Jensen, as she'd promised, had already spoken with him.

Louise drew a heavy circle around his address, which she'd written on a notepad. His real name was Finn Anderson, and he lived close to Toftegårds Square.

The voices distracted her again. "What's going on out there?" she yelled. She walked over to kick the door shut, but as she raised her foot, she heard Michael Stig say, "He's being brought before a judge in an hour."

Their eyes met as she stood awkwardly on one leg. She lowered her foot and walked out in the hall, and the officers surrounding Stig retreated a step.

This isn't a coincidence, their being outside the office, she thought. She regretted taking the bait, but now it was too late. "Who are you talking about?"

She stood face-to-face with Stig, and he looked at her as if he hadn't noticed her before. He smiled. "Matter of fact, I was just on my way to tell you about the breakthrough on the Karoline Wissinge case. How about a cup of coffee?"

Louise wanted to kick him in the shins. Like hell he was on his way to see her—he'd planned this little charade so she would come out to him.

She was about to say no, but she surprised herself by inviting him into her office.

She dragged a cushioned chair over to her desk and pointed at it. "What happened?"

He slid down in the chair, his arm and leg dangling spiderlike over the seat and armrest. "Anders Hede was arrested early this morning."

"Anders Hede?" The name rang a bell, but she couldn't place him.

"Martin Dahl's boyhood buddy from Frederikshavn. Dahl came in yesterday, said Hede has been acting strange lately. Keeping to himself, nervous. Dahl leaned on him hard to get him to say if he was in trouble again, but he kept denying it."

Louise was having trouble breathing, as if her windpipe was blocked. Had a young, pregnant woman been killed because her boyfriend's old friend was a piece of shit? "And?"

"They were in town Friday night, good and drunk. As you

know. That's when Hede admitted someone was threatening him, had been for quite a while. And he thought the only way out was to either give up and take his medicine or leave the country."

"So, what, he didn't do either?" Louise said. "Did he forget to pay again?"

Stig shook his head. "Hede claims that Klaus West had his men pay him a visit to find out who he was buying from."

"I thought he bought from West. Isn't that who he owed money to, back then?"

"Yeah, but the men said that West stopped selling to him a long time ago, and they wanted the name of Hede's dealer."

Louise held her forehead.

"The last three months someone's been calling him, telling him he'd get hit where it hurts most if he didn't talk."

"So where does he get his drugs from?" she asked.

"From West, he says."

"Is Hede lying, or did West and his gorillas forget who they sold to?"

"We don't have any evidence that West is behind it. Anders Hede has been buying from the same source for the last two years. Every time he's bought the same amount, and it's always the same drug."

"Green dust," Louise said.

He nodded. "About nine months ago, when the first arrests were made in the drug case, a new middleman showed up. It's the same number Anders Hede messages when he wants to buy. Always done precisely the same way. He swears he isn't buying from other sources. He doesn't dare to, either, after the beating he took when he was late in paying. He has no idea why they're so riled up."

"He could be buying somewhere else, too," Louise suggested. "Maybe he doesn't want to admit it because he's afraid of getting his ass kicked again. You think they killed his best friend's girl-friend to show him they were serious?"

Stig nodded. "Martin Dahl's afraid that's how it happened. We're charging Hede as an accessory to murder."

Louise shut her eyes for a moment and thought of Karoline's parents. They'd lost their youngest son because one of his friends drove way too fast. And now they might have to live with the fact that their daughter chose a man whose boyhood pal couldn't shield his friends from the type of people he was dealing with.

"Things are piling up for good old Klaus West. The sale of nar-cotics alone can put him behind bars for several years, plus the murders of the two reporters, and if it turns out that Karoline Wissinge is added to the tab, it looks like the king is about to fall big-time."

"That sounds too cynical."

"Dear little Rick. Cynicism isn't a bad word in these circles. I'm not blaming you for your female intuition not working, but this is how the world is. Unfortunately, it's not unlikely that West had a few of his boys show Anders Hede what happens when you don't cooperate. It would be too simple to just kill him. This is some-thing he'd have to live with; it would hurt more. I spoke with Jensen from Narcotics, she's the one in charge of the investigation of the drug case—"

"I know who she is." Louise wanted to cram all the macho opin-ions of broad-shouldered, athletic Michael Stig right up his ass, but she fought back her rage.

He ignored her. "We can interrogate Klaus West tomorrow. You get the first shot at him, then it's Narcotics' turn. But it's not even certain he knows who Karoline Wissinge is, even though his boys are behind her murder. Probably he was just told that some-body wasn't playing ball, and he gave the okay to have it taken care of."

"By the same ones who took care of Frank Sørensen and Søren Holm?"

"That's entirely possible. Suhr just formed a team to work on narrowing down who it could be."

He stood up and walked to the door. "You seem to have a pretty good relationship with her parents. Don't you think it's a good idea that you explain this to them?"

Without waiting for an answer, he walked out and left the door open.

Bastard! The word popped up behind her closed eyes. It fit Klaus West, who cold-bloodedly took the lives of other people; it fit Anders Hede, a coward who didn't dare say he had a new dealer; and it fit Michael Stig, who without blinking put it on her to tell the parents that their daughter was a victim in a case where a slap or maybe a hard right to the jaw would have sufficed. Would have scared the person they wanted to scare.

The knock on the door annoyed Camilla. She was struggling with the article about Klaus West and the secret apartment. First Høyer had exploded when she told him she had something new on the case.

"You're not writing one word about that case!" he'd yelled so loudly that the whole building must have heard. But after she explained that the police had been there when she met with the Finn, and that it had led to finding the apartment, he calmed down a bit. "All right. This is it, though, the last article you're writing about it."

His hair stuck out every which way, and his face was still gray. Camilla had nodded and promised him it would be, then she'd gone into her office and sat down at her computer.

Nothing new had come from the police, and every time she called Suhr, his phone was busy. She decided that if she didn't hear from him before seven, she'd stop by Police Headquarters.

The person outside knocked again. "Yes! What?" she snapped.

A man Camilla guessed to be in his late forties stepped in her office. He held out his hand. "John Bro."

If he'd heard the irritation in her voice, he showed no sign of it. Without waiting for an invitation, he sat down.

Camilla leaned back. She had no idea who this man was or what he wanted, but his aura of authority interested her and kept her from throwing him out.

"I'm a defense attorney," he said. "My client has asked me to look you up."

Still puzzled, she shook her head. "I'm a little bit busy," she said, trying to sound friendly. "I've got an article to finish. We can make an appointment later this week."

She reached for her calendar, but before she could grab it he said, "Klaus West wants me to speak with you."

Camilla stopped. Ohhhh, *that* John Bro. Finally, she recognized him. He wore a suit and tie whenever he was on TV or his photo was in the paper, but now he looked shabby in his sweater and worn jeans. The star lawyer. "Klaus West," she repeated softly, noticing how the name filled the room. He knew she'd told the police. A jolt of fear left her nearly breathless, but she put on a brave face. "About what?"

He studied her for a moment, leaned back in the chair, and peered around the office. At the loose curtains beside the windows, the two tall bookshelves filled with dictionaries and folders of old clippings and press material. He stopped at the drawings Markus had made. They were taped to the edge of her desk, hanging down like trimming.

"My client believes you can help us."

She raised her eyebrows in surprise. Instinctively her guard was up. Something was going on here; Klaus West had no reason at all to think she would help him. A bouquet of flowers wasn't going to buy her cooperation. "I don't know Klaus West, and he doesn't know me."

The lawyer eyed her. "I trust his judgment," he said, ignoring her remark. "My client is going to be charged with two counts of murder for hire...though now it looks like three counts."

Camilla was about to say something, but he raised his hand. "He's being accused of arranging the sale of a large number of narcotics. These charges are very serious. Here." He tossed a plastic folder over to her. "We've gone through every charge in the indictment and refuted each one. We can prove my client didn't commit these crimes."

"I'd like for you to speak with my boss, Terkel Høyer. This isn't something I can get involved in." Despite saying this, she took the folder and sat with it on her lap.

Again, he ignored her. "I have a deal for you. We'll give you a wildly explosive story. If you're not interested, we'll take care of it ourselves." He kept his voice even, neutral.

Slowly her brain began to wake up. "Take care of *what* yourselves?"

"Someone is using him as a scapegoat."

Camilla had to smile at that. It was a little late to start blaming other people.

"My client is responsible for the drug commonly referred to as green dust."

Camilla tried to break in, but again he stopped her. "And he is ready to make a full confession, once we find out how his drug keeps showing up, again and again, when he knows it's no longer on the market. The police found some records in his apartment. They're connected with the sale he believes was made without his consent."

Bro pointed to the papers he'd given her. "It's not difficult for others to take up where he left off."

Camilla laid the folder on her desk. "If that's actually what happened."

"That's precisely it. The green dust, as you presumably already know, has a very faint green color. It's almost impossible to make it with exactly the same shade of color every time."

"He mixed the green color in with the heroin and then cut it with talcum powder," she said.

Bro nodded. At least she understood some of it.

"Imagine five kilos of powdered sugar, colored light green. You can come very close to replicating the color, but you're never going to get the exact same nuance. That's how we know this heroin out on the street is part of the same shipment my client is willing to take responsibility for. But we don't understand where the hell it's coming from. My client knows exactly what happened to the five kilos he converted to green dust. The last kilo was confiscated a week ago during a raid in an Østerbro apartment. Two more kilos ended up with the police earlier this year, and the rest was injected by addicts."

Camilla sat with her mouth open. She was still certain he was making a last-ditch attempt to dodge the blame, but the story fascinated her. "And you believe him!"

"It's not a question of if I believe him. It's a question of what can be proven." Again, he showed no emotion as he spoke.

Camilla shut up and let him talk.

"West is absolutely certain the green heroin being sold on the street today is part of what was confiscated. He believes the same lackeys are selling it, because several of his connections still think he's the one they're dealing with."

She needed time to digest all this information. "And that means?"

"That means we need to find out how the green drug keeps showing up. It's not difficult to imagine that Frank Sørensen and Søren Holm found out what was going on!"

"This is one damn strange story. What is it you think I can help you with?"

Camilla looked away. She still wasn't convinced, but deep inside she heard that familiar voice chanting: This could be *your* story, this could be *your* story...

"I want you to help me find out who's trying to pin all this on my client. Until I know who's pulling the strings, I can't determine if it's something I can use in defending my client."

"What precisely is it you want me to do?"

"I'm assuming you have sources. You could start by finding out if they know something. And my client can say that he watched you and your police friend in action at the King's Bar. Maybe together you can loosen up some tongues."

They shook hands and he left.

Camilla was confused. And also flattered that John Bro had come to her for help. Her heart was hammering; this is probably how soccer players felt the first time they were picked for the national team.

She closed her eyes and leaned back. Høyer's insistence on taking over these articles was forgotten. Completely.

Louise poured herself a large glass of red wine and held it carefully in both hands as she walked into the living room. She shut off the kitchen light with her elbow.

Rain spattered against the window; the light from the streetlamp outside was distorted by the drops running down the glass. Traffic was thin. She shivered when the sound of tires on wet asphalt reminded her of how cold it had been lately. Occasional sunny days had brought spring within arm's length, but the cheery mood was broken when the sky hung low and leaden.

She pulled her legs up under her, grabbed her phone, and tried calling Peter again. No luck, only voice mail. She tossed the phone down, took a sip of wine, and leaned her head back on the sofa. Her thoughts fluttered around like gigantic moth wings, threatening to escape.

The examination of the butterfly knife hadn't given them all that much, but it had definitely been used to kill Frank Sørensen. They found traces of blood and tissue from his spinal cord. Flemming had driven from the Department of Forensic Medicine to Forensic Services to give his assessment. He had confirmed that the knife was consistent with his measurements of the puncture wound. The slender knife handle, however, had been wiped clean of fingerprints.

Louise forced herself to concentrate, to look at the big picture of everything that had happened the previous twenty-four hours. Of what looked like the end of both murder cases, if it did turn out that Karoline Wissinge's murder had been a cynical demonstration of the drug kingpin's power.

She'd been fighting off her desperation for a while now, a vague yet urgent feeling that earlier in the evening had made their big breakthrough seem less important. Now it threatened to overtake her.

She emptied the glass, then slid down and buried her face in the soft, sand-colored pillows. And cried.

She'd been on her way to the lunchroom to eat dinner with some of her colleagues. The mood was hectic but cheerful, now that the case was nearing an end. Several of them had stopped by her office to pat her on the back and say a few words about what had happened the night before at Cafe Svejk. Occasionally she'd felt the joy and relief that comes from solving a case, yet she couldn't let go of Michael Stig telling her to explain it all to the parents.

Outside the lunchroom, they had run into Toft, who said that Heilmann's husband had died late Tuesday evening. Her colleagues went on in to eat, but Louise stood there thinking about how Heilmann had chosen to be with her man. And Louise hadn't.

She wiped her nose on her sleeve and buried her face in the sofa again. Peter wasn't dying; the situation was totally different.

Louise kept fighting off her self-recriminations until the phone rang. She glanced around, confused. It was still raining. She had no idea how long she'd been crying. It could have been the middle of the night. "Hello."

"We have to meet tomorrow."

Camilla sounded frenzied. Louise swung her legs down off the sofa and banged her knee against the coffee table. Her leg prick-led. "What's happened?"

"I just had a visit from John Bro, the defense attorney. Klaus West isn't behind the two murders."

Louise ruffled her hair and pushed her empty wineglass off to the side. "All the evidence points directly at Klaus West." Yet she felt an unease rising behind her exhaustion.

"I have information that says different. Someone is trying to pin it on him."

Louise was about to say that West was likely also behind the murder of Karoline, but she held back.

"And I'm going to find out who!"

"Leave it alone, Camilla. The police have him. There's no more you can do. Of course, Bro is doing everything he can; that's what he's paid to do. Why do you think he approached you and not your boss?"

Silence. Louise couldn't stop herself. "Because you're less ex-perienced and the easiest one to convince to fight for his fucking guilty client. It's called being naïve. Good night."

She hung up, annoyed yet more nervous now. Camilla had stirred something in her, the same misgiving she'd felt while

listening to Stig's cynical theory about Karoline's murder stem-
ming from the cynical narcotics racket. There was a logical flaw in
both situations that she couldn't put her finger on.

She yawned and realized she was too exhausted to think clearly.
It would have to wait until tomorrow. If she still felt something
didn't add up in the morning, she would go through everything
one more time.

22

No one can get hold of narcotics confiscated by the police."
Jørgensen laid both hands on the desk, leaned forward, and
stared right between Camilla's eyes to make sure his words had
soaked in.

Louise sighed and cursed that defense lawyer for waving the in-
famous red flag in front of her friend's face.

Camilla had been sitting in their office when they came back
from lunch, and she'd refused to leave, even though Louise and
Jørgensen told her in no uncertain terms that they were busy.

"So, okay, let's say it's impossible. Can you imagine something
disappearing between the time it's found until it's registered?"

Jørgensen sighed heavily. Louise looked back and forth between them. She'd withdrawn from the conversation, because she
didn't know enough about the procedures having to do with confiscated narcotics. Several times during the last hour she'd tried to
make Camilla understand she was being manipulated.

"In principle, it's a possibility," Jørgensen said.

The small hairs on Louise's arm rose. She tried to catch Jørgensen's eye to get him to stop answering questions. He needed to wind up their little chat and politely usher Camilla out.

Camilla had been pacing the floor, but now she sat down and nodded for him to continue.

"You can't rule out an officer sticking something in his pocket when nobody's looking. But we're talking about small amounts, taken from people on the street."

Louise watched them again for a moment, then she took a deep breath. "Camilla, would you please, please stop! Does Høyer even know what you're up to?"

Camilla shot her an annoyed look and raised her palm to shut her up.

"Then I'd better call and tell him you're sitting here." She was tired of Camilla always ignoring everyone when she'd made up her mind about something.

"You can't stick a kilo of heroin in your pocket," Jørgensen said, then looked over at Louise. "This is one stubborn friend you've got here."

He smiled at Camilla. "That must have been quite a bouquet he sent you!"

Camilla was about to answer that, but instead she spread her arms wide and peered angrily at Louise. Her cheeks reddened when Jørgensen laughed.

"That has nothing to do with this," Camilla snapped. "But if it's true that someone is trying to frame the wrong person, you'd have to step in."

Louise was glad she hadn't said *frame someone who's innocent*. Klaus West would never be innocent. "Well, we'd have to step in, just like we have to listen to this version of events. It's just that there's nothing to support it, while there's a lot that tells us it's not right."

Louise thought a moment. She'd dismissed the idea last night, but her nagging unease had led her to telling Jørgensen about Camilla's call.

"Interesting," he'd said. He'd also listened patiently when Camilla showed up and claimed that Klaus West wasn't the one they should be focusing on.

"How are the narcotics you seize stored?" Camilla asked, to get Jørgensen back on track.

"We have a large storage room in the basement under head-quarters here, where we keep everything confiscated or seized, like stolen goods, evidence, fenced articles. We also have a special narcotics storage room. Only the superintendent of our service department and the head of Narcotics have the code and key. Occasionally things disappear from the storage room. Also from our own."

Jørgensen nodded toward the hall, at Department A's locked room for stolen goods.

"But no seized narcotics can be removed from the narcotics storage room, once they've been locked up? What happens to them? They don't stay in there forever?"

She spoke softly, as if she were afraid her least movement would stop him.

"They're destroyed just like the other things. Though some things are sold at the police auction."

Camilla opened her mouth but suddenly froze. As if she forgot what she was going to say. "Destroyed?" she finally said.

"They're taken out to be incinerated. Usually after a drug trial is over."

Camilla was nearly panting. Louise had watched Jørgensen closely as he spoke, wondering why he was being so open with information that not even she knew about. She hoped Camilla would respect that this was confidential information.

"Narcotics are regarded as controlled waste. Which means that when the drugs are driven out to be destroyed, the police keep an eye on them from the time they leave the storage room until they're incinerated."

Camilla stared at him. "Maybe someone out there thinks it's a shame to burn it all, and they take it home instead."

Jørgensen shook his head. "Documents are also controlled waste. Whenever it's time to burn them, we call and make an appointment to take them in to be incinerated." He spoke like a schoolteacher to his class. "When narcotics are destroyed, we show up unannounced. Two plainclothes officers and two officers from Narcotics deliver them in one of our trucks. They guard them all the way up to the top of the building, then witness them being dumped directly into the flames. No one can come near the place."

The silence that followed felt like a vacuum into which his words had disappeared.

"Okay." Camilla's voice was hoarse, and she cleared her throat and studied the toes of her boots before slumping in her chair. "How many people know about the method of disposal?"

"Not many, I think. It's not something people talk about."

She nodded, and after a few moments she thanked him and left.

"Feel better now?" Louise asked as they stood out in the hallway.

Camilla shrugged. "I don't really know. I can see it can't be done, apparently."

Louise followed her to the stairway.

"Maybe the bouquet was a little bit too impressive!" Camilla said, with a tinge of irony. "So, what's the situation on the case right now?"

"We have the presumed murder weapon and the six hundred grams of heroin found in his apartment, plus a witness who did business with him. And all we have is West's word that there were only five kilos of green dust. If he actually blended twenty or fifty kilos, I get it that he's claiming it was five kilos!"

Camilla stopped and leaned against the wall. "I feel dizzy suddenly."

Louise grabbed her arm and led her over to a bench along the wall. "Just let it go. You're not going to get anything out of it. They're not giving you any space in the paper, and it's a good case we have; it's going fine. If it's any consolation, he won't be sentenced for anything we can't prove he did."

Camilla leaned her head against her friend's shoulder. "I didn't even think about how he could have fixed up fifty kilos instead of five!" She held her breath and slowly let it out. "God, I've been naïve. You're absolutely right!"

Louise put her arm around her shoulder. "Yeah, you are a bit gullible, but it's good you know it, because it's almost impossible for anyone to convince you."

"What the hell am I going to say when his attorney calls and asks how it's going?"

"Call him yourself and tell him you're not going to be involved," said Louise, her voice firm. "He's not the one in charge here. Tell him you're out, or you could refer him to Høyer."

"I'm still going to talk to Birte Jensen; I can just as well tell her what John Bro is up to. I'm meeting her in a few minutes."

Camilla checked her watch. Almost three o'clock.

"What about Markus?"

"I'll pick him up later. I'd better call the paper and tell them I won't be in the rest of the day."

Louise hugged her before she left.

"I'm glad you told me this." Jensen looked serious as she gazed at the stack of documents on the desk in front of her. "It's taken us a long time to get to this point. West has been a player for years, and we haven't been able to touch him, but now it's over. You can hardly blame him for doing what he can to convince people he's innocent."

"Have you checked into the possibility of what Bro is claiming? Could it in any way be someone here selling the heroin that's been seized?"

"Camilla Lind." Jensen's voice was icy. "I've been following this man for years. He's guilty as sin, and you're just the latest in a line of people he's charmed."

Camilla turned her head instinctively, as if she'd been slapped. Her throat tightened, and she was about to defend herself when Jensen pushed the documents aside and leaned forward.

"I have great respect for your reporting, even though we've only just begun working together. I like the way you go after stories, and I owe you for your help."

Camilla looked in surprise at Jensen; she wasn't sure she understood. Her anger at being humiliated a second ago tapered off.

"This evening I'm taking two of my people along to Anders Hede's apartment on Østerbro. He's the man Department A is holding in connection with the murder of Karoline Wissinge. He ordered fifty grams of heroin last week. It's being delivered this evening, and we're going to be there when it is. You're welcome to come along."

Jensen's eyes bored right through Camilla. Made her feel small. She wasn't sure she wanted in on this. "Can I write about it?"

Jensen thought for a moment, then she nodded. "Don't mention it to anyone before we go. We never tell when we're going to make a raid. But afterward it's all yours."

Camilla thought about Høyer, hoping he would forgive her when she came in with a front-page story.

"Then you can compare what happens to the fantasy West is telling."

She hunched her shoulders when a chill ran down her spine. This could be her story. She would be at the forefront, be mentioned on the TV evening news. "Okay."

"Be at St. Kjeld's Square at ten. Wait for us in front of the basement restaurant; we'll pick you up there."

23

Louise's chair rocketed back when she stood up. "I'm not going out to her parents'!"

Suhr looked startled.

"He can go out there himself. But you owe them the courtesy of waiting until you're absolutely certain that's why she was killed."

"We also owe them the courtesy of letting them know of developments in the case, and right now Anders Hede's drug suppliers are the only ones who have a motive! They planned and carried out Karoline's murder."

"Please, please wait to say anything to them; the motive's too iffy."

"Hede's best friend is Martin Dahl. And Dahl's weakest spot is his girlfriend. He'll never forgive Hede, ever."

Louise crossed her arms and nodded. Several times that afternoon and evening, Stig had asked her to drive out and inform the parents. Finally, she'd exploded and marched into Suhr's office.

"We need to loosen some tongues," he said. "Surely we can find these guys threatening Hede, and then we put the screws to them. It's better the parents are prepared before they read about it in the paper."

"All right, how about this. I'll talk to them when you have something that makes us 100 percent sure we have it right. Have you completely cleared Lasse Møller?"

Suhr raised his eyebrows in surprise. "I thought you knew. There had been some mix-up with the bank, but after Toft asked them to have another look, they confirmed that Møller used his debit card and PIN at one fifteen a.m. at Pussy Galore. Besides that, we have two more witnesses who say he arrived right before they left, which was just past one. He's not a suspect now."

Louise sighed. Not because she was disappointed to hear he'd been cleared, but because it seemed so hopeless. "What does Martin Dahl have to say?"

"One minute he wants to rip Hede apart, the next minute he feels guilty that their friendship indirectly killed his girlfriend and their unborn child. It's not so strange he didn't dare mention his suspicion at first, but of course he couldn't keep it to himself. We've been questioning him all day; he's been given something to calm him down. Right now, he's in the National Hospital for crisis counseling with Jakobsen."

Louise gazed at his desk, at the soft light from the PH lamp. Earlier she'd met Toft escorting him down the hall. Dahl looked crushed, and he hadn't recognized her when she said hello.

She noticed Suhr watching her.

"We don't believe Martin killed her," he said, anticipating her next question. Which she was getting ready to ask.

She shook her head. Martin hadn't been on her list, either. She always tried to keep an open mind about suspects, but she couldn't help having favorites.

It was ten p.m., and she'd gone through and filed the officers' reports on the people they'd talked to in the surrounding apartment buildings on Vestergade. She suppressed a yawn and stood up. "Time to go home. See you tomorrow."

The next morning the investigation team would be meeting with Forensics and the police prosecutor. They hoped they had enough to retain Klaus West in connection with the murders of the two reporters. They had the murder weapon and the witness statement tying him to the first crime scene, and they'd also found the key to his apartment on his key chain. That was the biggest success of the day. Without the key, it would have taken only a few minutes for his lawyer to sow doubt about him living in the apartment.

She turned around when she reached the doorway. "What the hell are we going to do if we can't find more evidence against him?"

Suhr's hands rested on his stomach. "There's not much else we can do. But people might be more willing to talk if he's in custody."

"I don't understand why they wiped the fingerprints off the knife instead of just throwing it away somewhere."

She'd been turning that over in her mind. Either West and his people had felt so confident that they didn't think it was important, or else some complete idiot had killed the two reporters and then brought the murder weapon back to the apartment without thinking.

"But at least we know the killer is part of West's circle. Not someone he hired from outside. It could also be a sign of their sense of superiority to the police. West thinks he's untouchable. The knife isn't a problem to him as long as it can't be connected to whoever used it."

Louise shrugged. It wouldn't be the first time a criminal had been smart enough to avoid being charged.

The rain had stopped, and the streetlamp's glare reflected off the puddles on the street. Camilla leaned up against a wall beside the basement restaurant. Would Jensen pick her up in a police car? She wasn't sure.

She shivered, even though she was wearing jeans, a sweater, and a thick windbreaker she'd found in the closet. Her toes were freezing in her light blue sneakers. She should have worn boots. Think about nice, simple things, she told herself. Markus, who was already asleep when she left; Christina, who had canceled a movie date to watch him; a coat she'd seen in a women's magazine. Then she gave up. Her nervousness had started as a small lump inside after leaving Jensen's office, and it had grown since then.

She didn't know what to expect, but she felt certain everyone would be under pressure, since the drug case presumably was winding up.

Even before leaving home she'd understood that the people the police were looking for could be the killer or killers, or at least could lead them to whoever was. It could turn violent. And lurking in the back of her mind was her humiliation over being so naïve, now that everything could be traced back to Klaus West.

She studied the streets leading to the roundabout. Traffic was light. Every time she heard a car engine, she straightened up. It must be at least ten past ten; she reached in her pocket for her phone, but after checking all her pockets she remembered laying it on the bed while changing clothes. Damn!

Camilla walked a short way down the street, but then she hurried back; she didn't want to attract attention. Someone was headed toward her—male or female? All she could see was a dark figure. She leaned against the wall again.

A few cars approached the roundabout. One of them sped past

her; the other parked about twenty meters away. After a few moments, the driver got out and approached her.

Camilla relaxed when she saw it was Birte Jensen.

"Sorry. We had to get the final details sorted out. I have two more cars parked at the other end of the street. He lives in number six. Third building." She pointed.

This was a bigger operation than Camilla had expected; earlier that day, Jensen had talked about bringing along two of her people. She took a deep breath to calm her nerves. All she'd be doing was observing.

"You and I will enter through the courtyard, the others from the street. But we have plenty of time; we're not moving in until eleven."

"Okay. What exactly is going to happen?"

Jensen smiled at her. "You're freezing. Come on, let's hop in the car. I brought along coffee. And I can fill you in briefly."

On the way to the car, Camilla noticed Jensen had changed into dark pants, with a short, black down coat and black gloves. Classy, Camilla thought. A female police leader could look good even when out on an operation. It wasn't at all like Louise's heavy police coat and clunky boots.

"Have you followed up on anything since John Bro came in to see you?"

Jensen started the car and switched on the heater, then she turned and grabbed a basket with a thermos and cups.

Camilla shook her head, but then she realized Jensen might not have seen that in the dark. "No, and I won't as long as we get something out of this tonight."

Jensen poured her a cup of coffee, carefully handed it to her, and set the thermos down. "Of course. We're open to other theories, too; it has to be looked into."

They sat quietly and stared at the wall in front of them. The car clock showed 10:27 p.m.

Camilla had the feeling she was being observed. She held on to the plastic cup, even though it burned her fingers. Steam rose up and warmed her face. Her nose ran; she was still cold. Briefly she thought about bringing her notepad out and doing a short interview with Jensen. There might not be time later. "Will we join the others before they go up to the apartment?"

Jensen shook her head. "Drink your coffee. When you've warmed up, we'll go into the courtyard and get ready. Two officers will take the front stairs to the apartment, another will stand out in front, and the last one will join us and we'll go up the back steps and through the kitchen."

Camilla nodded. She blew on the hot coffee and drank it greedily. Adrenaline began flowing; the welcome buzz calmed her down. It was going to be exciting! And there was no sense thinking about the dressing-down Høyer would give her. She smiled at the thought of the photo editor yelling and screaming about not bringing along a photographer. But she was sure her boss would back her up this time and agree the story was fantastic even without photos. The thought of the front-page headlines quieted her nerves.

Jørgensen was speaking softly on the phone when Louise returned to the office to shut down her computer and grab her coat and bag. He looked serious. "Jesus Christ, they've got to stop…," she overheard, though she tried hard to appear not to be listening.

He hung up, and she glanced over at him. His face was pale, his eyes unfocused.

"What's going on?"

"Trouble over in Narcotics."

"What's that got to do with you?"

"Apparently it's something that goes back to when I was there." She frowned.

"That defense attorney, John Bro, requested they go through all the records of seized narcotics within the past year. Two registered numbers are missing."

Before Louise could ask, he said, "Two bags. When seized drugs come into the station, they're weighed and examined to determine what they are. Heroin, cocaine, amphetamines. Then they're bagged up and labeled."

He glanced at Louise to make sure she was following. She nodded.

"Then someone writes a report, and the bag is numbered before it's taken down and stored with the rest of the drugs."

"So, what's missing?"

"Two bags, three kilos of heroin."

He let that hang in the air for a moment. "One point two million kroner!"

Louise took a deep breath. "Didn't you just sit here and explain how that could never happen?"

He nodded slowly.

"Let me guess. The heroin has a faint tinge of green."

He pushed his chair back against the wall and sat with his elbows on his knees, his head in his hands. "The chief wants everyone in the department questioned. The superintendent of the service department and his people have also been called in."

"Relax, aren't the head of Narcotics and the superintendent the only ones with the key and code?"

He nodded again. "And that's the damn problem."

"What does Jensen say?"

He shrugged. "No one can find her." He stood up and walked out.

She was calm when she shut the car door behind her, though she had to lean against the fender a moment because the cold made her dizzy.

They walked down the dark street. Camilla was careful not to step into a puddle on the sidewalk. The big arched entrance to the courtyard wasn't lit, and they had to take a few moments to get their bearings.

"This way, over here." Jensen walked on, Camilla fumbling along behind her. She glimpsed the wall along the long, narrow paved courtyard and the iron railing cordoning off the basement stairs. The dark silhouette looked like a shed.

"Are you here?"

"Yes." Camilla breathed deeply and concentrated. "Which floor does Anders Hede live on?"

She couldn't hear Jensen's answer, so she repeated the question a bit louder. The policewoman pulled on her arm, knocking her off balance. "Keep it down!" she whispered.

Camilla whispered back, "Will they tell us when they go in?"

Jensen had pulled her over to the wall, close to the shed, which was probably used either for bicycles or trash cans. From the faint sour odor, Camilla guessed trash cans.

"They'll let me know."

Camilla couldn't see her face, yet she sensed her vividly. Why was it difficult to keep her eyes open? She gave in and leaned against the wall to rest a moment until the action started.

Would it be okay to sit down? Something told her more than fifteen minutes had passed since they left the car. "You think something's wrong, since they haven't come yet?"

"No. They're not coming; that's never been the plan."

The voice came from somewhere over her head, though Camilla couldn't say where. She didn't recognize it, either. It was cold and impersonal, like an echo bouncing off the walls of the surrounding buildings. She struggled to get up, but her legs wouldn't obey.

This was how it had happened. After being drugged, they'd

been stabbed. Faces danced across her line of vision, smiling and waving at her. She tried in vain to smile and wave back. "They found out you're the one who took the heroin."

Camilla said this to herself and felt a shadow looming over her.

"No one will ever know. Too bad, isn't it?"

Everything feminine about the voice had disappeared, leaving only the raw words behind. Camilla felt warm breath. She managed to focus on the blurry face in front of her.

"I'm in charge. I decide who has to pay and who gets off the hook. When someone tries to stop me, obviously I have to act. If Frank hadn't suspected more people were involved in the green heroin, I wouldn't have had to do anything about it."

Camilla heard scorn in the voice, though she was nearly unconscious.

"You reporters are so goddamn smart. But not smart enough when someone sticks a good story in front of your nose."

Nausea overwhelmed Camilla. She leaned to the side and threw up. Rocked back and forth as if she were seasick and rolling with the waves. The world seemed to be drifting in fog.

"Søren Holm was so high-and-mighty when he confronted me on Vestergade. All his ridiculous accusations, bragging about finding the apartment that we couldn't. Ha!"

The laughter rang hollow in Camilla's ears.

"The witnesses said Holm and I were absorbed in each other. That was when I stuck the needle in him. Even though he suspected me, he drank the cup of coffee I offered him. Just like Frank Sørensen. Idiots!"

Camilla gave up trying to follow along.

24

Louise was packing up when her cell phone rang. Camilla's home number. Thoughts flew through her head before she answered, the worst being that the lawyer had contacted her again.

"Hi."

The voice startled her. "This is Christina. I'm sorry to bother you, but I'm here at home with Markus and I can't get hold of Camilla."

Louise sat down, confused now. And worried; she heard crying in the background, and Christina sounded panicky. "Has something happened?"

"Markus is sick. He's burning up with fever; I took his temperature and it's over 102."

"Where's Camilla?"

"At work. She called this afternoon and asked if I could stay with Markus until she got home."

The crying in the background faded out. What the hell was Camilla doing? Her son was sick! "She's not at the paper?"

"No, I called her office but no one answered, and she doesn't have her cell phone; it's here on her bed."

"Did you try calling the paper directly, reception?"

"I only have the one number."

"I'll try to find her," Louise said, "and if I can't, I'll come over. Call emergency for an on-call doctor."

She punched the number for the newspaper and asked the receptionist if any of the crime staff were in.

"Everyone's gone for the day."

"I'd like to speak to Terkel Høyer."

"He'll be in again tomorrow. I can't give you his private number."

"I'm calling from the Copenhagen Police, Homicide Division. It's vital that I get hold of him."

She was about to hang up and call the phone carrier directly, when to her surprise the woman said, "Of course."

Louise wrote down the number and called it. She heard the voice of a girl who sounded much too young to be up so late. "Hello."

"Hello, my name is Louise Rick, may I speak to your father?"

"Mmmm...Daaaddy!" The girl laid the phone down with a thunk.

Høyer didn't sound surprised she was calling him at home. "Camilla called at four and said she wasn't coming back in. Something about a meeting at day care. I didn't ask her to work this evening, either."

Louise rocked back and forth on her toes. She thanked him and hung up.

Jørgensen came back in. She sat down, aware she was overreacting. She loosened her hair tie and lowered her head between her legs, shook her hair out until it fell like a curtain to the floor. Blood ran to her head.

The phone rang, and she banged her head on her desk when she straightened up. She swore as she rushed to pick up. "Department A, Louise Rick."

"Camilla Lind is lying in the courtyard behind Nygårdsvej 6."

Before Louise could hear background noise or any indication of where the call came from, the man hung up. He'd spoken quietly but clearly.

She jumped to her feet. "Camilla's been murdered!" She felt nauseous, frightened, cold; Jørgensen followed her as she ran down the hall and barged into Suhr's office. She tried to speak, but suddenly she was out of breath, as if she'd been punched. She doubled over and let out a half-choked sound. Someone lifted her up by her armpits and sat her down in a chair. She lashed out; they didn't have time to sit around, they had to go, but she couldn't speak. Again, it felt as if she were being punched.

"We have to go, Nygårdsvej 6, Camilla's lying in the courtyard," she finally managed to say. The pain in her gut spread throughout her body, and she breathed silently and deeply, again and again as she looked up at Suhr with Jørgensen kneeling beside the chair, his hand on her arm.

Suhr picked up his office phone. "Send an ambulance to Nygårdsvej 6; there's a woman on the ground in the courtyard."

"Let's get out there," Louise said, her panic attack over. "Who's got a car?"

"I have the keys to a patrol car," Jørgensen said, briefly explaining that Stig had talked him into delivering it back to the garage—for once something good had come from Stig's laziness.

They ran down the hallway, Suhr at the rear. Louise remembered Markus and Christina, but the on-call doctor surely was there by now, and he and the babysitter would have to handle the situation.

Jørgensen switched on the siren and flashing blue lights. He seemed calm enough as he pulled out from the curb and roared down the street, but from the back seat, Louise saw the veins standing out on his temple.

Suhr turned and looked at her. "Who called?"

"I don't know. A man. All he said was that Camilla Lind was lying in the courtyard of Nygårdsvej 6."

"Then it must be someone who knows her?"

Louise shrugged. Her thoughts were jumbled. In her mind's eyes she saw Holm lying in the autopsy room. Cold steel, glaring white light. She swallowed, tasted salt water in her saliva. She held back her nausea. "I feel like I know that voice."

The police radio sent out short messages, but she wasn't listening. "Shouldn't we be thinking about backup?"

Jørgensen glanced over at Suhr, who growled shortly before grabbing the microphone and asking for two patrol cars.

The ambulance's blue flashing lights reflected faintly out onto the street. It had backed into the courtyard and was blocking the entrance; Louise, Suhr, and Jørgensen had to squeeze their way past. A spotlight illuminated a portion of the narrow courtyard.

Louise shook off the arm that had been supporting her since they left the car. She broke into a run but stopped short of the corner where three people stood leaning over a wheeled stretcher. She could barely make out the motionless figure lying there.

"Wait over here." The ambulance driver grabbed her arm. Louise tried to break free, but he tightened his grip and led her away. Suhr came over and stood beside them.

"Let's go!" one of the three shouted as he pushed the stretcher over to the ambulance.

Suhr followed along beside the stretcher. "What's happening, what's her condition?"

"Is she dead?" Louise yelled, annoyed that her boss didn't ask the question directly.

Jørgensen joined them and put his arm around Louise. This time she didn't shake him off.

"One of them is, the other's unconscious; we're taking her to the National Hospital."

Louise tried to catch Suhr's eye to see if he understood what the ambulance doctor meant.

"Come on, let's go!" The doctor hopped in and sat beside the stretcher. Another siren announced a second ambulance, which backed in after the intensive care unit ambulance carefully drove out and switched on its siren and lights. More people showed up.

"Louise!" Suhr's voice pierced through her fog. "Jørgensen will drive you to the hospital." He looked at her seriously. "We have to be there if Lind regains consciousness. Hopefully she'll be able to tell us what happened."

If she regains consciousness!

Louise nodded. Jørgensen took her arm and they walked out. She spied Flemming Larsen standing at the entrance, speaking to a tech. Flemming took a step toward her to say something, but she turned and hurried away. She didn't want to hear the pathologist say anything that could connect him with Camilla.

25

They parked outside the trauma center and ran in, hesitating only a moment as the glass doors slid open.

"We're with Camilla Lind; she's just been brought in from Nygårdsvej," Jørgensen said to the white-coated woman approaching them.

"Have a seat over there." She pointed at two chairs in the hall beside the revolving door. "We need to contact her next of kin."

"I'm her next of kin." Louise stood up before realizing what she'd said. The family, they needed to call Camilla's family. Her knees gave way, and she had to sit back down.

"Do you have her parents' number?" Jørgensen asked.

"I can find her mother's."

Louise sat for a moment, staring straight ahead at a spot on the wall. She had to pull herself together, for Chrissake! Her voice thundered inside her head and spread throughout her body. She cursed her emotional reaction, threw her weakness aside, imagined a tremor passing through her as her strength returned. "What the hell happened? I'm sorry, I still don't understand what's going on, how bad is she?" She turned to her partner.

"I don't know," he said.

It was a relief to hear he was also in the dark about Camilla. She walked over to the woman behind the glass windows. "How is she?"

The woman looked up. "I'm sorry, all I know is that she was unconscious when they brought her in. As soon as the doctor comes out, we'll talk to him."

Louise wrote down the number and address of Camilla's mother. "But she lives in Jutland."

The woman nodded.

Louise called Christina to find out how Markus was and to tell her that neither she nor Camilla would be coming home. The on-call doctor had told Christina to keep an eye on Markus and give him something to drink. His temperature had fallen somewhat, and now he was on the sofa, sleeping under a quilt.

They waited. More patients came in, but they were sent to the waiting room. Louise and Jørgensen were alone in the hall. She closed her eyes for a moment, or maybe longer, she wasn't sure. She opened them at the sound of footsteps. A man wearing a coat approached them; not a doctor, she thought, and she closed her eyes again.

He stopped in front of them. "Are you Louise Rick?"

Jørgensen started to stand up, but Louise stopped him. She recognized the man, even though she'd only seen him at a distance. The Finn.

"Yes."

That voice..."You're the one who called!"

His face was blank. "I'd like to talk to you."

Louise stood up and nodded. "I'll find us a place."

She went back over to the woman, while Jørgensen stayed with the Finn. They could use the lounge. Louise stood by the revolving door and waved them over. Jørgensen hesitated a moment before joining them, and the Finn didn't object.

They were offered coffee, and it was brought to them at the long table in the lounge.

The Finn looked Louise right between the eyes. "I killed her."

Her mouth dropped open; short bursts of emotions rammed into her one after another. "Killed her? Camilla?"

He frowned. "No. Birte Jensen."

"We have no idea what happened," Jørgensen said. "We have an unconscious woman in here, that's all we know. Could you take it from the beginning?"

The Finn glanced at him before turning back to Louise. "She's the one who killed the two reporters. It just took me too long to figure it out."

He sighed heavily, then sipped at his coffee. "And she was going to kill Camilla Lind."

Jørgensen took over again. "What makes you believe the head of Narcotics wanted to kill Camilla Lind?"

"I suppose because Lind suspected what was going on, just like the other two."

"And what *was* going on?"

The Finn closed his eyes and held his head in his hands for a few moments. "She cheated me. I've been helping her this past year. I thought we were trying to nail Klaus West, but it turned out that *she* was West."

"Don't you think we should continue this at Police Headquarters?" Jørgensen pushed his chair back to stand up.

"I'll go in with you, but I'd like to tell you what happened first."

Louise tried to pull herself together to follow what he was saying.

"I've worked with Jensen off and on for several years. She scratched my back, I scratched hers. Last spring, she asked me to help with Klaus West, and there's nothing I'd rather see than that man getting what's coming to him."

The Finn paused a moment. "He killed my sister." His voice was calm, but his eyes flared with hatred.

"They'd made a few arrests. One guy was dealing for West. They gave me his cell phone and a locker key he had in his pocket when they nabbed him."

Louise's muscles knotted as she listened. She leaned back in her chair and stretched to loosen up.

"Jensen said the drugs were being delivered to a storage locker on Vestergade. My job was to pick the drugs up and sell them. I was given the names and numbers of several customers, and what was left over I sold to some old connections I have. The money was to be stashed back in the locker. The idea was that people in her department could keep an eye on who was buying."

He looked away. "At least that's what she wanted me to think. And I swallowed it. But she's the one who stashed the drugs in the locker and then told me to go get them. And who picked up the money later on."

He sat up. "I'm sorry about what happened to your friend."

"How do you know Camilla Lind is my friend?"

He smiled weakly. "It's pretty obvious, after your performance at the King's Bar. You talked to my friend. Like I told Lind, he wanted to find out who you two were. When you asked about me, he figured you knew my sister. That's why he agreed to pass along Camilla's phone number. Then when I told Jensen about it, she said the dark-haired woman must be you."

The woman at reception knocked and stuck her head inside. "We have news."

Louise jumped up and followed her.

Camilla lay with an IV in her arm and a plastic tube in her nose. Her eyes were closed when Louise came in and introduced herself to the two doctors beside her bed. They smiled at her, which Louise took as a good sign.

"She's regaining consciousness," one of them whispered, leading Louise a few steps away. "A moment ago, she mumbled something. It sounded like 'the goddamn bitch.'" His face was a question mark.

"That sounds about right," she said. She stepped back over to the bed and laid her hand on Camilla's cheek. "The bitch is gone. You can come out now."

Louise brushed the strands of blond hair off her face. Camilla had a large abrasion on one cheek and a long cut on her chin. "It's over," she said softly as she caressed her friend's cheek.

"She killed them." Camilla's voice was hoarse and weak, wheezy. She opened her eyes and felt around for Louise's hand.

Louise choked up. Her friend seemed so frail, which her angry words only served to underscore.

"Markus?" Camilla blinked a few times and fought to keep her eyes open.

"Christina is staying with him." Louise saw no need to tell her about the boy's fever and calling the doctor.

Camilla sighed and closed her eyes.

"It'll be a few hours before she really wakes up," one of the doctors said. He told Louise that she could stay in the room with her friend.

"I'll just step out and tell the others, then I'll be back," she said.

When she returned to the lounge, Suhr was sitting with a steaming cup of coffee, listening to the Finn's story. He looked up at Louise.

"I'm staying with Camilla tonight," she said.

He nodded. "Is she awake?"

"Not really, but she had enough spunk in her to call Birte Jensen a bitch, so she's getting there."

He smiled.

26

Peter ripped the lid off one of the large pizza boxes. The steam rose and clouded up under the lamp above the coffee table. "Ham or pepperoni?"

"Ham," Markus squealed. He lay under the blanket at one end of the sofa.

"Pepperoni for me," Camilla said from the other end. She looked at her son. The hospital had given her strict orders to rest, and she and Markus had been installed in Louise's guest room for the weekend. She had suffered a few heavy blows to the head, and even though the drug she'd been given was almost out of her body, her headache persisted.

"When did the hospital release you?" Peter said.

"We were at Police Headquarters at one. They offered to let me stay at the hospital to give my statement, but I wanted to get home."

"What the hell possessed you to go into that courtyard alone?"

Peter leaned forward to hear her story. Louise had already heard it so many times that she didn't want to listen. It was horrible, and she was angry at Camilla for being so irresponsible. At the same time, she was so relieved that Camilla was all right. She almost sobbed at the thought of her friend ending up with her spinal cord severed.

Markus had taken his pizza and cola into the bedroom to lie in the big bed and watch cartoons on TV.

"I wasn't alone. I was there with Jensen, to follow the police operation and find out who was behind all this."

Louise could hear Camilla still believed she'd acted sensibly.

"But there wasn't any police operation," Peter said. He'd just flown back from Aberdeen, and he still didn't know all the details.

"I couldn't know that." Now Camilla didn't sound so self-assured. She stared at the ceiling, her pizza untouched.

Peter took Markus's spot on the sofa. "How did she drug you?"

"It was in the coffee I drank. I'm not clear on what happened after we left the car. I was excited about being in on the action, I remember that, but everything changed in the courtyard. Jensen started acting weird. I couldn't recognize her voice, didn't understand what she said, and then I got scared. But it was the drug kicking in. Then I realized that if John Bro was right, she could have taken the heroin out of the storage room."

Louise went out to put water on. She brought three coffee cups back and set them on the coffee table. "Did you even see the Finn?"

"No. I could feel my face on the asphalt, but I didn't hear anything. And that's all I remember."

Louise sat down. "The Finn said that Bro contacted him earlier in the day." She filled Peter in on who Bro was.

"He knew the Finn was involved in dealing the heroin," she said to Camilla. "The Finn was the connection between Jensen and all the buyers."

Camilla sighed heavily. "Apparently, Bro convinced the Finn that Klaus West wasn't the one delivering the heroin to the locker on Vestergade. That it had to come from someone in the police. That's when the Finn suspected Jensen was using him, and it made him furious. All he'd wanted was to destroy West. He followed Jensen when she left headquarters. At the time, he didn't know she was meeting me; he'd just decided to tail her, to see if he could confirm his suspicion."

"She must have gone home for the syringe and the knife," Peter said. "Surely she was smart enough to not have them in her office."

Louise shrugged. "The knife could have come from our storage room; we've confiscated plenty of knives. Jensen's learned about forensic pathology over the years—that helped her. You have to know some anatomy to be able to cut a spinal cord." She thought of the talks pathologists gave occasionally at headquarters. "But anyway, it was all well thought out. The victim dies within five or ten minutes, and there's not much blood. And to be on the safe side, she gave them an overdose."

She pushed aside her plate with the dry edges of pizza crust, stood up, and went out to get the coffee. The apartment was quiet except for the cartoon voices squawking from the bedroom. When she came back, she set the cups in place and filled them.

Peter eyed Louise. "Did the Finn know she was a murderer, too?"

"When Jensen and Camilla got out of the car, he was just a few steps ahead of them, watching closely. He hid in the shed with the trash cans, and he heard everything they said."

Camilla had already heard the Finn's story, but she was all ears.

"He heard Jensen say that Camilla was too insignificant to stop her. And that's when he realized what was about to happen."

Peter hadn't touched his coffee. He was fascinated by the drama that had played out while he'd been negotiating his salary with the Scottish production manager.

"The Finn snuck out of the shed and saw her pull a syringe from her pocket. By then you were already on the ground." Louise glanced at Camilla. "He attacked her from behind and grabbed the syringe and stuck her in the neck with it. She died of an overdose."

The story hung heavily in the air for a few moments.

"Why did she do it?"

The same question had been asked repeatedly all day at Police Headquarters.

Louise took several moments to sort things out in her mind. "She was rich; it couldn't have been the money. The most logical answer is that she was on some power trip, she did it because she could. She juggled nonexistent evidence and witness statements without anyone suspecting her. She had it all thought out, and she manipulated the Finn and Camilla, knowing that if they both supported the narrative she'd created, it would be believable."

Peter nodded in agreement.

"Klaus West wasn't in the Royal Hotel the evening Frank Sørensen was murdered. The raid did take place, they seized a large cache of drugs, and because she was the one who claimed she'd seen him, it was a lot more credible. She used people. No one wondered about her being in the storage room, there was nothing strange about it."

Camilla rubbed her forehead, clearly tired now. "One hell of a game she was playing."

"Anders Hede was just a small fish. He had nothing to do with any heroin to be delivered yesterday. But when she said it was going to happen, no one doubted her."

"No, no one would, would they." Peter gave Camilla a friendly clap on the knee.

Louise thought about all the pieces that had fallen into place that day. "She must have been the one who planted the six hundred grams of heroin in the apartment West used for his base. And the butterfly knife. Of course, it had been wiped clean of fingerprints. It takes a sharp person to plan and execute all that."

"It's crazy, insane," Camilla said. "What did she have against Klaus West? It sounds so personal."

"He claims he's never had anything to do with her. But with his record, it's logical to suspect him of this kind of thing."

They all jumped when the door buzzer rang. Peter went out in the hall to see who it was.

"Pretty impressive," Camilla said. "I remember thinking she had style. That must've been right before I fainted."

Louise heard Peter talking to someone out in the hall. He shut the door, and a few seconds later he came in with a forest of a bouquet, twenty times as big as the ones he occasionally pulled together himself to give her.

"'To Camilla Lind, *Morgenavisen*'s most beautiful employee. Get well soon!'"

He laid it on her blanket, and instantly she was hidden underneath it. "This is incredible! Wow!"

She stuck her head into the flowers.

"The champagne man," Louise said. Then she remembered she'd never told Peter about the evening at the bar. "Klaus West," she added. She regretted saying where Camilla could be found.

Her friend set the bouquet on the floor while Peter went out to find a bucket large enough.

"Who was it sitting and crying in the hall outside your office today?" Camilla asked. "You were talking to him when I came out of the bathroom."

Louise's face clouded over. "Jesper Mørk. He was Karoline Wissinge's boyfriend in nursing school."

"Come on, let's hear it!" Camilla said.

"He was brought in early this morning, and as I understand it from what Suhr said, he confessed immediately."

Peter called out from the kitchen, asking them if he should open a bottle of wine.

"Yeah, but bring along a cola for the patient," Louise said.

"Well, what happened?" Camilla said.

"The day before Karoline's murder, she had lunch with him. When we arrested him, he said she'd gotten pregnant back when they were together, but she had an abortion because she'd met someone else. Which ended their relationship. He was still in love with her, though."

Peter set a glass in front of Louise.

"Then last Friday they were sitting together in the hospital cafeteria, and he begged her again to leave her boyfriend and come back to him. They'd had that conversation several times, and she'd always refused. Then she told him she was pregnant, that she was looking forward to telling her boyfriend. It must have been too much for him, way too much, because he was waiting for her when she came home late Saturday night. He talked her into taking a walk with him."

"She must have wondered what he wanted," Camilla said.

"He admitted to Stig that she tried to cheer him up when he accused her of breaking his heart. And he still claims that deep down she still loved him."

"He sounds crazy. Do you have anything that supports his confession?"

"They found Karoline's bag in his apartment. And he was the one who wrote the card I found with the flowers at the crime scene. 'Thy will be done.' Because she wanted a child with someone else and not him, he thought it was God's will that she should die!"

"Unbelievable!"

"Yeah, scary, isn't it? He's being evaluated mentally. It didn't seem to matter to him whether he was caught or not. We found two cigarette butts at the crime scene, and he said he was smoking while they sat and talked. I'd be surprised if one of them isn't his."

"This world is filled with lunatics!" Camilla said. She leaned back on the sofa, her eyelids drooping. "How the hell did you find out it was him?"

"Last night in the hospital, I was sitting there looking at the whiteboard above your bed. And I remembered I'd seen one like it, just bigger, in the lounge on Mørk's ward. The writing on the whiteboard was the same block lettering as on the card I found. So this morning I called the ward's head nurse, Anna Wallentin, and she checked the work schedule. Mørk had taken a night shift the day before we were there, and he was the one who'd written on the whiteboard."

Camilla looked impressed. "What did Stig say when you told him?"

Louise grunted. "What do you think? He said there was no way the motive could be a broken love affair."

"Wow, you're the one who's a bit touchy now, aren't you?"

"Look who's talking! At least I haven't threatened to resign because I couldn't get along with my colleagues."

Their phone rang. Peter walked over and answered it, then he held his hand over the receiver and looked at Camilla. "It's a journalist from the news department at Danish Broadcasting. The story is going to be on the evening news, and he wants to know if he can do a phone interview with you."

Camilla sat up and stared at him.

"No, absolutely not," Louise said. "It's not going to happen."

"Yes," Camilla yelled, "of course I'll do it."

"What about the Finn?" Peter said, after Camilla had walked out to the bathroom to freshen up before speaking to the journalist. "He's looking at a long prison sentence."

Louise shrugged. "That's hard to say. He did save Camilla's life, and the question is, will he be charged with acting as a middleman for Birte Jensen. It doesn't look like he made any money at all, and he was collaborating with the police. I really don't know what's in store for him."

She yawned. The cartoon show was over, and they hadn't heard a peep out of Markus. She guessed he'd fallen asleep.

Peter took their plates out to the kitchen and opened the dishwasher. "I better get home. I have to get up early, and I still have to pack."

She looked at him in surprise. "Pack?"

"My contract says I'm starting April 1. That's Wednesday."

"You're starting on Wednesday? But you don't have to go home now to pack your clothes, and there's not so much else you'll be taking along right now, is there?"

He looked serious now. "I'm subleasing my apartment. I've thought this over, a lot. When I get back from Aberdeen at the end of September, I want to move in with you. And if that's not what you want, I'm afraid it's over between us."

Slowly his words began to sink in.

"I want to be with you, I don't want there to be any doubt about that. But since you're not ready to make a sacrifice for me in the short term, maybe it's just not in the cards for us to be together forever."

Louise thought about Heilmann, who hadn't been in doubt about what was most important to her. She spoke quietly. "I am willing to make sacrifices for you. But I also need to do my job, and anyway, you're coming back."

She reached for his hand. "Exactly," Peter said. "And when I do, you'll have made your decision."

He kissed her cheek, and they agreed to talk on Saturday.

The door closed behind him as Camilla came out of the bathroom.

"Where's he going?"

"He has to go home and sleep. He's going back to Aberdeen on Wednesday, and he's got a lot to take care of this weekend, but he said to say goodbye and give you a kiss on the forehead."

Camilla's phone rang, and she hurried to answer it.

AUTHOR'S NOTE

The Midnight Witness is a work of fiction. The characters are solely the product of my imagination and bear no resemblance to any persons living or dead. The world I've built up around the events in this book naturally resembles the real world, but I've permitted myself the artistic freedom to change certain details. *Morgenavisen* and the King's Bar, for example, exist only within these pages.

It was vital for me to gain firsthand knowledge of the sort of people I've written about. My heartfelt thanks go out to those who were kind enough to spend time helping me in my research. Without them it would have been impossible to create Louise Rick's world. Any errors in the book are exclusively my own.

—Sara Blaedel

ACKNOWLEDGMENTS

From my very first publication and onward, I've been a stickler for thorough research, which is essential if the goal is storytelling that is believable, authentic, and realistic. I've had enormous help along the way. Special thanks go to my now old friends at Copenhagen's Police Headquarters, without whose help the framework around Louise Rick wouldn't hold. A big, fat, massive thank-you to Tom Christensen, Flying Squad, who has been with me all along the way, and has generously contributed with talk and details as the book was in process. Deep gratitude for your time and compassion.

Heartfelt thanks go, as always, to my brilliant friend, forensic expert, Steen Holger Hansen, who is there to help out when a plot needs to be spun together. Without you there would be no books.

Great thanks to my talented Danish editor, Lisbeth Møller Madsen, and to my publisher, People's Press. It's a pleasure to work with you.

A billion thanks to my wonderful, supersmart American editor, Lindsey Rose, and to the spectacular, endlessly committed team at Grand Central. It is a thrill, an honor, and an enormous joy to work with you all. I appreciate every single effort you've made on my behalf. So happy to be here.

Thank you so very much to my fabulous and savvy American agent, the unparalleled Victoria Sanders, who works magic for me, and to your incredibly wonderful associates, the lovely and talented Bernadette Baker-Baughman and Jessica Spivey, whose great work, all around the world, leaves me filled with gratitude and aware of just how fortunate I am.

Thank you to clever and tireless Benee Knauer, who knows what I am thinking and what I mean, and how to capture it perfectly. It means so much to know you are there, to have you behind and beside me.

I want to express my heartfelt appreciation to the American crime-writing community and to my dear American readers. I cannot sufficiently convey how much your warm welcome has meant to me; you have made my dream come true. I love this country so much, and I'm delighted to call it my second home.

My warmest thanks must go to my son, Adam, whom I love with all my heart, and who has traveled every step of the way with me on this indescribable journey.

If you enjoy Sara Blaedel's Louise Rick suspense novels, you'll love her Family Secrets series.

An unexpected inheritance from a father she hasn't seen since childhood pulls a portrait photographer from her quiet life into a web of dark secrets and murder in a small Midwestern town...

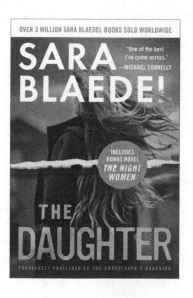

Please see the next page for an excerpt from
***THE DAUGHTER*.**

Available Now.

1

"What do you mean you shouldn't have told me? You should have told me thirty-three years ago."

"What difference would it have made anyway?" Ilka's mother demanded. "You were seven years old. You wouldn't have understood about a liar and a cheat running away with all his winnings; running out on his responsibilities, on his wife and little daughter. He hit the jackpot, Ilka, and then he hit the road. And left me—no, he left *us* with a funeral home too deep in the red to get rid of. And an enormous amount of debt. That he betrayed me is one thing, but abandoning his child?"

Ilka stood at the window, her back to the comfy living room, which was overflowing with books and baskets of yarn. She looked out over the trees in the park across the way. For a moment, the treetops seemed like dizzying black storm waves.

Her mother sat in the glossy Børge Mogensen easy chair in the corner, though now she was worked up from her rant, and her knitting needles clattered twice as fast. Ilka turned to her. "Okay," she said, trying not to sound shrill. "Maybe you're right. Maybe I wouldn't have understood about all that. But you didn't think I was too young to understand that my father was a coward, the way he suddenly left us, and that he didn't love us anymore. That he was an incredible asshole you'd never take back if he ever showed up on our doorstep, begging for forgiveness. As I recall, you had no trouble talking about that, over and over and over."

"Stop it." Her mother had been a grade school teacher for twenty-six years, and now she sounded like one. "But does it make any difference? Think of all the letters you've written him over the years. How often have you reached out to him, asked to see him? Or at least have some form of contact." She sat up and laid her knitting on the small table beside the chair. "He never answered you; he never tried to see you. How long did you save your confirmation money so you could fly over and visit him?"

Ilka knew better than her mother how many letters she had written over the years. What her mother wasn't aware of was that she had kept writing to him, even as an adult. Not as often, but at least a Christmas card and a note on his birthday. Every single year. Which had felt like sending letters into outer space. Yet she'd never stopped.

"You should have told me about the money," Ilka said, unwilling to let it go, even though her mother had a point. Would it really have made a difference? "Why are you telling me now? After all these years. And right when I'm about to leave."

Her mother had called just before eight. Ilka had still been in bed, reading the morning paper on her iPad. "Come over, right now," she'd said. There was something they had to talk about.

Now her mother leaned forward and folded her hands in her lap, her face showing the betrayal and desperation she'd endured. She'd kept her wounds under wraps for half her life, but it was obvious they had never fully healed. "It scares me, you going over there. Your father was a gambler. He bet more money than he had, and the racetrack was a part of our lives for the entire time he lived here. For better and worse. I knew about his habit when we fell in love, but then it got out of control. And almost ruined us several times. In the end, it did ruin us."

"And then he won almost a million kroner and just disappeared." Ilka lifted an eyebrow.

"Well, we do know he went to America." Her mother nodded. "Presumably, he continued gambling over there. And we never heard from him again. That is, until now, of course."

Ilka shook her head. "Right, now that he's dead."

"What I'm trying to say is that we don't know what he's left behind. He could be up to his neck in debt. You're a school photographer, not a millionaire. If you go over there, they might hold you responsible for his debts. And who knows? Maybe they wouldn't allow you to come home. Your father had a dark side he couldn't control. I'll rip his dead body limb from limb if he pulls you down with him, all these years after turning his back on us."

With that, her mother stood and walked down the long hall into the kitchen. Ilka heard muffled voices, and then Hanne appeared in the doorway. "Would you like us to drive you to the airport?" Hanne leaned against the doorframe as Ilka's mother reappeared with a tray of bakery rolls, which she set down on the coffee table.

"No, that's okay," Ilka said.

"How long do you plan on staying?" Hanne asked, moving to the sofa. Ilka's mother curled up in the corner of the sofa, covered herself with a blanket, and put her stockinged feet up on Hanne's lap.

When her mother began living with Hanne fourteen years ago, the last trace of her bitterness finally seemed to evaporate. Now, though, Ilka realized it had only gone into hibernation.

For the first four years after Ilka's father left, her mother had been stuck with Paul Jensen's Funeral Home and its two employees, who cheated her whenever they could get away with it. Throughout Ilka's childhood, her mother had complained constantly about the burden he had dumped on her. Ilka hadn't known until now that her father had also left a sizable gambling debt behind. Apparently, her mother had wanted to spare her, at least to some degree. And, of course, her mother was right. Her father *was* a coward and a selfish jerk. Yet Ilka had never completely accepted his abandonment of her. He had left behind a short letter saying he would come back for them as soon as everything was taken care of, and that an opportunity had come up. In Chicago.

Several years later, after complete silence on his part, he wanted a divorce. And that was the last they'd heard from him. When Ilka was a teenager, she found his address—or at least, an address where he had once lived. She'd kept it all these years in a small red treasure chest in her room.

"Surely it won't take more than a few days," Ilka said. "I'm planning to be back by the weekend. I'm booked up at work, but I found someone to fill in for me the first two days. It would be a great help if you two could keep trying to get hold of Niels from North Sealand Photography. He's in Stockholm, but he's supposed to be back tomorrow. I'm hoping he can cover for me the rest of the week. All the shoots are in and around Copenhagen."

"What exactly are you hoping to accomplish over there?" Hanne asked.

"Well, they say I'm in his will and that I have to be there in person to prove I'm Paul Jensen's daughter."

"I just don't understand why this can't be done by e-mail or fax," her mother said. "You can send them your birth certificate and your passport, or whatever it is they need."

"It seems that copies aren't good enough. If I don't go over there, I'd have to go to an American tax office in Europe, and I think the nearest one is in London. But this way, they'll let me go through his personal things and take what I want. Artie Sorvino from Jensen Funeral Home in Racine has offered to cover my travel expenses if I go now, so they can get started with closing his estate."

Ilka stood in the middle of the living room, too anxious and restless to sit down.

"Racine?" Hanne asked. "Where's that?" She picked up her steaming cup and blew on it.

"A bit north of Chicago. In Wisconsin. I'll be picked up at the airport, and it doesn't look like it'll take long to drive there. Racine is supposedly the city in the United States with the largest community of Danish descendants. A lot of Danes immigrated to the region, so it makes sense that's where he settled."

"He has a hell of a lot of nerve." Her mother's lips barely moved. "He doesn't write so much as a birthday card to you all these years, and now suddenly you have to fly over there and clean up another one of his messes."

"Karin," Hanne said, her voice gentle. "Of course Ilka should go over and sort through her father's things. If you get the opportunity for closure on such an important part of your life's story, you should grab it."

Her mother shook her head. Without looking at Ilka, she said, "I have a bad feeling about this. Isn't it odd that he stayed in the undertaker business even though he managed to ruin his first shot at it?"

Ilka walked out into the hall and let the two women bicker about the unfairness of it all. How Paul's daughter had tried to reach out to her father all her life, and it was only now that he was gone that he was finally reaching out to her.

2

The first thing Ilka noticed was his Hawaiian shirt and longish brown hair, which was combed back and held in place by sunglasses that would look at home on a surfer. He stood out among the other drivers at Arrivals in O'Hare International Airport who were holding name cards and facing the scattered clumps of exhausted people pulling suitcases out of Customs.

Written on his card was "Ilka Nichols Jensen." Somehow, she managed to walk all the way up to him and stop before he realized she'd found him.

They looked each other over for a moment. He was in his early forties, maybe, she thought. So, her father, who had turned seventy-two in early January, had a younger partner.

She couldn't read his face, but it might have surprised him that the undertaker's daughter was a beanpole: six feet tall without a hint of a feminine form. He scanned her up and down, gaze settling on her hair, which had never been an attention-getter. Straight, flat, and mousy.

He smiled warmly and held out his hand. "Nice to meet you. Welcome to Chicago."

It's going to be a hell of a long trip, Ilka thought, before shaking his hand and saying hello. "Thank you. Nice to meet you, too."

He offered to carry her suitcase. It was small, a carry-on, but she gladly handed it over to him. Then he offered her a bottle of water. The car was close by, he said, only a short walk.

Although she was used to being taller than most people, she always felt a bit shy when male strangers had to look up to make eye contact. She was nearly a head taller than Artie Sorvino, but he seemed almost impressed as he grinned up at her while they walked.

Her body ached; she hadn't slept much during the long flight. Since she'd left her apartment in Copenhagen, her nerves had been tingling with excitement. And worry, too. Things had almost gone wrong right off the bat at the Copenhagen airport, because she hadn't taken into account the long line at Passport Control. There had still been two people in front of her when she'd been called to her waiting flight. Then the arrival in the US, a hell that the chatty man next to her on the plane had prepared her for. He had missed God knew how many connecting flights at O'Hare because the immigration line had taken several hours to go through. It turned out to be not quite as bad as all that. She had been guided to a machine that requested her fingerprints, passport, and picture. All this information was scanned and saved. Then Ilka had been sent on to the next line, where a surly passport official wanted to know what her business was in the country. She began to sweat but then pulled herself together and explained that she was simply visiting family, which in a way was true. He stamped her passport, and moments later she was standing beside the man wearing the colorful, festive shirt.

"Is this your first trip to the US?" Artie asked now, as they approached the enormous parking lot.

She smiled. "No, I've traveled here a few times. To Miami and New York."

Why had she said that? She'd never been in this part of the world before, but what the hell. It didn't matter. Unless he kept up the conversation. And Miami. Where had that come from?

"Really?" Artie told her he had lived in Key West for many years. Then his father got sick, and Artie, the only other surviving member of the family, moved back to Racine to take care of him. "I hope you made it down to the Keys while you were in Florida."

Ilka shook her head and explained that she unfortunately hadn't had time.

"I had a gallery down there," Artie said. He'd gone to the California School of the Arts in San Francisco and had made his living as an artist.

Ilka listened politely and nodded. In the parking lot, she caught sight of a gigantic black Cadillac with closed white curtains in back, which stood first in the row of parked cars. He'd driven there in the hearse.

"Hope you don't mind." He nodded at the hearse as he opened the rear door and placed her suitcase on the casket table used for rolling coffins in and out of the vehicle.

"No, it's fine." She walked around to the front passenger door. Fine, as long as she wasn't the one being rolled into the back. She felt slightly dizzy, as if she were still up in the air, but was buoyed by the nervous excitement of traveling and the anticipation of what awaited her.

The thought that her father was at the end of her journey bothered her, yet it was something she'd fantasized about nearly her entire life. But would she be able to piece together the life he'd lived without her? And was she even interested in knowing about it? What if she didn't like what she learned?

She shook her head for a moment. These thoughts had been swirling in her head since Artie's first phone call. Her mother thought she shouldn't get involved. At all. But Ilka disagreed. If her father had left anything behind, she wanted to see it. She wanted to uncover whatever she could find, to see if any of it made sense.

"How did he die?" she asked as Artie maneuvered the long hearse out of the parking lot and in between two orange signs warning about roadwork and a detour.

"Just a sec," he muttered, and he swore at the sign before deciding to skirt the roadwork and get back to the road heading north.

For a while they drove in silence; then he explained that one morning her father had simply not woken up. "He was supposed to drive a corpse to Iowa, one of our neighboring states, but he didn't show up. He just died in his sleep. Totally peacefully. He might not even have known it was over."

Ilka watched the Chicago suburbs drifting by along the long, straight bypass, the rows of anonymous stores and cheap restaurants. It seemed so overwhelming, so strange, so different. Most buildings were painted in shades of beige and brown, and enormous billboards stood everywhere, screaming messages about everything from missing children to ultracheap fast food and vanilla coffee for less than a dollar at Dunkin' Donuts.

She turned to Artie. "Was he sick?" The bump on Artie's nose—had it been broken?—made it appear too big for the rest of his face: high cheekbones, slightly squinty eyes, beard stubble definitely due to a relaxed attitude toward shaving, rather than wanting to be in style.

"Not that I know of, no. But there could have been things Paul didn't tell me about, for sure."

His tone told her it wouldn't have been the first secret Paul had kept from him.

"The doctor said his heart just stopped," he continued. "Nothing dramatic happened."

"Did he have a family?" She looked out the side window. The old hearse rode well. Heavy, huge, swaying lightly. A tall pickup drove up beside them; a man with a full beard looked down and nodded at her. She looked away quickly. She didn't care for any sympathetic looks, though he, of course, couldn't know the curtained-off back of the hearse was empty.

"He was married, you know," Artie said. Immediately Ilka sensed he didn't like being the one to fill her in on her father's private affairs. She nodded to herself; of course he didn't. What did she expect?

"And he had two daughters. That was it, apart from Mary Ann's family, but I don't know them. How much do you know about them?"

He knew very well that Ilka hadn't had any contact with her father since he'd left Denmark. Or at least she assumed he knew. "Why has the family not signed what should be signed, so you can finish with his…estate?" She set the empty water bottle on the floor.

"They did sign their part of it. But that's not enough, because you're in the will, too. First the IRS—that's our tax agency—must determine if he owes the government, and you must give them permission to investigate. If you don't sign, they'll freeze all the assets in the estate until everything is cleared up."

Ilka's shoulders slumped at the word "assets." One thing that had kept her awake during the flight was her mother's concern about her being stuck with a debt she could never pay. Maybe she would be detained; maybe she would even be thrown in jail.

"What are his daughters like?" she asked after they had driven for a while in silence.

For a few moments, he kept his eyes on the road; then he glanced at her and shrugged. "They're nice enough, but I don't really know them. It's been a long time since I've seen them. Truth is, I don't think either of them was thrilled about your father's business."

After another silence, Ilka said, "You should have called me when he died. I wish I had been at his funeral."

Was that really true? Did she truly wish that? The last funeral she'd been to was her husband's. He had collapsed from heart failure three years ago, at the age of fifty-two. She didn't like death, didn't like loss. But she'd already lost her father many years ago, so what difference would it have made watching him being lowered into the ground?

"At that time, I didn't know about you," Artie said. "Your name first came up when your father's lawyer mentioned you."

"Where is he buried?"

He stared straight ahead. Again, it was obvious he didn't enjoy talking about her father's private life. Finally, he said, "Mary Ann decided to keep the urn with his ashes at home. A private ceremony was held in the living room when the crematorium delivered the urn, and now it's on the shelf above the fireplace."

After a pause, he said, "You speak English well. Funny accent."

Ilka explained distractedly that she had traveled in Australia for a year after high school.

The billboards along the freeway here advertised hotels, motels, and drive-ins for the most part. She wondered how there could be enough people to keep all these businesses going, given the countless offers from the clusters of signs on both sides of the road. "What about his new family? Surely they knew he had a daughter in Denmark?" She turned back to him.

"Nope!" He shook his head as he flipped the turn signal.

"He never told them he left his wife and seven-year-old daughter?" She wasn't all that surprised.

Artie didn't answer. *Okay*, Ilka thought. *That takes care of that.*

"I wonder what they think about me coming here."

He shrugged. "I don't really know, but they're not going to lose anything. His wife has an inheritance from her wealthy parents, so she's taken care of. The same goes for the daughters. And none of them had ever shown any interest in the funeral home."

And what about their father? Ilka thought. *Were they uninterested in him, too?* But that was none of her business. She didn't know them, knew nothing about their relationships with one another. And for that matter, she knew nothing about her father. Maybe his new family had asked about his life in Denmark, and maybe he'd given them a line of bullshit. But what the hell, he was thirty-nine when he left. Anyone could figure out he'd had a life before packing his weekend bag and emigrating.

Both sides of the freeway were green now. The landscape was starting to remind her of late summer in Denmark, with its green fields, patches of forest, flat land, large barns with the characteristic bowed roofs, and livestock. With a few exceptions, she felt like she could have been driving down the E45, the road between Copenhagen and Ålborg.

"Do you mind if I turn on the radio?" Artie asked.

She shook her head; it was a relief to have the awkward silence between them broken. And yet, before his hand reached the radio, she blurted out, "What was he like?"

He dropped his hand and smiled at her. "Your father was a decent guy, a really decent guy. In a lot of ways," he added, disarmingly, "he was someone you could count on, and in other ways he was very much his own man. I always enjoyed working with him, but he was also my friend. People liked him; he was interested in their lives. That's also why he was so good at talking to those who had just lost someone. He was empathetic. It feels empty, him not being around any longer."

Ilka had to concentrate to follow along. Despite her year in Australia, it was difficult when people spoke English rapidly. "Was he also a good father?"

Artie turned thoughtfully and looked out his side window. "I really can't say. I didn't know him when the girls were small." He kept glancing at the four lanes to their left. "But if you're asking me if your father was a family man, my answer is, yes and no. He was very much in touch with his family, but he probably put more of himself into Jensen Funeral Home."

"How long did you know him?"

She watched him calculate. "I moved back in 1998. We ran into each other at a local saloon, this place called Oh Dennis!, and we started talking. The victim of a traffic accident had just come in to the funeral home. The family wanted to put the young woman in an open coffin, but nobody would have wanted to see her face. So I offered to help. It's the kind of stuff I'm good at. Creating, shaping. Your father did the embalming, but I reconstructed her face. Her mother supplied us with a photo, and I did a sculpture. And I managed to make the woman look like herself, even though there wasn't much to work with. Later your father offered me a job, and I grabbed the chance. There's not much work for an artist in Racine, so reconstructions of the deceased was as good as anything."

He turned off the freeway. "Later I got a degree, because you have to have a license to work in the undertaker business."

They reached Racine Street and waited to make a left turn. They had driven the last several miles in silence. The streets were deserted, the shops closed. It was getting dark, and Ilka realized she was at the point where exhaustion and jet lag trumped the hunger gnawing inside her. They drove by an empty square and a nearly deserted saloon. Oh Dennis!, the place where Artie had met her father. She spotted the lake at the end of the broad streets to the right, and that was it. The town was dead. Abandoned, closed. She was surprised there were no people or life.

"We've booked a room for you at the Harbourwalk Hotel. Tomorrow we can sit down and go through your father's papers. Then you can start looking through his things."

Ilka nodded. All she wanted right now was a warm bath and a bed.

"Sorry, we have no reservations for Miss Jensen. And none for the Jensen Funeral Home, either. We don't have a single room available."

The receptionist drawled apology after apology. It sounded to Ilka as if she had too much saliva in her mouth.

Ilka sat in a plush armchair in the lobby as Artie asked if the room was reserved in his name. "Or try Sister Eileen O'Connor," he suggested.

The receptionist apologized again as her long fingernails danced over the computer keyboard. The sound was unnaturally loud, a bit like Ilka's mother's knitting needles tapping against each other.

Ilka shut down. She could sit there and sleep; it made absolutely no difference to her. Back in Denmark, it was five in the morning, and she hadn't slept in twenty-two hours.

"I'm sorry," Artie said. "You're more than welcome to stay at my place. I can sleep on the sofa. Or we can fix up a place for you to sleep at the office, and we'll find another hotel in the morning."

Ilka sat up in the armchair. "What's that sound?"

Artie looked bewildered. "What do you mean?"

"It's like a phone ringing in the next room."

He listened for a moment before shrugging. "I can't hear anything."

The sound came every ten seconds. It was as if something were hidden behind the reception desk or farther down the hotel foyer. Ilka shook her head and looked at him. "You don't need to sleep on the sofa. I can sleep somewhere at the office."

She needed to be alone, and the thought of a strange man's bedroom didn't appeal to her.

"That's fine." He grabbed her small suitcase. "It's only five minutes away, and I know we can find some food for you, too."

The black hearse was parked just outside the main entrance of the hotel, but that clearly wasn't bothering anyone. Though the hotel was apparently fully booked, Ilka hadn't seen a single person since they'd arrived.

Night had fallen, and her eyelids closed as soon as she settled into the car. She jumped when Artie opened the door and poked her with his finger. She hadn't even realized they had arrived. They were parked in a large, empty lot. The white building was an enormous box with several attic windows reflecting the moonlight back into the thick darkness. Tall trees with enormous crowns hovered over Ilka when she got out of the car.

They reached the door, beside which was a sign: JENSEN FUNERAL HOME. WELCOME. Pillars stood all the way across the broad porch, with well-tended flower beds in front of it, but the darkness covered everything else.

Artie led her inside the high-ceilinged hallway and turned the light on. He pointed to a stairway at the other end. Ilka's feet sank deep in the carpet; it smelled dusty, with a hint of plastic and instant coffee.

"Would you like something to drink? Are you hungry? I can make a sandwich."

"No, thank you." She just wanted him to leave.

He led her up the stairs, and when they reached a small landing, he pointed at a door. "Your father had a room in there, and I think we can find some sheets. We have a cot we can fold out and make up for you."

Ilka held her hand up. "If there is a bed in my father's room, I can just sleep in it." She nodded when he asked if she was sure. "What time do you want to meet tomorrow?"

"How about eight thirty? We can have breakfast together."

She had no idea what time it was, but as long as she got some sleep, she guessed she'd be fine. She nodded.

Ilka stayed outside on the landing while Artie opened the door to her father's room and turned on the light. She watched him walk over to a dresser and pull out the bottom drawer. He grabbed some sheets and a towel and tossed them on the bed; then he waved her in.

The room's walls were slanted. An old white bureau stood at the end of the room, and under the window, which must have been one of those she'd noticed from the parking lot, was a desk with drawers on both sides. The bed was just inside the room and to the left. There was also a small coffee table and, at the end of the bed, a narrow built-in closet.

A dark jacket and a tie lay draped over the back of the desk chair. The desk was covered with piles of paper; a briefcase leaned against the closet. But there was nothing but sheets on the bed.

"I'll find a comforter and a pillow," Artie said, accidentally grazing her as he walked by.

Ilka stepped into the room. A room lived in, yet abandoned. A feeling suddenly stirred inside her, and she froze. He was here. The smell. A heavy yet pleasant odor she recognized from somewhere deep inside. She'd had no idea this memory existed. She closed her eyes and let her mind drift back to when she was very young, the feeling of being held. Tobacco. Sundays in the car, driving out to Bellevue. Feeling secure, knowing someone close was taking care of her. Lifting her up on a lap. Making her laugh. The sound of hooves pounding the ground, horses at a racetrack. Her father's concentration as he chain-smoked, captivated by the race. His laughter.

She sat down on the bed, not hearing what Artie said when he laid the comforter and pillow beside her, then walked out and closed the door.

Her father had been tall; at least that's how she remembered him. She could see to the end of the world when she sat on his shoulders. They did fun things together. He took her to an amusement park and bought her ice cream while he tried out the slot machines, to see if they were any good. Her mother didn't always know when they went there. He also took her out to a centuries-old amusement park in the forest north of Copenhagen. They stopped at Peter Liep's, and she drank soda while he drank beer. They sat outside and watched the riders pass by, smelling horseshit and sweat when the thirsty riders dismounted and draped the reins over the hitching post. He had loved horses. On the other hand, she couldn't remember the times—the many times, according to her mother—when he didn't come home early enough to stick his head in her room and say good night. Not having enough money for food because he had gambled his wages away at the track was something else she didn't recall—but her mother did.

Ilka opened her eyes. Her exhaustion was gone, but she still felt dizzy. She walked over to the desk and reached for a photo in a wide mahogany frame. A trotter, its mane flying out to both sides at the finishing line. In another photo, a trotter covered by a red victory blanket stood beside a sulky driver holding a trophy high above his head, smiling for the camera. There were several more horse photos, and a ticket to Lunden hung from a window hasp. She grabbed it. Paul Jensen. Charlottenlund Derby 1982. The year he left them.

Ilka didn't realize at the time that he had left. All she knew was that one morning he wasn't there, and her mother was crying but wouldn't tell her why. When she arrived home from school that afternoon, her mother was still crying. And as she remembered it, her mother didn't stop crying for a long time.

She had been with her father at that derby in 1982. She picked up a photo leaning against the windowsill, then sat down on the bed. "Ilka and Peter Kjærsgaard" was written on the back of the photo. Ilka had been five years old when her father took her to the derby for the first time. Back then, her mother had gone along. She vaguely remembered going to the track and meeting the famous jockey, but suddenly the odors and sounds were crystal clear. She closed her eyes.

"You can give them one if you want," the man had said as he handed her a bucket filled with carrots, many more than her mother had in bags back in their kitchen. The bucket was heavy, but Ilka wanted to show them how big she was, so she hooked the handle with her arm and walked over to one of the stalls.

She smiled proudly at a red-shirted sulky driver passing by as he was fastening his helmet. The track was crowded, but during the races, few people were allowed in the barn. They were, though. She and her father.

She pulled her hand back, frightened, when the horse in the

stall whinnied and pulled against the chain. It snorted and pounded its hoof on the floor. The horse was so tall. Carefully she held the carrot out in the palm of her hand, as her father had taught her to do. The horse snatched the sweet treat, gently tickling her.

Her father stood with a group of men at the end of the row of stalls. They laughed loudly, slapping one another's shoulders. A few of them drank beer from bottles. Ilka sat down on a bale of hay. Her father had promised her a horse when she was a bit older. One of the grooms came over and asked if she would like a ride behind the barn; he was going to walk one of the horses to warm it up. She wanted to, if her father would let her. He did.

"Look at me, Daddy!" Ilka cried. "Look at me." The horse had stopped, clearly preferring to eat grass rather than walk. She kicked gently to get it going, but her legs were too short to do any good.

Her father pulled himself away from the other men and stood at the barn entrance. He waved, and Ilka sat up proudly. The groom asked if he should let go of the reins so she could ride by herself, and though she didn't really love the idea, she nodded. But when he dropped the reins and she turned around to show her father how brave she was, he was back inside with the others.

Ilka stood up and put the photo back. She could almost smell the tar used by the racetrack farrier on horse hooves. She used to sit behind a pane of glass with her mother and follow the races, while her father stood over at the finish line. But then her mother stopped going along.

She picked up another photo from the windowsill. She was standing on a bale of hay, toasting with a sulky driver. Fragments of memories flooded back as she studied herself in the photo. Her father speaking excitedly with the driver, his expression as the horses were hitched to the sulkies. And the way he said, "We-e-e-ell, shall we…?" right before a race. Then he would hold his hand out, and they would walk down to the track.

She wondered why she could remember these things, when she had forgotten most of what had happened back then.

There was also a photo of two small girls on the desk. She knew these were her younger half sisters, who were smiling broadly at the photographer. Suddenly, deep inside her chest, she felt a sharp twinge—but why? After setting the photo back down, she realized it wasn't from never having met her half sisters. No. It was pure jealousy. They had grown up with her father, while she had been abandoned.

Ilka threw herself down on the bed and pulled the comforter over her, without even bothering to put the sheets on. She lay curled up, staring into space.

3

At some point, Ilka must have fallen asleep, because she gave a start when someone knocked on the door. She recognized Artie's voice.

"Morning in there. Are you awake?"

She sat up, confused. She had been up once in the night to look for a bathroom. The building seemed strangely hushed, as if it were packed in cotton. She'd opened a few doors and finally found a bathroom with shiny tiles and a low bathtub. The toilet had a soft cover on its seat, like the one in her grandmother's flat in Bagsværd. On her way back, she had grabbed her father's jacket, carried it to the bed, and buried her nose in it. Now it lay halfway on the floor.

"Give me half an hour," she said. She hugged the jacket, savoring the odor that had brought her childhood memories to the surface from the moment she'd walked into the room.

Now that it was light outside, the room seemed bigger. Last

night she hadn't noticed the storage boxes lining the wall behind both sides of the desk. Clean shirts in clear plastic sacks hung from the hook behind the door.

"Okay, but have a look at these IRS forms," he said, sliding a folder under the door. "And sign on the last page when you've read them. We'll take off whenever you're ready."

Ilka didn't answer. She pulled her knees up to her chest and lay curled up. Without moving. Being shut up inside a room with her father's belongings was enough to make her feel she'd reunited with a part of herself. The big black hole inside her, the one that had appeared every time she sent a letter despite knowing she'd get no answer, was slowly filling up with something she'd failed to find herself.

She had lived about a sixth of her life with her father. *When do we become truly conscious of the people around us?* she wondered. She had just turned forty, and he had deserted them when she was seven. This room here was filled with everything he had left behind, all her memories of him. All the odors and sensations that had made her miss him.

Artie knocked on the door again. She had no idea how long she'd been lying on the bed.

"Ready?" he called out.

"No," she yelled back. She couldn't. She needed to just stay and take in everything here, so it wouldn't disappear again.

"Have you read it?"

"I signed it!"

"Would you rather stay here? Do you want me to go alone?"

"Yes, please."

Silence. She couldn't tell if he was still outside.

"Okay," he finally said. "I'll come back after breakfast." He sounded annoyed. "I'll leave the phone here with you."

Ilka listened to him walk down the stairs. After she'd walked over to the door and signed her name, she hadn't moved a muscle. She hadn't opened any drawers or closets.

She'd brought along a bag of chips, but they were all gone. And she didn't feel like going downstairs for something to drink. Instead, she gave way to exhaustion. The stream of thoughts, the fragments of memories in her head, had slowly settled into a tempo she could follow.

Her father had written her into his will. He had declared her to be his biological daughter. But evidently, he'd never mentioned her to his new family, or to the people closest to him in his new life. Of course, he hadn't been obligated to mention her, she thought. But if her name hadn't come up in his will, they could have liquidated his business without anyone knowing about an adult daughter in Denmark.

The telephone outside the door rang, but she ignored it. What had this Artie guy imagined she should do if the telephone rang? Did he think she would answer it? And say what?

At first, she'd wondered why her father had named her in his will. But after having spent the last twelve hours enveloped in memories of him, she had realized that no matter what had happened in his life, a part of him had still been her father.

She cried, then felt herself dozing off.

Someone knocked on the door. "Not today," she yelled, before Artie could even speak a word. She turned her back to the room, her face to the wall. She closed her eyes until the footsteps disappeared down the stairs.

The telephone rang again, but she didn't react.

Slowly it had all come back. After her father had disappeared, her mother had two jobs: the funeral home business and her teaching. It wasn't long after summer vacation, and school had just begun. Ilka thought he had left in September. A month before she turned eight. Her mother taught Danish and arts and crafts to students in several grades. When she wasn't at school, she was at the funeral home on Brønshøj Square. Also on weekends, picking up flowers and ordering coffins. Working in the office, keeping the books when she wasn't filling out forms.

Ilka had gone along with her to various embassies whenever a mortuary passport was needed to bring a corpse home from outside the country, or when a person died in Denmark and was to be buried elsewhere. It had been fascinating, though frightening. But she had never fully understood how hard her mother worked. Finally, when Ilka was twelve, her mother managed to sell the business and get back her life.

After her father left, they were unable to afford the single-story house Ilka had been born in. They moved into a small apartment on Frederikssundsvej in Copenhagen. Her mother had never been shy about blaming her father for their economic woes, but she'd always said they would be okay. After she sold the funeral home, their situation had improved; Ilka saw it mostly from the color in her mother's cheeks, a more relaxed expression on her face. Also, she was more likely to let Ilka invite friends home for dinner. When she started eighth grade, they moved to Østerbro, a better district in the city, but she stayed in her school in Brønshøj and took the bus.

"You *were* an asshole," she muttered, her face still to the wall. "What you did was just completely inexcusable."

The telephone outside the door finally gave up. She heard soft steps out on the stairs. She sighed. They had paid her airfare; there were limits to what she could get away with. But today was out of the question. And that telephone was their business.

Someone knocked again at the door. This time it sounded different. They knocked again. "Hello." A female voice. The woman called her name and knocked one more time, gently but insistently.

Ilka rose from the bed. She shook her hair and slipped it behind her ears and smoothed her T-shirt. She walked over and opened the door. She couldn't hide her startled expression at the sight of a woman dressed in gray, her hair covered by a veil of the same color. Her broad, demure skirt reached below the knees. Her eyes seemed far too big for her small face and delicate features.

"Who are you?"

"My name is Sister Eileen O'Connor, and you have a meeting in ten minutes."

The woman was already about to turn and walk back down the steps, when Ilka finally got hold of herself. "I have a meeting?"

"Yes, the business is yours now." Ilka heard patience as well as suppressed annoyance in the nun's voice. "Artie has left for the day and has informed me that you have taken over."

"*My* business?" Ilka ran her hand through her hair. A bad habit of hers, when she didn't know what to do with her hands.

"You did read the papers Artie left for you? It's my understanding that you signed them, so you're surely aware of what you have inherited."

"I signed to say I'm his daughter," Ilka said. More than anything, she just wanted to close the door and make everything go away.

"If you had read what was written," the sister said, a bit sharply, "you would know that your father has left the business to you. And by your signature, you have acknowledged your identity and therefore your inheritance."

Ilka was speechless. While she gawked, the sister added, "The Norton family lost their grandmother last night. It wasn't unexpected, but several of them are taking it hard. I've made coffee for four." She stared at Ilka's T-shirt and bare legs. "And it's our custom to receive relatives in attire that is a bit more respectful."

A tiny smile played on her narrow lips, so fleeting that Ilka was in doubt as to whether it had actually appeared. "I can't talk to a family that just lost someone," she protested. "I don't know what to say. I've never—I'm sorry, you have to talk to them."

Sister Eileen stood for a moment before speaking. "Unfortunately, I can't. I don't have the authority to perform such duties. I do the office work, open mail, and laminate the photos of the deceased onto death notices for relatives to use as bookmarks. But you will do fine. Your father was always good at such conversations. All you have to do is allow the family to talk. Listen and find out what's important to them; that's the most vital thing for people who come to us. And these people have a contract for a pre-paid ceremony. The contract explains everything they have paid for. Mrs. Norton has been making funeral payments her whole life, so everything should be smooth sailing."

The nun walked soundlessly down the stairs. Ilka stood in the doorway, staring at where she had vanished. Had she seriously inherited a funeral home? In the US? How had her life taken such an unexpected turn? What the hell had her father been thinking?

She pulled herself together. She had seven minutes before the Nortons arrived. "Respectful" attire, the sister had said. Did she even have something like that in her suitcase? She hadn't opened it yet.

But she couldn't do this. They couldn't make her talk to total strangers who had just lost a relative. Then she remembered she hadn't known the undertaker who helped her when Erik died either. But he had been a salvation to her. A person who had taken care of everything in a professional manner and arranged things precisely as she believed her husband would have wanted. The funeral home, the flowers—yellow tulips. The hymns. It was also the undertaker who had said she would regret it if she didn't hire an organist to play during the funeral. Because even though it might seem odd, the mere sound of it helped relieve the somber atmosphere. She had chosen the cheapest coffin, as the undertaker had suggested, seeing that Erik had wanted to be cremated. Many minor decisions had been made for her; that had been an enormous relief. And the funeral had gone exactly the way she'd wanted. Plus, the undertaker had helped reserve a room at the restaurant where they gathered after the ceremony. But those types of details were apparently already taken care of here. It seemed all she had to do was meet with them. She walked over to her suitcase.

Ilka dumped everything out onto the bed and pulled a light blouse and dark pants out of the pile. Along with her toiletry bag and underwear. Halfway down the stairs, she remembered she needed shoes. She went back up again. All she had was sneakers.

The family was three adult children—a daughter and two sons— and a grandchild. The two men seemed essentially composed, while the woman and the boy were crying. The woman's face was stiff and pale, as if every ounce of blood had drained out of her. Her young son stared down at his hands, looking withdrawn and gloomy.

"Our mother paid for everything in advance," one son said when Ilka walked in. They sat in the arrangement room's comfortable armchairs, around a heavy mahogany table. Dusty paintings in elegant gilded frames hung from the dark green walls. Ilka guessed the paintings were inspired by Lake Michigan. She had no idea what to do with the grieving family, nor what was expected of her.

The son farthest from the door asked, "How does the condolences and tributes page on your website work? Is it like anyone can go in and write on it, or can it only be seen if you have the password? We want everybody to be able to put up a picture of our mother and write about their good times with her."

Ilka nodded to him and walked over to shake his hand. "We will make the page so it's exactly how you want it." Then she repeated their names: Steve—the one farthest from the door—Joe, Helen, and the grandson, Pete. At least she thought that was right, though she wasn't sure because he had mumbled his name.

"And we talked it over and decided we want charms," Helen said. "We'd all like one. But I can't see in the papers whether they're paid for or not, because if not we need to know how much they cost."

Ilka had no idea what charms were, but she'd noticed the green form that had been laid on the table for her, and a folder entitled "Norton," written by hand. The thought struck her that the handwriting must be her father's.

"Service Details" was written on the front of the form. Ilka sat down and reached for the notebook on the table. It had a big red heart on the cover, along with "Helping Hands for Healing Hearts."

She surmised the notebook was probably meant for the relatives. Quickly, she slid it over the table to them; then she opened a drawer and found a sheet of paper. "I'm very sorry," she said. It was difficult for her not to look at the grandson, who appeared crushed. "About your loss. As I understand, everything is already decided. But I wasn't here when things were planned. Maybe we can go through everything together and figure out exactly how you want it done."

What in the world is going on? she thought as she sat there blabbering away at this grieving family, as if she'd been doing it all her life!

"Our mother liked Mr. Jensen a lot," Steve said. "He took charge of the funeral arrangements when our father died, and we'd like things done the same way."

Ilka nodded.

"But not the coffin," Joe said. "We want one that's more upscale, more feminine."

"Is it possible to see the charms?" Helen asked, still tearful. "And we also need to print a death notice, right?"

"Can you arrange it so her dogs can sit up by the coffin during the services?" Steve asked. He looked at Ilka as if this were the most important of all the issues. "That won't be a problem, will it?"

"No, not a problem," she answered quickly, as the questions rained down on her.

"How many people can fit in there? And can we all sit together?"

"The room can hold a lot of people," she said, feeling now as if she'd been fed to the lions. "We can squeeze the chairs together; we can get a lot of people in there. And of course you can sit together."

Ilka had absolutely no idea what room they were talking about. But there had been about twenty people attending her husband's services, and they hadn't even filled a corner of the chapel in Bispebjerg.

"How many do you think are coming?" she asked, just to be on the safe side.

"Probably somewhere between a hundred and a hundred and fifty," Joe guessed. "That's how many showed up at Dad's services. But it could be more this time, so it's good to be prepared. She was very active after her retirement. And the choir would like to sing."

Ilka nodded mechanically and forced a smile. She had heard that it's impossible to vomit while you're smiling, something about reflexes. Not that she was about to vomit; there was nothing inside her to come out. But her insides contracted as if something in there was getting out of control. "How did Mrs. Norton die?" She leaned back in her chair.

She felt their eyes on her, and for a moment everyone was quiet. The adults looked at her as if the question weren't her business. And maybe it was irrelevant for the planning, she thought. But after Erik died, in a way it had been a big relief to talk about him, how she had come home and found him on the kitchen floor. Putting it into words made it all seem more real, like it actually had happened. And it had helped her through the days after his death, which otherwise were foggy.

Helen sat up and looked over at her son, who was still staring at his hands. "Pete's the one who found her. We bought groceries for his grandma three times a week and drove them over to her after school. And there she was, out in the yard. Just lying there."

Now Ilka regretted having asked.

From underneath the hair hanging over his forehead, with his head bowed, the boy scowled at his mother. "Grandma was out cutting flowers to put in vases, and she fell," he muttered.

"There was a lot of blood," his mother said, nodding.

"But the guy who picked her up promised we wouldn't be able to see it when she's in her coffin," Steve said. He looked at Ilka, as if he wanted this confirmed.

Quickly she answered, "No, you won't. She'll look fine. Did she like flowers?"

Helen smiled and nodded. "She lived and breathed for her garden. She loved her flower beds."

"Then maybe it's a good idea to use flowers from her garden to decorate the coffin," Ilka suggested.

Steve sat up. "Decorate the coffin? It's going to be open."

"But it's a good idea," Helen said. "We'll decorate the chapel with flowers from the garden. We can go over and pick them together. It's a beautiful way to say good-bye to the garden she loved, too."

"But if we use hers, will we get the money back we already paid for flowers?" Joe asked.

Ilka nodded. "Yes, of course." Surely it wasn't a question of all that much money.

"Oh God!" Helen said. "I almost forgot to give you this." Out of her bag she pulled a large folder that said "Family Record Guide" and handed it over to Ilka. "It's already filled out."

In many ways, it reminded Ilka of the diaries she'd kept in school. First a page with personal information. The full name of the deceased, the parents' names. Whether she was married, divorced, single, or a widow. Education and job positions. Then a page with familial relations, and on the opposite page there was room to write about the deceased's life and memories. There were sections for writing about a first home, about becoming a parent, about becoming a grandparent. And then a section that caught Ilka's attention, because it had to be of some use. Favorites: colors, flowers, season, songs, poems, books. And on and on it went. Family traditions. Funny memories, role models, hobbies, special talents. Mrs. Norton had filled it all out very thoroughly.

Ilka closed the folder and asked how they would describe their mother and grandmother.

"She was very sociable," Joe said. "Also after Dad died. She was involved in all sorts of things; she was very active in the seniors' club in West Racine."

"And family meant a lot to her," Helen said. She'd stopped crying without Ilka noticing. "She was always the one who made sure we all got together, at least twice a year."

Ilka let them speak, as long as they stayed away from talking about charms and choosing coffins. She had no idea how to wind up the conversation, but she kept listening as they nearly all talked at once, to make sure that everything about the deceased came out. Even gloomy Pete added that his grandmother made the world's best pecan pie.

"And she had the best Southern recipe for macaroni and cheese," he added. The others laughed.

Ilka thought again about Erik. After his funeral, their apartment had felt empty and abandoned. A silence hung that had nothing to do with being alone. It took a few weeks for her to realize the silence was in herself. There was no one to talk to, so everything was spoken inside her head. And at the same time, she felt as if she were in a bubble no sound could penetrate. That had been one of the most difficult things to get used to. Slowly things got better, and at last—she couldn't say precisely when—the silence connected with her loss disappeared.

Meanwhile, she'd had the business to run. What a circus. They'd started working together almost from the time they'd first met. He was the photographer, though occasionally she went out with him to help set up the equipment and direct the students. Otherwise, she was mostly responsible for the office work. But she had done a job or two by herself when they were especially busy; she'd seen how he worked. There was nothing mysterious about it. Classes were lined up with the tallest students in back, and the most attractive were placed in the middle so the focus would be on them. The individual portraits were mostly about adjusting the height of the seat and taking enough pictures to ensure that one of them was good enough. But when Erik suddenly wasn't there, with a full schedule of jobs still booked, she had taken over. Without giving it much thought. She did know the school secretaries, and they knew her, so that eased the transition.

"Do we really have to buy a coffin, when Mom is just going to be burned?" Steve said, interrupting her thoughts. "Can't we just borrow one? She won't be lying in there very long."

Shit. Ilka had blanked out for a moment. Where the hell was Artie? Did they have coffins they loaned out? She had to say something. "It would have to be one that's been used."

"We're not putting Mom in a coffin where other dead people have been!" Helen was indignant, while a hint of a smile appeared on her son's face.

Ilka jumped in. "Unfortunately, we can only loan out used coffins." She hoped that would put a lid on this idea.

"We can't do that. Can we?" Helen said to her two brothers. "On the other hand, if we borrow a coffin, we might be able to afford charms instead."

Ilka didn't have the foggiest idea if her suggestion was even possible. But if this really was her business, she could decide, now, couldn't she?

"We *would* save forty-five hundred dollars," Joe said.

Forty-five hundred dollars for a coffin! This could turn out to be disastrous if it ended with them losing money from her ignorant promise.

"Oh, at least. Dad's coffin cost seven thousand dollars."

What is this? Ilka thought. *Are coffins here decorated in gold leaf?*

"But Grandma already paid for her funeral," the grandson said. "You can't save on something she's already paid for. You're not going to get her money back, right?" Finally, he looked up.

"We'll figure this out," Ilka said.

The boy looked over at his mother and began crying.

"Oh, honey!" Helen said.

"You're all talking about this like it isn't even Grandma; like it's someone else who's dead," he said, angry now.

He turned to Ilka. "Like it's all about money, and just getting it over with." He jumped up so fast he knocked his chair over; then he ran out the door.

His mother sent her brothers an apologetic look; they both shook their heads. She turned to Ilka and asked if it were possible for them to return tomorrow. "By then we'll have this business about the coffin sorted out. We also have to order a life board. I brought along some photos of Mom."

Standing now, Ilka told them it was of course fine to come back tomorrow. She knew one thing for certain: Artie was going to meet with them, whether he liked it or not. She grabbed the photos Helen was holding out.

"They're from when she was born, when she graduated from school, when she married Dad, and from their anniversary the year before he died."

"Super," Ilka said. She had no idea what these photos would be used for.

The three siblings stood up and headed for the door. "When would you like to meet?" Ilka asked. They agreed on noon.

Joe stopped and looked up at her. "But can the memorial service be held on Friday?"

"We can talk about that later," Ilka replied at once. She needed time to find out what to do with 150 people and a place for the dogs close to the coffin.

After they left, Ilka walked back to the desk and sank down in the chair. She hadn't even offered them coffee, she realized.

She buried her face in her hands and sat for a moment. She had inherited a funeral home in Racine. And if she were to believe the nun in the reception area laminating death notices, she had accepted the inheritance.

She heard a knock on the doorframe. Sister Eileen stuck her head in the room. Ilka nodded, and the nun walked over and laid a slip of paper on the table. On it was an address.

"We have a pickup."

Ilka stared at the paper. How was this possible? It wasn't just charms, life boards, and a forty-five-hundred-dollar coffin. Now they wanted her to pick up a body, too. She exhaled and stood up.

ABOUT THE AUTHOR

Sara Blaedel's suspense novels have enjoyed incredible success around the world: fantastic acclaim, multiple awards, and runaway number one bestselling success internationally. In her native Denmark, Sara was voted most popular novelist for the fourth time in 2014. She is also a recipient of the Golden Laurel, Denmark's most prestigious literary award. Her books are published in thirty-seven countries. Her series featuring police detective Louise Rick is adored the world over, and Sara has just launched her new Family Secrets suspense series to fantastic acclaim.

Sara Blaedel's interest in story writing, and especially crime fiction, was nurtured from a young age. The daughter of a renowned Danish journalist and an actress whose career included roles in theater, radio, TV, and movies, Sara grew up surrounded by a constant flow of professional writers and performers visiting the Blaedel home. Despite her struggle with dyslexia, books gave Sara a world in which to escape when her introverted nature demanded an exit from the hustle and bustle of life. Sara tried a number of careers, from a restaurant apprenticeship to graphic design, before she started a publishing company called Sara B, where she published Danish translations of American crime fiction.

Publishing ultimately led Sara to journalism, and she covered a wide range of stories, from criminal trials to the premiere of *Star Wars: Episode I*. It was during this time—and while skiing in Norway—that Sara started brewing the ideas for her first novel. In 2004 Louise and Camilla were introduced in *Grønt Støv* (*Green Dust*), and Sara won the Danish Academy for Crime Fiction's debut prize.

Originally from Denmark, Sara has lived in New York, but now spends most of her time in Copenhagen. When she isn't busy committing brutal murders on the page, she is an ambassador with Save the Children and serves on the jury of a documentary film competition.